A Dark and
Stormy Tea

Titles by Laura Childs

Tea Shop Mysteries

DEATH BY DARJEELING
GUNPOWDER GREEN
SHADES OF EARL GREY
THE ENGLISH BREAKFAST MURDER
THE JASMINE MOON MURDER
CHAMOMILE MOURNING
BLOOD ORANGE BREWING
DRAGONWELL DEAD
THE SILVER NEEDLE MURDER
OOLONG DEAD
THE TEABERRY STRANGLER
SCONES & BONES

AGONY OF THE LEAVES
SWEET TEA REVENGE
STEEPED IN EVIL
MING TEA MURDER
DEVONSHIRE SCREAM
PEKOE MOST POISON
PLUM TEA CRAZY
BROKEN BONE CHINA
LAVENDER BLUE MURDER
HAUNTED HIBISCUS
TWISTED TEA CHRISTMAS
A DARK AND STORMY TEA

Scrapbooking Mysteries

KEEPSAKE CRIMES
PHOTO FINISHED
BOUND FOR MURDER
MOTIF FOR MURDER
FRILL KILL
DEATH SWATCH
TRAGIC MAGIC
FIBER & BRIMSTONE

SKELETON LETTERS
POSTCARDS FROM THE DEAD
GILT TRIP
GOSSAMER GHOST
PARCHMENT AND OLD LACE
CREPE FACTOR
GLITTER BOMB
MUMBO GUMBO MURDER

Cackleberry Club Mysteries

EGGS IN PURGATORY
EGGS BENEDICT ARNOLD
BEDEVILED EGGS
STAKE & EGGS
EGGS IN A CASKET

SCORCHED EGGS
EGG DROP DEAD
EGGS ON ICE
EGG SHOOTERS

Anthologies

DEATH BY DESIGN
TEA FOR THREE

Afton Tangler Thrillers
writing as Gerry Schmitt

LITTLE GIRL GONE
SHADOW GIRL

A DARK AND STORMY TEA

Tea Shop Mystery #24

LAURA CHILDS

BERKLEY PRIME CRIME
New York

BERKLEY PRIME CRIME
Published by Berkley
An imprint of Penguin Random House LLC
penguinrandomhouse.com

Copyright © 2022 by Gerry Schmitt & Associates, Inc.
Excerpt from *Lemon Curd Killer* copyright © 2022 by Gerry Schmitt & Associates, Inc.
Penguin Random House supports copyright. Copyright fuels creativity, encourages diverse
voices, promotes free speech, and creates a vibrant culture. Thank you for buying an
authorized edition of this book and for complying with copyright laws by not reproducing,
scanning, or distributing any part of it in any form without permission. You are supporting
writers and allowing Penguin Random House to continue to publish books for every reader.

BERKLEY and the BERKLEY & B colophon are registered trademarks and
BERKLEY PRIME CRIME is a trademark of Penguin Random House LLC.

Library of Congress Cataloging-in-Publication Data

Names: Childs, Laura, author.
Title: A dark and stormy tea / Laura Childs.
Description: New York: Berkley Prime Crime, [2022] | Series: Tea shop mystery; #24
Identifiers: LCCN 2021061891 (print) | LCCN 2021061892 (ebook) |
ISBN 9780593200896 (hardcover) | ISBN 9780593200902 (ebook)
Subjects: LCGFT: Novels.
Classification: LCC PS3603.H56 D37 2022 (print) |
LCC PS3603.H56 (ebook) | DDC 813/.6—dc23
LC record available at https://lccn.loc.gov/2021061891
LC ebook record available at https://lccn.loc.gov/2021061892

Printed in the United States of America
1st Printing

A DARK AND
STORMY TEA

1

❧

At five thirty on a Monday afternoon, it was full-on dark when Theodosia Browning, proprietor of the Indigo Tea Shop, stepped out the back door of the Heritage Society. Pushing back a lock of curly auburn hair, she scanned the western sky, hoping for a faint smudge of orange to light the way home. When she didn't find it, she set off at a fast clip, chiding herself for staying so late.

Still, Charleston's venerable Heritage Society was sponsoring a Maritime History Seminar this Wednesday, and as luck would have it, Theodosia and her team had been tapped to cater an afternoon tea for visiting scholars.

Gotta hurry back. Drayton will be waiting, Theodosia told herself as she snugged her coat collar up against a cold wind. Overhead, trees thrashed as rain began to pelt down, stinging her face like icy needles.

Awful weather for early March. Especially when Charleston should be bursting with azaleas and pink camellias.

Now thunder rumbled overhead, low and slow, as if pin after pin were being knocked down in a cosmic bowling alley.

Theodosia hurried across King Street and hesitated. She glanced around at enormous two-hundred-year-old homes that sat on their haunches like nervous cats, then shivered as sheets of rain slashed down. Because the shortest distance between two points was a straight line, she knew a shortcut down Gateway Walk, a tangled trail that wound through the back side of the Historic District, would save her an entire block of slopping through puddles. And with this weather system blowing in so hard and strong, the decision was a no-brainer.

Of course, Gateway Walk was probably deserted right now, Theodosia told herself as she hurried through a pair of ancient wrought-iron gates and headed down a narrow, winding path. With this foul, unseasonable weather, there'd be no tourists snapping photos, none of the usual ghost-walk tours with guides spinning eerie tales about haunted graves and wafting white specters.

Tall boxwood hedges closed in as Theodosia skimmed along slippery cobblestones. Great gray wisps of fog rolled across her path like ghostly ocean waves, driven in by the wind off Charleston Harbor a few blocks away. Charleston, a city that was already slightly ethereal due to high humidity, salt-laden sea air, and antique glowing streetlamps, became positively spooky when the fog swirled in.

Of course it's spooky, Theodosia told herself. *Even this pathway is purported to be a prime viewing area for ghostly phenomena. Which, by the way, I don't happen to subscribe to.*

Theodosia had traveled these hidden paths and walkways dozens of times, always reveling in their sumptuous gardens, Greek statuary, hidden grape arbors, and pattering fountains. But tonight she had to admit the atmosphere did feel slightly different.

And for good reason.

Always a gracious and posh dowager, Charleston was on edge right now. A dangerous killer the local press had dubbed Fogheel

Jack had been skulking down its hidden lanes and alleys. After a seven-year hiatus, this madman had suddenly reappeared in Charleston to strangle an unsuspecting young woman with a twist of sharp wire.

Now residents hurried home from work in a wash of blue twilight and locked their doors before total darkness descended. Visitors who'd come to languish in luxury at Charleston's historic inns and feast at four-star restaurants that specialized in grilled redfish, blue crab, and fresh oysters were warned not to wander too far from the relatively safe confines of the Historic District. Around the City Market, Waterfront Park, and White Point Gardens, the Charleston police had stepped up patrols and officers rode two to a cruiser.

No. Theodosia shook her head to dispel the notion of danger and told herself she'd be fine. Better than fine. Even though she was surrounded by live oaks, palmettos, and crumbling stone walls, she was only three blocks away—actually, make that two and a half—from busy Church Street and the welcoming warmth of her tea shop. And once she reached the front door of that cozy little establishment, she'd be perfectly safe. Drayton Conneley, her dear friend and tea sommelier, would be waiting with a fresh-brewed pot of Darjeeling, eager to hear final details about their catering job. Haley, her young chef extraordinaire, would probably be tucked upstairs in her apartment along with Teacake, her little orange-and-brown RagaMuffin cat.

Theodosia could almost feel the warmth of the Indigo Tea Shop settle around her shoulders like a cashmere blanket, could practically inhale its rich aromas. So nothing to worry about, right?

Then why do I feel so unsettled?

Theodosia knew the practical, rational answer. It was because of Fogheel Jack. He was the mysterious unknown killer who'd murdered two women some seven years ago and was apparently back for a return engagement. Even her customers, sipping tea and nibbling fresh-baked scones at her quasi-British, slightly French-inspired tea shop, furtively whispered his name.

Who was he?

Where was he?

When would he strike next?

The *Post and Courier* had made no bones about last week's murder, a headline boldly declaring "Fogheel Jack Is Back!" That murder had taken place in a small park over near the university, the strangling an almost exact reenactment of the two seven-year-old, still-unsolved crimes.

Fogheel Jack. That's what rabid journalists had called him back then. And the name had stuck. Obviously.

Some of the TV stations had gone so far as to speculate that this brutal killer had been roaming the country and returned to Charleston because he found it to be more to his liking, a kind of preferred hunting ground.

Enough of that nonsense, Theodosia told herself as she chugged along. Last week's murder had happened miles from here. So there was no way . . .

A faint sound up ahead. The scrape of shoe leather on pavement?

Theodosia slowed, listened carefully, then stopped dead in her tracks. Cocked her head and listened harder.

But the only thing she heard was the constant pounding of rain and the occasional whoosh of cars over on Archdale Street.

I'm being silly. Acting like a fraidy-cat.

Resuming her pace, Theodosia headed down the final passageway. This was normally a gorgeous place to sit and watch sunlight play on palmetto trees and purple wisteria. To watch butterflies and honeybees cavort. Not happening today. Instead, she hurried past fog-strangled clumps of azaleas as thunder rumbled overhead and rain pelted down. Blinking, wiping her eyes, she found it difficult to navigate the narrow path let alone avoid its deepening puddles.

Theodosia cautioned herself to hold steady. After all, St. Philip's Graveyard was just ahead. After that she'd be home free.

Unfortunately, she had to contend with this blinding rain and doggone fog.

Theodosia ducked her head and continued on as damp vines clutched at her ankles. Finally, through a scrim of shifting fog, a moldering tomb came into view. Then another seemed to pop up. And even though this was most definitely a creepy graveyard (ghost hunters claimed they'd seen glowing orbs here), Theodosia had never been so happy to see it.

The brick path doglegged left and Theodosia followed it around a square marble tomb with a kneeling angel on top. Cold, wet, feeling like a drowned rat, she couldn't wait to . . .

Another noise.

Theodosia's shoulders hunched reflexively as she came to an abrupt stop.

Is someone besides me wandering around in this miserable weather? A graveyard visitor or lost tourist?

She waited nervously as electricity seemed to thrum the air like so many high-tension wires.

What to do?

An answering slash of lightning lit the boiling clouds overhead. And illuminated a strange tableau taking place some thirty feet in front of her.

Two figures. Locked in some kind of unholy embrace. As if caught and buffeted in the eye of a hurricane.

Then utter darkness enveloped the scene and rain drummed down even harder.

Her heart practically blipping out of her chest, Theodosia wondered what she'd just witnessed. Lovers' quarrel? Crazy horse-play? Someone being attacked?

Lightning strobed and crackled again, yielding a startling revelation. One of the figures was now stretched out atop a low tomb.

Behavioral experts say that faced with imminent danger, most everyone has an immediate fight-or-flight reaction. Theodosia didn't opt for either of these. Instead, she shouted, "Hey there!" Tried to make her voice sound loud and authoritative.

A hooded figure in a long black shiny coat rose slowly and turned to face her. The image suddenly struck her as somber and frightening, like a creature out of a horror film. Or the Headless Horseman character from "The Legend of Sleepy Hollow." She stared, trying desperately to make out the man's face—she thought it was a man—but was only able to discern dark hollows for eyes and a horizontal slash of thin lips.

"What are you . . . ?" she shouted again, even though it was difficult to make herself heard above the onslaught of the storm.

Then Theodosia was struck silent as the man lifted a gleaming blade and tilted it in her direction. It was a strange gesture. He could have been threatening her; he could have been offering a benediction.

The air felt charged with danger as Theodosia slowly spread her arms wide, as if in surrender, and took a step backward.

That's when the man turned and slipped away into the shadows.

Unnerved, Theodosia waited a few moments and then crept forward. Really, what *had* just happened? What had she witnessed?

Slowly, cautiously, her heart beating like the wings of a frightened dove, Theodosia advanced on the small dark figure that had been flung carelessly across the tomb. It looked . . . almost like a bundle of rags. Was it a person? She thought so.

Peering at the crumpled figure, she said, "Hello? Do you need help?"

There was no answer.

She took another step forward.

That's when it all changed for Theodosia. That's when she saw streaming rivulets of blood mingled with rain as it hammered down.

2

Flustered and trying to fight off the blind panic that threatened to engulf her, Theodosia fumbled for her phone and managed to punch in 911. When a dispatcher came on the line, her words poured out in a torrent.

"There's been a murder! At least I *think* it's a murder. In St. Philip's Graveyard. I need help!"

"Where are you?" the dispatcher asked. A male voice, all business but concerned-sounding, too.

"I just told you. St. Philip's Graveyard."

She heard mumbling in the background, several voices all merged together, and someone saying *ten-fifty-three* and *a possible one-eighty-seven*. Police codes, she guessed. Then the dispatcher was right back with her.

"An alert's been sent; help is on the way," he said. "But you *must* remain on the line, do you understand?"

"Okay . . . okay," Theodosia said. She was trying to stay calm, to sound as if she was in control of her faculties, but it was difficult. Rain continued to pour down, seeping under her collar and running down the back of her neck, chilling her to the bone. She was also standing in total darkness, surrounded by ancient, crumbling statuary and tombstones. A carved skull stared at her with hollow eyes. A lamb with a missing head stood guard just to her left. And of course there was that poor body. With so much blood leaking out.

"Are you still there?" the dispatcher asked. "Talk to me. I need to know that you're okay."

"I'm here, I'm okay," Theodosia said as she clutched her phone with a cold, deathlike grip.

"There's a cruiser two minutes out, so you need to hang in there as best you can." Against the constant drip, drip, drip of rain he sounded worried.

Theodosia nodded, even though she knew the dispatcher couldn't see her.

"Okay," she said finally. "I'm still here."

"Are you in any physical danger?"

Theodosia looked around. "Right now? I don't think so. But . . ."

She ground her teeth together as her curiosity reared up hard and fast, getting the better of her. Clouding her judgment.

She crept forward, the heels of her loafers sinking into soft, dark moss as she edged across soggy ground. Then she stopped and peered speculatively at the woman. She'd been flung haphazardly across a low pockmarked marble tombstone, almost as if she'd been put there on display. As if her killer wanted to say, *Look what I did.*

The scene was macabre. The woman's face and arms looked bleached white, like bones picked clean. And every time lightning flashed, and wind ruffled the woman's clothing and hair, it was like watching a herky-jerky old-time black-and-white movie.

But wait . . .

It took Theodosia a few moments to become fully aware of the khaki book bag with a purple emblem, sodden and half-hidden under the woman.

"Dear Lord," she said, her voice low and hoarse. "Could it be Lois?" Lois Chamberlain was the retired librarian who owned Antiquarian Books, a few doors down from the Indigo Tea Shop. She sold khaki book bags that looked a lot like this one.

Theodosia lifted her cell phone and spoke into it again. "I think . . . I think I might know her."

"You recognize the victim?" the dispatcher asked. Surprise along with a hint of doubt had crept into his voice.

"I recognize the book bag anyway."

"Uh-huh."

"I'm afraid it might be Lois Chamberlain from Antiquarian Books," Theodosia said. Then the lightning strobed again, set to the tune of a kettle-drum thunderclap, and she saw long reddish blond hair hopelessly tangled and streaked with blood.

"Or maybe . . . her daughter?"

Could that be Cara? Theodosia wondered.

"Officers are thirty seconds out," the dispatcher said in her ear. "Two cars coming." He seemed more concerned with their timely arrival than the dead body Theodosia was staring at. "Are you hearing sirens yet?"

As if on cue, dual high-pitched wails penetrated her consciousness.

"I hear them, yes. They're getting close."

Then they were more than close. Gazing across a tumble of moss-encrusted tombstones through swirls of fog, Theodosia saw the first cruiser turn off Church Street and bounce up and over the curb. Without cutting its speed, the car skidded across the sidewalk, maneuvered around the side of the church, and churned its way toward the graveyard. Slewing across wet grass, the car rocked to a stop just as its reinforced front bumper hit a tilting tombstone with a jarring *clink*.

A second cruiser followed as lights pulsed, sirens blared, and a crackly voice yelled at her over a loudspeaker.

It was kind of like Keystone Cops, only it wasn't.

Guns drawn, serious-looking uniformed officers sprang from both vehicles.

"Here. Over here," Theodosia called out. She raised her hands in the air to let them know she was an unarmed civilian. "I'm the one who called it in." *So please don't shoot me.*

The EMTs arrived right on their heels. Siren screaming, red lights flashing, jumping from the ambulance and rushing to tend to the victim. They cleared her airway, used a ventilator bag, did chest compressions, administered some sort of injection to try to jump-start her heart. Nothing seemed to work. The woman— Cara?—appeared to be dead.

"Soft tissue trauma compounded by a hyoid fracture," one of the EMTs murmured. "Ligature cut deep. Not much we could do."

One of the officers, a man who'd been holding a flashlight so the EMTs could work, walked over to Theodosia. His name tag read DANA.

"You're sure she's been . . . ?" Theodosia touched a hand to the side of her own neck to indicate a strangulation.

"Looks like," Officer Dana said.

Theodosia's face was a pale oval lit only by bouncing flashlights and the glowing blue and red bars on the cruisers. "So it could have been . . . ?" Her voice trailed off again.

Officer Dana aimed suspicious cop eyes at her. "You're thinking Fogheel Jack? Let's hope not."

But Theodosia knew it probably was. She'd been born with masses of curly auburn hair, blue eyes that practically matched her sapphire earrings, an expressive oval face, beaucoup smarts, and a curiosity gene that simply wouldn't quit. Right now her smarts and her curiosity gene were ramping up big-time, telling her this was definitely the brutal handiwork of the killer known as Fogheel Jack.

Another officer, Officer Kimball, walked over to them as he spoke into his police radio. He said, "K," into the radio, then looked at Officer Dana. "We need to lock down the scene until they send an investigator."

Theodosia took a step forward. "Pete Riley?" Her voice sounded soft and muted amid the clank of activity and barked orders.

Officer Dana looked at her sharply. "You know him?"

"He's my boyfriend."

"I don't know who got the callout tonight," Officer Kimball said. He sounded unhappy and resigned, as if he'd rather be any-place else. "We'll have to wait and see." He sighed. "Anyhoo, Crime Scene's on its way."

"I'll get some tape from the vehicle," Officer Dana offered.

Halfway through stringing yellow-and-black crime scene tape from a grave to a mausoleum and then winding it around another grave, Officer Dana glanced up at a large figure that was bobbing toward them. The figure slipped behind a tall obelisk, then re-emerged again.

"Looks like the big boss himself came out," Officer Dana said.

Theodosia peered through dark swaying strands of Spanish moss and decided that could mean only one thing.

"Detective Tidwell," she murmured, just as Detective Burt Tidwell, head of the Charleston Police Department's Robbery and Homicide Division, appeared. He was dressed in a baggy brown suit the color of sphagnum moss. What little hair he had left was acutely disheveled, his eyes were magpie beady, and his oversized belly jiggled. As he drew closer, Theodosia saw a soup stain marring his ugly green tie.

"You," Tidwell said when he caught sight of Theodosia. Clearly they knew each other.

Theodosia gave a half shrug. "I was taking a shortcut back to my tea shop and I . . ." Her voice trailed off as Tidwell held up a hand. Then she cleared her throat and said, "I think I know her."

That grabbed Tidwell's attention. He peered at Theodosia from beneath heroic bushy eyebrows and said, "You *recognize* the victim?"

"I think it might be Cara Chamberlain, Lois's daughter."

"The bookstore lady," Tidwell murmured. Besides being a meticulous, boorish, ill-tempered investigator, he was extremely bright and well-read. "You're sure it's Lois's daughter? Are you able to make a positive ID?"

"I think so."

His head shook, setting off a jiggle of jowls. "You need to be absolutely sure before we do any kind of notification."

"Then I don't . . ."

Theodosia's words were once again cut short, this time by the arrival of the Crime Scene team. Their shiny black van pulled up next to the police cruisers. Men in black jumpsuits got out and immediately established a hard perimeter—setting up lights on tripods and even more yellow crime scene tape. When the entire graveyard glowed a ghastly yellow, they began to record the scene, using still cameras as well as video cameras.

"Any footprints?" Tidwell asked. "Can you pull plaster casts?"

The tech looked skeptical. "Dunno. There are a few prints, but they're already mushy and filled with rain."

Theodosia stood there feeling helpless and bedraggled. Her normally curly hair was plastered to her head and she'd crossed her arms in a futile attempt to stay warm. Still, a keen intellect shone in her eyes as she watched the proceedings.

Strangely, the night was shaping up for even more action. A shiny white van with a satellite dish on top had just rolled in. Theodosia figured it was TV people who'd tuned in on their scanner and gotten wind of the murder.

"Oh, hell's bells," Tidwell said when he saw the van. "The media jackals have arrived."

"What have we got? Lemme through, lemme through," came the high-pitched, semi-authoritative voice of Monica Garber. She was the lead investigative reporter at Channel Eight, a tenacious pit bull of a woman who lived for the thrill of sinking her teeth into a fast-breaking story.

Officer Kimball held up a hand and tried to block her, said, "Ma'am, you need to stay back."

"Stuff it," Monica Garber snarled as she sailed right past him. She was in her mid-thirties—around Theodosia's age—attractive in a hard-edged way, and always projected her own brand of on-air sassiness. Tonight she was tricked out in a form-fitting hot pink blazer, tight black jeans, and short black boots. Her long dark hair swished damply about her shoulders.

Theodosia didn't think Monica Garber would be particularly thrilled when she discovered who the victim was. Cara Chamberlain was a journalism student who'd taken the semester off to do a news internship at Channel Eight. Thus, she was practically one of their own.

How would Monica Garber handle her emotions when she realized the victim was Cara?

Turned out, not very well.

Once Monica had pushed her way past the police line and registered that it was Cara lying there, she promptly fainted. Would have fallen and split her skull open on a hump-backed tombstone had not Bobby, her cameraman, lunged forward and caught her at precisely the last second.

"Nuh, I'm okay," Monica protested when she regained consciousness a few moments later. Then, as she looked over at the body, her eyes rolled back in her head and her knees wobbled like a Jell-O ring being passed around a Thanksgiving table.

"Get her out of here!" Tidwell shouted.

Bobby the cameraman and the young man who'd been manning the boom microphone got on either side of a shaky, protesting Monica Garber and half carried, half dragged her away.

"Good," Tidwell said. "Now, if only this tedious rain would let up. I have additional personnel on the way and we need to . . ." He half spun, noticed Theodosia again, seemed to seriously study her, and said, "Miss Browning. A favor if you will."

3

"*There you are,*" Drayton exclaimed as the door to the Indigo Tea Shop burst open. "I was wondering what could've . . ."

His words suddenly evaporated as Theodosia hurried in, followed by Detective Tidwell; his assistant, Glen Humphries; and two uniformed officers.

"What?" Drayton said, his voice rising, high-pitched and sharp, like a surprised crow. The normally unflappable Drayton Conneley was suddenly flapping.

"There's a problem," Tidwell said as he shouldered his way into the tea shop, glanced around, and seemed pleased that it was warm, dry, and unoccupied.

"There's been a murder," Theodosia said. Why beat around the bush when the media had already latched on to this terrible story and would no doubt whip things into a frenzy?

"Oh no." Drayton touched a hand to his heart. Then, when he saw the look of anguish on Theodosia's face, he said, "Is it someone we know?"

"Cara. Lois's daughter."

Drayton's mouth opened and closed without uttering a single peep. Then he said, "Antiquarian Books Lois? That can't be."

"I'm afraid it's so," Tidwell said.

Drayton raised both hands as if to invoke divine intervention. When nothing happened, he said, "What can I . . . ? What can we . . . ?"

"I told them they could use the tea shop as a makeshift command post," Theodosia said. "It's pouring outside. Really coming down hard."

"Certainly," Drayton said. "So I should . . . what? Brew some tea? Round up a few scones?" He stood there, anxious and worried, a sixty-something gent who'd been working almost nine hours straight. Still, in his tweed jacket and bow tie, he looked perfectly turned out, as if he'd just stepped out of a Savile Row tailor's shop.

"Would you?" Tidwell asked as his men spread out, grabbed chairs, and sat down heavily at one of the large tables. "I'm afraid that, besides all of us, there are more people on the way."

More people meant more drama. But it also gave Theodosia and Drayton something to do, a chance to burn off pent-up nervous energy by prepping both food and tea for their impromptu guests. Theodosia grabbed two dozen eggnog scones from the cooler, warmed them up, then arranged them on two large trays. She added a stack of small plates, a dozen butter knives, and silver bowls filled with generous scoops of Devonshire cream and raspberry jam.

Drayton got busy at the front counter, brewing pots of Darjeeling and Assam tea, sending out great steaming clouds that gently perfumed the air.

When Theodosia emerged from the kitchen carrying the food, Drayton was already pouring tea for a dozen members of Tidwell's law enforcement team, many newly arrived and sprawled out at various tables.

Her boyfriend, Pete Riley, was among them. Tall, serious-looking, but with a boyish demeanor about him, Riley had an aristocratic nose, high cheekbones, and blue eyes a shade lighter than Theodosia's. He was also one of the up-and-coming detectives on Charleston's police force. Theodosia, of course, simply thought of him as Riley, her Riley. And he called her Theo. It was as easy as that because it suited them.

"Hey," Theodosia said, setting down one of the trays in front of him.

Riley offered a faint smile, caught her hand and squeezed it, then focused on what Detective Tidwell had to say.

Theodosia listened in on the conversation as well.

Tidwell was standing in the center of the tea shop, gathering information from all the involved officers. As he asked questions and jotted notes, he seemed to be weighing some kind of decision.

A few minutes later, Jesse Trumbull, the CPD's public information officer, flew through the door. He was stocky and slightly muscle-bound, the way free-weight lifters often get. His dark brown hair was worn in a crew cut, his hazel-brown eyes darted about worriedly, and he looked a little dazed by all the excitement.

"Good, you're here," Tidwell said to Trumbull. "We're going to need a carefully worded press release ASAP." His mouth pulled into an unconscious grimace and he added, "You've got your work cut out for you tonight."

This was it, Theodosia decided. This was when they made the call on whether there really was a serial killer stalking the women of Charleston. This was when they'd make a decision to alert the media—and thus all of Charleston. The moment felt absolutely terrifying. Still, being in the nerve center, surrounded by this hubbub of activity, felt strangely exhilarating, too.

"You're making the call?" Officer Dana asked Tidwell.

"It appears to be the same MO, so I'm making the call,"

Tidwell said. He looked reluctant but decisive. "But we have to make sure next of kin have been notified," he cautioned.

Glen Humphries looked up from a sheaf of papers. "They've been notified."

"Okay, then," Tidwell said. "Okay."

"If we're going ahead with this, I need as many details as possible," Trumbull said. "Because anything we release to the media is surely going to get blown out of proportion."

"It's already out of proportion," Tidwell said.

There was a flurry of activity then. Lots of low mumbles as the officers put their heads together. Cell phones burped and beeped. Tension hung heavy in the air. Finally, Trumbull began tapping away on his iPad as he talked nonstop into two cell phones at once.

Shaking her head, feeling dazed and more than a little sick at heart, Theodosia went into the kitchen to grab another dozen scones. In the back hallway she encountered a worried-looking Haley.

"What's going on?" Haley asked. She was dressed in blue jeans and a yellow T-shirt that said TAKE IT ONE STEEP AT A TIME. Her long blond hair curled around a youthful face that was scrubbed clean and never seemed to need a speck of makeup. Her feet were bare, toenails painted pale peach, and she cradled her cat, Teacake, in her arms.

"There's been a murder," Theodosia said.

"Where?" Fear flickered in Haley's eyes. "Here?"

"In the graveyard, behind St. Philip's Church."

"Who?"

"Cara Chamberlain."

Haley's eyes were suddenly huge with alarm. "Lois's daughter? Oh no." She digested the terrible news for a few moments, then said, "Was it, you know, that creeper the newspaper's been talking about?"

"Fogheel Jack? That's what the police are speculating," Theodosia said.

"Wow." Haley peered around Theodosia at the gaggle of law enforcement that had taken over the tea shop. "How come the police are here? Wait, are you involved in this?"

"I'm afraid I discovered Cara's body."

This time Haley's hand flew to her mouth. "Are you okay?"

"I'm fine."

"Is there anything I can do?"

"I don't think so. Just . . . go back upstairs to your apartment." Theodosia bent forward and gave Haley a reassuring hug. Gave the cat one, too. "And be safe."

Walking back into the tea room, Theodosia grabbed a pale blue teapot, rounded a table, and poured a second—or maybe it was a third—refill for Detective Tidwell.

"I have a question," she said.

Tidwell's head tilted sideways to acknowledge her.

"How could this murder . . . this death . . . have happened so fast?"

This time Tidwell swiveled in his chair to meet her eyes.

"Whoever did this knows his business," Tidwell said.

"But how . . . ?" Theodosia was still confused.

"A carotid artery will collapse under five and a half to twenty pounds of pressure," Tidwell said. "The human trachea collapses under thirty-three pounds of pressure. Loss of either vital structure leads to almost instantaneous death."

"Dear Lord," Drayton muttered under his breath. He'd edged his way over to listen in.

"So the killer used some kind of wire?" Theodosia asked. She knew her question was macabre but needed to ask it anyway.

"That's what accounts for such a deep cut," Tidwell said. "Five dollars' worth of galvanized wire from the hardware store attached to two pieces of wood yields a working garrote."

"A handyman's special," Riley said, causing Theodosia to flinch. When he saw her reaction, he murmured, "Sorry."

"Sure," she said. "But he also had a knife."

"Not surprising," Tidwell said in a manner that was meant to dismiss her.

Moving to the next table, where Jesse Trumbull was typing out his press release, Theodosia said, "More tea?"

Trumbull looked up with a friendly smile. "Love some. Especially if it'll help keep me going."

Theodosia glanced at the screen of his iPad. "Writing a press release about something like this can't be easy. Though it looks as if you're making good progress."

"Me and this iPad, we're attached at the hip," Trumbull said. "And yes, it can sometimes be a crappy job when you've got to write about the latest disaster." He looked over as the front door opened and a man peered in. He clearly wasn't law enforcement because he was dressed head to toe in khaki and had an out-of-style, too-long gray ponytail that trailed down his back, large horsey teeth, and small eyes with pinprick pupils.

Tidwell noticed him at the same time and shouted, "No!" Then to Officer Dana, "Get that idiot out of here."

Mr. Ponytail took a step forward and said, "Come on, guys, just a few quick questions, huh? I'm on deadline."

"You're always on deadline," Tidwell responded, then promptly ignored the man.

"Who's that?" Theodosia asked as Officer Dana hustled the man out.

Trumbull rolled his eyes. "He's a freelance crime reporter by the name of Robert Basset. The guy's been shadowing us ever since last week's murder. Besides being the worst kind of pest, he's a stringer for a couple of national gossips rags. The *Star Tattler* and *World Examiner*."

"And he covers crime? Specializes in it?"

"The guy's *addicted* to crime stories. Because he's independent, he spends most of his time crisscrossing the country, searching out all sorts of crazy stories."

"By 'crazy stories' you mean . . ."

"The worst of the worst. Serial killers, female ax murderers, hostage situations, child kidnappings, loonies, extraterrestrials, you name it. Some wackadoodle pops up on Basset's radar and suddenly he's all over him like shine on a cheap suit." Trumbull let loose a disdainful snort. "We call him the Basset Hound."

By eight thirty it was all over. Tidwell and his crew had gone, leaving tables pushed together, chairs tipped back, and the tea shop strewn with debris.

"They're like bad roommates," Drayton observed. "They show up, eat, drink, and then leave without helping us clean up."

"Can you blame them?" Theodosia said. "They're trying to catch a killer."

"I suppose." Drayton grabbed a teapot that was still half-full of Assam and poured out a cup of tea for each of them. He carried the cups to one of the cleaner tables and they both sat down. Then he gazed at Theodosia and asked, "Were you scared?"

"You mean when I stumbled upon Cara's body? Yes, I suppose I was. A little."

"It's a good thing you didn't attempt any sort of move against that . . . that madman. Or you could have ended up one of his victims as well."

"Maybe." Theodosia was brave, but she wasn't foolish. When someone dangerous challenged her, she was darn well going to be careful. Or, worst-case scenario, turn tail and run like crazy. Yup, there was a reason she jogged and stayed in shape.

"This Fogheel Jack character is one of the worst things that's ever happened to our city," Drayton said. "I mean"—he leaned forward, a look of indignation on his lined face, his voice practically shaking—"Charleston is supposed to be a bastion of civility."

"Right," Theodosia said. "Until we're not."

4

It wasn't exactly business as usual this Tuesday morning, but Theodosia did her best to keep up the pretense. The Indigo Tea Shop still looked adorable with its exposed beams, stone fireplace, slightly rustic tables and chairs, blue toile curtains, and wood-plank floors. One brick wall was covered with handmade grapevine wreaths decorated with bone china teacups. A French chandelier dangled overhead and cute little hurricane lamps spilled warm puddles of light across each table.

The atmosphere within, like the weather outside, remained subdued, however. Theodosia readied the tables so they could accommodate their usual influx of morning customers, and Drayton was at his post behind the front counter selecting and brewing tea. Still, teakettles warbled their morning salutations, cups and saucers rattled cheerily, and the air was redolent with the scent of fresh-baked apple scones, lemon tea bread, and cardamom tea.

"Is Haley okay?" Drayton asked. He was perusing his floor-to-ceiling racks of tea tins. His fingers touched a gold tin filled with gunpowder green, lingered, then moved on to a dark green tin of tippy Yunnan.

"If her scones and tea bread are any indication of her mental status, I'd say Haley's doing just fine," Theodosia said. "She was rattled last night by the murder and all the police being here, but this morning she seems to be over it."

"Well, *I'm* not over it," Drayton said.

Theodosia studied him. Drayton did seem a bit tense.

"No, I daresay you're not."

"And the weather's still awful. All this rain and fog. Not very conducive for our Rhapsody in Blue Tea tomorrow. I was hoping for some springtime weather."

"Even with this gloomy weather, almost every seat's been reserved," Theodosia said. She glanced at the tables, where Shelley Dainty Rosebud teacups sat ready, bouquets of pink asters bobbed their shaggy heads, and white votive candles flickered in glass holders. And smiled. Even when everything was head over tea-kettle, Theodosia remained a glass-half-full kind of person. Generally upbeat and optimistic. Looking for the good in people.

"Concerning our tea tomorrow, we're lucky we have a cadre of loyal customers," Drayton said.

Theodosia walked over to the counter where he was fussing with his teapots, rested her elbows on a pine plank, and gave Drayton a questioning look.

"Yes?" A short word that he elongated.

"Do you know the history behind this Fogheel Jack character?"

Drayton patted his bow tie, a blend of yellow and ochre silk that was as bright and luxuriant as a Painted Lady butterfly. "I know some of it."

"Tell me."

"Hmm. Then I suppose I should start at the very beginning," Drayton said.

Placing two Limoges cups and saucers on the counter, he filled them with Irish breakfast tea. He slid one cup across the counter to Theodosia and drew a deep breath.

"Fogheel Jack is basically an updated version of a killer known in Victorian England as Spring-heeled Jack," he said.

"Sounds like a Jack the Ripper–type killer," Theodosia said.

"A nasty killer, yes, but also a sort of Victorian boogeyman." Drayton took a sip of his tea and looked thoughtful. "You know, the subject of scary stories that were told to wide-eyed children around a glowing hearth. To keep them in line." He took another sip of tea. "Anyway, the legend—as well as the brutal murders—began in England in the late eighteen hundreds. Always young women, always late at night, usually in springtime. Hence the moniker Spring-heeled Jack."

"And this actually happened? It's historically factual?"

"It most certainly is. Almost a dozen murders—strangulations, if you want to get technical—were attributed to Spring-heeled Jack."

"Yet he was never apprehended?"

"The London police, Scotland Yard, never caught a whiff of him," Drayton said. "Then, after a while, Spring-heeled Jack hysteria began to die out. Presumably because Spring-heeled Jack aged and died himself. A few decades go by and, strangely enough, his legend washed up on our shores."

"How so?" Theodosia asked.

"In the nineteen fifties there was a sighting and a murder, in Lynn, Massachusetts. One eyewitness claimed the killer was dressed as a Victorian dandy."

"Weird."

"And then"—Drayton raised a single eyebrow—"a strange, foppishly dressed killer wreaked havoc in North Carolina in the early eighties."

"So how did the name *Fogheel Jack* come about?" Theodosia asked.

"Seven years ago, two brutal murders occurred in Charleston, just weeks apart." Drayton gazed at her intently. "Do you remember that strange meteorological event when an enormous bank of fog swirled in and literally swallowed Charleston?"

"Um . . . vaguely."

"Well, heavy dense fog swept in from the Atlantic and stuck around for several days. Flights were halted; so was shipping. I understand the fog stretched as far inland as Columbia."

Theodosia registered surprise. "That's over one hundred miles from here."

"Exactly."

"And that's when the two murders occurred?"

"Exact same time as the fog," Drayton said. "That's when a newspaper reporter with a knowledge of Victoriana and an overactive imagination dubbed our killer Fogheel Jack."

"Drawing on an old legend," Theodosia mused. "I guess I vaguely remember hearing about those murders. But I didn't pay much attention to them at the time."

"You were still slaving away in marketing back then."

"Writing and directing TV commercials, pinch-hitting at PR," Theodosia said. It hadn't been a happy time for her, churning away almost 24/7. Switching careers and opening the Indigo Tea Shop had proved infinitely more rewarding for body and soul.

"And then last week, with the killing of that young woman over in the university area, well, the idea got stirred up again."

"Reconstituted," Theodosia said. "Thus we have the return of Fogheel Jack. Jack 2.0."

"Looks like," Drayton said. "Did you watch the TV news this morning? Channel Eight?"

Theodosia shook her head. "Missed it. I was busy walking

Earl Grey and trying to dodge raindrops." Earl Grey was her dog, canine roommate, and jogging companion. He also snuck in occasional appearances at the Indigo Tea Shop.

"Well, Channel Eight made a huge deal about last night's murder being similar to the one last week. So they basically trumpeted the return of Fogheel Jack. They even called it *the second coming.*"

"That's guaranteed to scare the daylights out of every man, woman, and child and put law enforcement in a complete frenzy." Theodosia figured Jesse Trumbull must have written some terrifying press release.

Drayton raised his teacup in a mock salute. "I should say so." He glanced toward the front door and seemed to readjust his thinking. "Time to put out our sign?" They'd had a fanciful, hand-lettered sign made that said OPEN FOR TEA AND LIGHT LUNCHES.

Theodosia glanced at her watch. Five to nine.

"Looks like," she said. "But I'm not sure we'll be all that busy on a rainy morning like this."

"Hey, guys."

They both glanced over as Haley hurried out of the kitchen, carrying a tray of scones.

"Anybody interested in more bakery treats?" she asked.

"There's more?" Drayton said.

"I baked another pan of apple scones," Haley said. "Just in case we get busy."

"Excellent." Drayton took the tray from Haley and began stacking scones into a large glass pie saver, the better to tempt their regular customers as well as occasional walk-ins.

Haley pulled a four-by-six recipe card from her white chef's jacket and peered at it. "So along with the apple scones we've got cinnamon coffee cake and lemon tea bread for morning tea."

"And for lunch?" Theodosia asked.

"That's going to be seafood chowder with cheddar scones, cashew chicken salad tea sandwiches, mushroom-and-onion quiche, and a fig-and-goat-cheese salad," Haley said.

"Perfect," Theodosia declared. "I doubt our local Church Street shopkeepers who faithfully drop by for takeout will be able to resist those delicacies."

"Except for poor Lois," Haley said.

"Lois," Theodosia repeated. Haley had brought her back down to the sad reality of last night's murder.

"I suppose her bookshop will be closed for a good long while," Drayton said.

"No, Lois is at the bookshop right now," Haley said. "I don't think she's actually open for business, but she's there."

Theodosia and Drayton both stared at Haley in amazement.

Theodosia recovered first. "What?" she said.

"Yeah, I just tossed some cardboard boxes out in the alley and saw that Lois's car was parked a couple doors down. You know, snugged up against the back door of her bookshop." Haley grimaced. "She's there all right, but she hasn't turned on the lights."

"You mean Lois is sitting in the dark?" Theodosia asked. "All by herself?"

"Pretty sad, huh?" Haley said.

"It's downright morbid," Drayton said.

"I'm going to run over there right now," Theodosia said. "Take her some scones and a cup of tea. See what's . . . Drayton, can you . . . ?"

Drayton was already moving. "I'm on it."

Antiquarian Books was three doors down from the Indigo Tea Shop with the White Rabbit Children's Shop and Cabbage Patch Gift Shop tucked in between. It was still raining when Theodosia peeked in the bookstore window and saw nothing but displays of books. The back of the store remained dark, while a string of yellow streetlamps reflected back at her in the wavy glass.

Theodosia knocked on the front door. If Lois was inside, surely she'd answer. Right?

But she didn't.

Theodosia decided this was a situation that needed to be handled with kid gloves.

She knocked on the door again, then put her hand on the old-fashioned brass doorknob and rattled it. "Lois?" she called out. "It's Theodosia. Are you in there? Can I talk to you?"

Seconds ticked by, then almost a full minute. Finally, Lois opened the door. In her middle fifties, with a cherubic face and long gray hair worn in a single braid down her back, Lois Chamberlain looked as if she'd aged a decade overnight.

"Hi," was all she said.

"Oh, Lois," Theodosia said. "I'm so sorry." She put her arms around Lois and hugged her. Felt the weariness and sadness that welled up inside the poor woman. Could almost feel defeat in her soul.

Lois allowed herself to be hugged, then pulled back and gave a weary smile. "Come in. Please come in."

Theodosia followed Lois into the bookstore. A small light glowed from behind the counter and the place smelled of cedar shelves and leather-covered books. Dozens of tall wooden shelves, all stocked floor to ceiling with new and used books, crowded around them companionably.

"I brought you some hot tea and fresh-baked scones," Theodosia said. She set her take-out bag down on the counter.

Lois nodded but made no move for it. "Kind of you."

"Is there anything I can do?" Theodosia felt helpless standing there. This poor woman had just lost her only daughter. She must be in agony.

Finally, Lois said, "Maybe you could . . . tell me about it?"

"Oh no." Theodosia was caring and honest to a fault, but that was the one thing she didn't want to do.

"When I spoke to the police an hour or so ago, they revealed that you were the one who found Cara. Is that true? It wasn't reported in the newspaper."

"I'm afraid that's correct. I was talking a shortcut back from the Heritage Society and . . . well . . . I became a sort of witness," Theodosia said.

"By *sort of*, you're saying you *didn't* see who did it? You don't know who murdered my poor baby girl?"

"Oh, Lois, I wish I did. Believe me, I'd do anything to help if I could!"

"I believe you."

"I had a general *impression* of the man," Theodosia said. "Which I shared with the police. As for specifics—there aren't any. It was storming, visibility was nil, and whoever it was wore a raincoat with a hood pulled up."

Lois stared at Theodosia with baleful eyes. "Why would Cara have been in that graveyard in the first place?"

Theodosia shook her head. "I have no idea." She figured that Cara must have been forced there against her will—dragged there by her killer—but didn't want to upset Lois any more by voicing such an awful notion.

"If only Cara hadn't signed up for that internship. Then maybe this never would have happened."

Lois's words puzzled Theodosia. "You think her internship had something to do with it?"

"Only because Cara was so ridiculously gung ho about all the current news stories."

Theodosia nodded. "When I talked to Cara this past Christmas I remember she was all excited about working at Channel Eight. But I can't imagine her job there would have put her in danger."

"I'm not so sure. Cara adored working with the Investigative Journalism Team. In fact, she thrived on it. But . . ." Lois pursed her lips and sighed deeply.

"But what?"

"Crazy me, I keep thinking—what if Cara *discovered* something? What if she was working on that Fogheel Jack story—I'm talking about that murder last week near the university—and then somehow got too close to it?"

"Oh no," Theodosia said. She doubted that the news director at Channel Eight would allow a lowly intern to work on a major story like that. Weren't interns mostly gophers and researchers? Sure they were. They fetched coffee and donuts. They scoured the Internet for facts and figures to feed to the *real* reporters, the paid professionals.

"Was Cara actually *working* on a story?" Theodosia asked.

"Knowing her, she was probably pitching a dozen different story ideas. Though I don't know if she'd been tapped to contribute to the Fogheel Jack story," Lois said. "I mean, she was an intern, just a kid with grandiose dreams. On the other hand, I know how Cara's mind works. She's always had a keen sense of the dramatic. And lately she'd been talking about how she wanted to sink her teeth into a good sensational story so she'd stand out and get recognized."

"She was young and eager, itching to make her mark," Theodosia said.

Lois dabbed at her eyes. "Which is why I keep thinking . . . what if Cara was murdered because she accidentally uncovered something? Some new information or . . ." Lois gulped. "What if she actually made contact with the killer?"

"I don't mean to be dismissive, but that sounds awfully far-fetched."

"I suppose." Lois sighed deeply. She dug the heels of her hands into her eyes, rubbed hard, dropped them, and gazed at Theodosia with a plaintive expression. "I realize I'm grasping at straws. But when I spoke with the police this morning they didn't have any suspects. Nobody on their radar. And now I'm just . . . I don't know . . . trying to, *hoping* to figure something out. Some reason for her murder. Some *clue*." She stopped, blew her nose into a tissue, and said, "So of course I immediately thought of you."

Theodosia took a surprised step backward. "Me?"

"And here you are. Like you've been delivered by the hand of providence."

Theodosia didn't quite know what to say.

Lois managed a shy, sad smile. "You realize that your friend Delaine Dish always jokes about how you're Charleston's very own Miss Marple."

"Delaine's famous for making some pretty crazy remarks." Fact was, Delaine was the town ditz. A true fashionista, a gifted entrepreneur, but a ditz all the same.

"This time I'd have to say Delaine was spot-on. As if it was meant to be," Lois continued.

"Wait . . . what?" Theodosia had a record-scratch moment. "Are you asking *me* to try to figure out who murdered Cara?"

Lois held up a hand. "No, please, nothing quite that heroic. I'm not asking you to *solve* Cara's murder or get involved in a seven-year-old mystery, but I was hoping maybe you could glean a few basic details. I mean . . . you found her. You were the one who saw, who confronted that . . . that *monster* who killed her!"

"Not really. It was pitch-black and raining hard. Like I said, the man wore a hood or some sort of cowl so I never caught a glimpse of his face." Theodosia lifted both hands in a gesture of helplessness. "There's no way I could identify him."

"I understand that, I really do. But I also know you're fairly well acquainted with Monica Garber, that hotshot TV reporter Cara was so fond of."

You mean the one who fainted last night?

"So I thought maybe you could nose around and talk to *her*," Lois continued. "Try to extract some inside information. Sometimes the media is privy to details that ordinary citizens are not."

And maybe I could get a tip from Riley as well? Theodosia wondered. *Well, I can't blame Lois for hoping he might let a few investigative details slip.*

"I still can't believe Channel Eight allowed Cara to work on actual stories," Theodosia said.

"You don't know Cara. She was one semester away from her degree in media and communications and bound and determined to make her mark as an investigative reporter. She kept a notebook, almost a scrapbook, of clippings on possible stories."

"Local stories?"

"I imagine they were."

Something pinged in Theodosia's brain. "Do you happen to have that notebook?" she asked.

"I don't have the notebook on me, but I could certainly get my hands on it." Lois's eyes blazed with hope. "Does this mean you'll look into Cara's murder?"

"Let me go through her notebook first, okay?"

"I'll go scrounge through her apartment and see if I can find it." Lois tried to muster a hopeful smile but failed miserably.

"Maybe I should be the one to check her apartment," Theodosia said. Her heart went out to Lois; the poor woman was so thoroughly distraught. "Going through Cara's belongings so soon might be awfully painful for you."

"You'd really do that for me?" Lois had already grabbed her purse off the counter and was digging through it.

"Of course."

"Here." Lois held out a brass key that dangled from a pink ribbon. "This is it. And let me jot down her address."

As Theodosia's fingers closed around the key, she prayed she wasn't getting in over her head. Yes, she was intrigued. Yes, she wanted to help. But last night's bizarre murder had frightened her to the bone.

"Before I go prowling through Cara's apartment looking for her notebook, I need to ask you a couple of questions," Theodosia said.

"Sure." Lois handed Theodosia a piece of paper with Cara's address written on it, then swiped at her eyes again. "What about?"

"Do you know what Cara was up to last night? Meeting friends, going to the gym, eating out, whatever?" Theodosia asked.

"I'm afraid not. Are you thinking about places where Cara may have met her killer?"

"Something like that. Okay, do you know anything about Cara's friends?"

"Most of her friends are at school up in Chapel Hill. I think she lost touch with most of her high school friends."

"Did Cara have a boyfriend?"

"She did mention a fellow she was dating, but I never met him," Lois said. "I don't even know his name, just that they broke up recently."

"Any idea why they parted ways?"

Lois shrugged. "Afraid not."

"Were you aware of any problems in Cara's life?"

Lois thought for a moment. "I don't think so. She loved working, thought her internship at Channel Eight was the absolute bomb."

"How about problems in *your* life? Anything unusual going on?"

Lois frowned. "What a weird question."

"I'm sorry, I—"

Lois held up a hand and waved it. "No, it's okay. I appreciate that you're asking tough questions, that you're taking this seriously. So what did you . . . ?"

"I asked about stressors in your life. Work, personal, or business." Theodosia knew there was an off-off chance that someone had wanted to get to Lois through Cara.

"Let me think for a minute. In my life? No, not really." Lois bounced an index finger against her bottom lip. "Unless you count . . . no."

"What?" Theodosia asked.

"The only thing I can think of right now is that my landlord offered to buy out my lease. Apparently there's a real estate developer who's super anxious to purchase this building. He wants to turn half of this block into high-end lofts. Luxury condos."

"There's a lot of that going around lately," Theodosia said. "So, has your landlord put pressure on you?"

"Not so much. The thing is, I have a five-year lease that isn't up for another three and a half years." She hesitated. "But I know the *developer* has been pressuring the landlord. You see, the developer's already purchased an adjoining property."

"Which building is that?"

"Around the corner where the Spice Bin is located. You know, that cute little shop that sells spices and olive oils. But they're really only a short-term pop-up store. In another six months they'll be gone. Probably move to another part of town or set up in the City Market over the summer."

"Okay, the real estate deal could be something."

"You think?" Lois said.

Theodosia was going to say, *Not really.* Instead she said, "Maybe." Then, "Who else did Cara hang out with?"

"I don't know."

"Do you think she was keeping something from you?"

"No." Lois blotted her nose and sniffled. "Well, maybe the boyfriend. I suppose he could be a factor."

Theodosia figured *factor* might be code for *suspect.* As she squeezed her fingers around the key to Cara's apartment, it felt cool to the touch and carried a hint of mystery.

"Then I need to snoop around and see if I can discover this boyfriend's name," Theodosia said. "Maybe have a talk with him."

"So you're really going to look into things?"

"I'm going to try."

Fresh tears sparkled in Lois's eyes. "Bless you."

5

"Good. You're back," Drayton said as he ducked out of the kitchen and met Theodosia in the back hallway.

"Are you telling me we're busy? Even with all this awful weather?" she asked.

"See for yourself."

Theodosia pushed aside the velvet celadon curtain and took a quick look into the tea room. Every table except one was occupied.

"Oh my, I'd better get cracking."

Drayton smiled. "Yes, you'd better."

Morning tea was Theodosia's favorite time at the Indigo Tea Shop. It was when Church Street regulars stopped by for their morning cuppa. When tourists wandered in, drawn by the aromatherapy-like scents of the various teas. And when innkeepers from the surrounding B and Bs recommended that their guests stop in for tea and scrumptious scones.

With an easy smile and a practiced hand at pouring tea, Theodosia bustled about the tea shop, taking orders, making gentle tea suggestions, and delivering Haley's fine baked goods.

"How did things go with Lois?" Drayton asked when Theodosia stopped by the counter to grab a pot of fresh-brewed Formosan oolong.

"She asked me to look into Cara's murder," Theodosia said.

"Of course she did." Drayton measured four spoonfuls of cinnamon spice tea into a green glazed teapot, added a pinch for the pot, and said, "So are you?"

"Well, it's macabre, but certainly fascinating."

"And knowing you, you're intrigued by the Fogheel Jack legend."

"Not so much intrigued as scared silly. If you could have been in the graveyard last night and seen that creature."

"No, thank you. I much prefer to stay behind my counter, where everything remains relatively safe and ordered."

The tea shop hummed along nicely until eleven o'clock. That's when Detective Tidwell walked in, glanced around, glowered, and made a stumbling beeline for the unoccupied table next to the stone fireplace.

Theodosia was at his side in a heartbeat.

"Has there been a break in the case? Have you caught someone?" she asked.

Tidwell's large head swiveled from side to side. "No," he said, drawing out the *o*.

"Then why are you here? Why aren't you out trying to catch Cara's killer?" Theodosia knew she was coming on strong but couldn't help herself. Her visit with Lois—and seeing Lois's palpable grief—was eating at her. To say nothing of her ordeal last night.

"Catching a killer isn't like looking for a lost dog," Tidwell replied. "You don't drive up and down every dark alley, whistling and calling their name. Evidence has to be collected, a case has to be built, before it can be solved."

"And that's what you're doing right now?"

"It will be when you answer a few more questions for me." He indicated the chair across from him. "Please. If you will."

Theodosia glanced around the tea shop. Everyone had been served; nobody seemed to need anything. So, yes, she had a few minutes. A precious few.

"Didn't you ask enough questions last night?" Theodosia asked as she slid into her chair.

Tidwell favored her with a perfunctory smile. "Probably not."

Theodosia leaned forward. "Then what?"

"Miss Browning. You're the only person I know who's had a brush with Fogheel Jack and lived to tell about it."

Theodosia felt the breath go out of her. She hadn't thought about it in those terms. But when Tidwell laid it out like that, the notion scared the living daylights out of her.

"Last night you gave me a general impression of what you witnessed," Tidwell said. "I'm hoping that, in the cold, clear light of day, your memory is somewhat improved."

"I'm afraid it's not."

"Hmm."

"Not what you were hoping to hear?"

Tidwell leaned forward. "Tell you what. Let's go over it again. And this time I want you to think long and hard about everything you saw—or thought you might have seen."

So they went over it, again and again, Tidwell always probing, asking questions, trying to draw out every nit and nat of information. And even though Theodosia tried to give him what he wanted, she could tell by the look on his face that he was disappointed.

"I'm sorry I couldn't give you a better description or information that was more concrete," Theodosia said. "But I tried, I truly did."

"Hmm," he said again.

"Listen, you've quizzed me from A to Z for the past ten minutes. Now I need some details, too. A little quid pro quo."

"Miss Browning, you always drive such a hard bargain."

"Right. So. Last night I got the impression from the crime scene techs that Cara had been strangled rather violently. What can you tell me about the ligature or wire or whatever it was?"

"I haven't received an exact COD from the crime lab."

"A COD?"

"Cause of death. But eyeballing the situation last night . . . it appeared to be piano wire."

"Is that consistent with the woman who was strangled last week over by the university?"

"For that the killer used florist's wire."

"You're sure it was the same person, the same killer?"

"Fairly sure, though there's always the possibility of a copycat."

"Does that happen often? Where you have a copycat killer?"

Tidwell pursed his lips and stared at her.

"You're not going to tell me, are you?"

"What good would it possibly accomplish?"

You have no idea, Theodosia thought.

"I have another question."

"I'm sure you do," Tidwell said.

"Since Cara was strangled as you say, why was her killer holding a knife?"

Tidwell stared at her.

Theodosia cupped a hand and wiggled her fingers. "Come on. This is a biggie, isn't it?"

Something shone in his eyes. Fear? Worry?

"There's an aspect of the murder you're not talking about," she pushed.

When Tidwell's eyes shifted from side to side, when he remained silent, Theodosia knew she was right.

"He does something to his victims, doesn't he? Marks them with his knife or does something else?"

"Yes," Tidwell whispered.

"Tell me."

"This time he cut off a lock of hair." Tidwell's right hand went to the side of his head and wavered there.

"You mean like a souvenir?"

"You can't breathe a word of this."

"I won't."

"Especially not to Lois."

"I wouldn't."

Theodosia's hands gripped the edge of the table as she leaned back in her chair. "And the woman who was killed last week? He took a lock of her hair as well?"

"He did."

"Holy crap," Theodosia said.

"You said a mouthful."

"Okay," Theodosia said. "The two strangulations that occurred . . . what? Seven years ago? Did he . . . ?"

"No."

"Huh." Theodosia thought for a few moments. "You were with the CPD back then. Did you work those cases? Are these new killings similar except for cutting off a lock of the victim's hair?"

"They're similar in nature."

"That doesn't tell me much."

"I don't intend to tell you much," Tidwell said. He set down his cup of tea and inclined his head in her direction. "I know you're a friend of Lois Chamberlain."

Theodosia shrugged. "I'm friends with lots of people."

"But she's already talked to you, hasn't she? Asked you to help? To worm your way into my investigation?"

"You're just rife with speculation, aren't you?"

"And I'm generally right." He lifted a single furry brow, his right one. "Aren't I?"

"Detective Tidwell," Theodosia said as she pushed back her chair and stood up. "That remains to be seen."

In the lull between morning tea and lunch, Theodosia decided she had to share Tidwell's findings with Drayton.

"A lock of hair?" Drayton looked taken aback. "Why would he do that?"

"I think it's like a souvenir. Something that the killer can treasure. I know this sounds gross, but it might help him look back fondly on his . . . handiwork."

"You mean *reminisce*?" Drayton looked horrified.

"Something like that."

"What else did Tidwell tell you?"

"Not much," Theodosia said. "Only that last week's victim was strangled with florist's wire and Cara was strangled with piano wire."

"So perhaps a piano-playing florist?" Drayton said. Then he shook his head. "Apologies, I don't mean to be droll about it. This is serious business. A tragedy."

"I've been thinking—that it's possible our two victims are somehow related. I don't mean genetically. What I'm wondering is—did they take the same yoga or Pilates class? Did they live close to each other? Maybe in the same apartment building? Perhaps they even knew each other? Or shopped at the same store? Or bought their caramel macchiatos at the same coffee shop?"

"You're looking for a connection," Drayton said.

"It seems like the logical place to start."

"Wait a minute. Are you trying to help Lois by feeding her relevant information, or are you trying to solve these murders?"

"Can't the two things be compatible?" Theodosia asked.

"Probably for you. But your Detective Riley might have a problem with it."

"Riley. Yeah, I hear you." Theodosia looked thoughtful. "I do need to walk a tricky tightrope with this, try and extract key information from Riley without letting on that I'm kind of working the case."

"*Kind of* working the case?" Drayton said.

"Okay, investigating on my own," Theodosia said. "I'll admit it. I am."

"I admire your fortitude for Lois's sake. But keep in mind, Fogheel Jack is a dangerous killer."

"One that Cara might have even known." Theodosia touched a hand to her forehead. "On the other hand, Cara's murder could have been crazy-insane randomness."

Drayton peered at her with a speculative look. "You saw his terrible handiwork firsthand last night. What did *you* think?"

Drayton's words caused Theodosia to look back, to recall the hazy memory that had haunted her dreams all last night. The man in the dark, shiny raincoat, rain dripping off its hood. The knife that gave an evil wink every time a bolt of lightning lit the sky.

"Not random," Theodosia said slowly. "But probably crazy-insane."

"Well, that narrows it down," Drayton said. "Not."

"Maybe it does. We just don't know how yet."

"If it's the same killer who struck last week near the university, if it's the same one from seven years ago, we know his taste for murder has been rekindled," Drayton said.

"When you put it that way, it sounds like some kind of fevered bloodlust."

Drayton looked apologetic. "I'm sorry. That did sound awfully grisly."

"Except you could be right," Theodosia said. "Except . . ."

"Except what?"

"With such a propensity for killing, with a hunger for murder, where does one begin to look?" Theodosia asked.

Drayton gazed at her. "Where do the *police* start looking or where do *you* start looking?"

"Um, the police?"

Drayton's eyelids fluttered. Of course he didn't believe her.

"If you wanted to flush out this demon," Drayton said. "And I'm speaking only hypothetically . . ."

"I know where you're going with this—you're wondering where *I'd* start looking," Theodosia said. She thought for a few moments, let his question rumble through her brain. "Okay, yeah. I'd probably begin by focusing on young-to-middle-aged unmarried men who are new to the city." She thought about the seven-year gap. "But not too young."

"I'm impressed," Dayton said. "That sounds like a fairly workable approach. By the way, do you know anyone who meets those criteria?"

Theodosia gave a laugh that turned into a bark. "My new neighbor."

"Mr. Robert Steele of the big stone mansion?"

"Actually, I'm happy to report that Steele has hightailed it off to London for a year."

"So who's living next door to you now in the old Granville Mansion?"

"Neighborhood gossip says the place has been leased to a young man, an author, who happens to be writing a book about true crime."

"How serendipitously bizarre," Drayton said. "Have you met this demented author yet?"

"Not yet. But I'll probably run into him eventually."

"Oh, you'll meet him," Drayton said. "Especially if he's writing a book on true crime. In fact, your author is probably sniffing after Fogheel Jack even as we speak." Drayton thought for a few moments. "He could even end up being your partner in crime."

"No," Theodosia said. "I don't think so."

6

Theodosia had just brought apple scones and slices of mushroom-and-onion quiche to table five when the front door flew open and Bob Basset came barreling into the tea shop, guns blazing. He glanced at the occupied tables, at the front counter, where Drayton was scooping tea into a Chinese Famille Rose teapot, then his eyes settled on Theodosia. Pasting a faux smile on his long face, he rushed toward her, right hand out, ready to shake hands and make nice.

"Hello, ma'am, Bob Basset here. Sorry we didn't get introduced when I stopped by last night. Mind if I ask a few questions? I understand you were a witness to the murder in that awful cemetery." His words tumbled out in a breathless torrent.

"Mr. Basset," Theodosia said as she shook his hand and studied him carefully. Bob Basset had a hangdog face that was slightly reminiscent of a basset hound. Plus, he was somewhat pear-shaped, as if his upper body had slid southward through no fault of its own. He reminded Theodosia of a prizewinning oversized gourd that you'd see on display at a county fair.

"Those are a lot of words you just threw at me. Slow down, please," Theodosia said.

Mollified by her words, Basset smiled. "I keep forgetting that I'm in the South now, where people move like molasses and everything takes three times as long to accomplish."

"We prefer to think of our culture as genteel and graceful, Mr. Basset."

Basset bobbed his head knowingly. "I can see that, I surely can. So kindly forgive all my random jib-jabbering. Guess I'm too used to dealing with hard-nosed newspaper editors and cops who lay out the facts bim-bam-boom. I'm a crime reporter, you see. A freelance professional who takes his job seriously."

"I've heard that about you," Theodosia said.

Basset offered a lopsided smile. "So you've been warned?"

"I have." When Theodosia saw his smile droop slightly, she added, "But in a good way."

Waving a hand, Basset said, "No matter. I realize I can be abrasive, but that's because I'm highly focused. Which lots of folks view as a plus. Say, do you mind if I record our conversation?" Basset set an old-fashioned cassette player on the closest table and pushed a button without waiting for Theodosia to answer. The tape player / recorder was a small black plastic machine that looked like a holdover from the eighties. Like he should be playing cassettes of the Carpenters or the Cowsills.

"Vintage," Theodosia said.

"Yeah, but it still works great." Basset sat down at the table. "So. Can we talk?"

Theodosia sat down across from him. "I don't mind if you record our conversation. But I have to be up front about the fact that I'm not really an eyewitness."

Basset's cassette continued to whirl. "But you were there last night," he prompted.

"It was my bad fortune to stumble onto what proved to be a terrible situation where a young woman was killed. A young woman whose mother happens to be a good friend of mine."

"Sad," Basset said, though he neither looked nor sounded sad. "So you came bopping into that creepy old cemetery and saw the whole situation explode?"

"It was dark, sheets of rain were literally pouring down, and I saw very little. Just . . . figures, kind of dancing together—or struggling—but only when there were quick bursts of lightning."

"Must have been doggone spooky."

"The outcome certainly was."

"Did you see a ghost? I heard a rumor there might have been some kind of ghostly presence. I researched some of the old legends that claim St. Philip's Graveyard is haunted."

"There were no ghosts present," Theodosia said. "Just a flesh-and-blood killer."

"That you're unable to identify?"

"All I saw was his basic outline, his shadow."

"But not his face. That's too bad."

"For who?" Theodosia asked.

"For me. For the police!"

Theodosia tapped the table. "Let me ask you something. Is Fogheel Jack the reason you're here in Charleston?"

"Absolutely," Basset said. "This could be the story of the century. Readers eat this stuff up."

"Somehow I doubt that." Theodosia stood up. "And now, if you'll excuse me, I need to get back to my luncheon guests."

"What else can you tell me?" Basset pleaded. "I have to have some kind of takeaway."

"Takeaway?" Drayton said from behind the counter. "How about a scone and a cup of tea to go?"

Basset scowled. "Not what I had in mind."

*   *   *

"He's a pushy chap, isn't he?" Drayton said once Basset had left. "With that faux-friendly patois." He was busy brewing a pot of jasmine tea.

Theodosia nodded. "Basset even admits to being abrasive, considers it a positive asset. I can see why he's earned his nickname the Basset Hound."

"Because he hunts out strange occurrences to write about?"

"More like he hounds people to death. Oh, and he asked about ghosts. Wanted to know if I'd seen a ghost last night."

"Well, that particular cemetery does have a certain reputation among amateur ghost hunters," Drayton said.

"Isn't that peachy," Theodosia said. "When Basset writes his story, half the city will think there's a serial killer on the loose; the other half will think there's a menacing ghost."

Drayton slid a Brown Betty teapot across the counter to Theodosia. "This is for table five. But it needs to steep another minute or so."

"No problem."

Theodosia poured tea, served lunch, cleared dishes, and stayed generally busy for the next hour or so. Then, when there were only two tables lingering over their tea and chocolate macarons, she moseyed back to the front counter.

"Today was fairly easy," she said to Drayton. "But tomorrow we've got our Rhapsody in Blue Tea, and then we're catering the Maritime History Seminar at the Heritage Society."

"And Saturday is our Murder Mystery Tea, the Murder at Chillingham Manor," Drayton said. "So it's going to be tight."

"It's always tight," Theodosia said. From the moment she'd refurbished the quaint little building on Church Street, she'd dealt with tight budgets and tight timelines. Which led to running a tight ship. Nothing was wasted; nothing was taken for granted. Which meant Theodosia, Drayton, and Haley operated like a well-oiled machine to take care of most everything—morning teatime, luncheons, afternoon tea, tea blending, retailing, and catering. On days when they were super stretched, Miss Dimple, their octogenarian bookkeeper, came in to help.

"Uh-oh," Drayton said. "We've got another customer peering in our window. Coming in from the rain and cold, I guess."

Theodosia spun around to look. "I think that's . . ."

Jesse Trumbull, the public information officer, suddenly burst through the front door, letting in a gush of damp air. He looked around, smiled as his eyes landed on Theodosia, and said, "Ah, there's a familiar face."

Theodosia cocked a finger at him and said, "Jesse . . . ?"

She was still fishing for his last name when he said, "Trumbull. Your friendly neighborhood public information officer. We spoke last night when I was here as part of the law enforcement scrum. And I daresay I've been fixated on your delicious scones ever since." He pantomimed a pat on his stomach. "Which is why I've come back. To hopefully grab some tea and scones to help keep me fortified." He looked around. "You do that, right?"

"Another candidate for takeout?" Drayton asked. "We not only love doing takeout; we do it in an infinite variety of ways. Fact is, I'm just brewing a fresh pot of Chinese Keemun. Might you be interested?"

"I am as long as its chockablock loaded with caffeine to keep me running at top speed," Trumbull said.

"So what exactly does a public information officer do?" Drayton asked as he poured tea into one of their indigo blue take-out cups. "Gets word out to the public?"

"To be honest, it's more about directing critical information to the media," Trumbull said.

Drayton snapped on a white lid and slid the cup across the

counter. "By *critical information* you mean the law enforcement version of what happened?"

Trumbull gave a lopsided grin. "Something like that, yeah." He glanced at Theodosia as he lifted a hand and pointed at Drayton. "Hey, this guy is good."

"So are you," Theodosia said. "That press release you wrote last night obviously went zinging through the ozone. Every TV and radio station seems to have picked it up."

"Newspapers, too," Drayton added.

"That's the job I've been hired to do," Trumbull said.

"You've always been a PR guy?" Theodosia asked.

"Kind of. I started out at a small PR firm over in Goose Creek, just handling a few local clients. You know, Realtors, lawyers, a radio station. Then I moved to Gainesville, Florida, where I worked on a newspaper. That was straight-ahead news reporting with the occasional feature story sprinkled in. Now I'm back in PR again. Well, media relations anyway."

"Theo used to do PR," Drayton said.

"Oh yeah?" Trumbull said. "Very cool. Say, thanks for last night, guys. It was kind of you to let us use your tea shop."

"You needed a command center that was dry and warm," Theodosia said. "We were happy to oblige. And I do have a personal interest in this case."

Trumbull's phone played a musical riff. He pulled it out of his jacket pocket, glanced at it, frowned, and said, "Oops, gotta bounce."

"Don't forget your scones!" Theodosia said, grabbing for one of their blue bags. "Let me package up a couple of scones for you."

"Thank you," Trumbull said as he watched her work. "And I do understand your interest in this case, so I'll try to keep you in the loop." He winked. "I mean, I can't give you precise details, but maybe I can kind of nudge things your way."

"That would be great," Theodosia said. "I'd really appreciate it." She tossed two more scones into the bag and handed it to him. "For the road."

Trumbull grinned. "Oh yum."

Haley had put together an afternoon tea special of cherry almond streusel scones with Devonshire cream and a fruit cup, so that's what they were serving to their customers when Bill Glass came schlumping in.

Glass was the brash, annoying publisher of a local tabloid known as *Shooting Star.* He was also the bane of Theodosia's existence because he pretended to be her friend while constantly ruffling her feathers.

Glass sidled up to the counter where Theodosia and Drayton were busy working. He was in his mid-forties, a little stocky, dark-haired, and had the hyped-up demeanor of a used-car salesman.

Drayton glanced up, saw Glass, and said, "What is this, Grand Central Station?"

Theodosia chuckled, while Glass took that as an invitation to launch a string of complaints.

"There's a reporter in town who's been tramping all over my turf and totally disrespecting me," Glass announced in what was definitely not his indoor voice.

Theodosia didn't have the heart to tell Glass that no one in Charleston respected him. That Glass was strangely similar to Bob Basset, except that Glass's stock-in-trade was local gossip and scandal. Who was divorcing whom? What nouveau riche social climber had been turned down by the board of the Snee Farm Country Club? Who overspent on a lavish party? What poor slob got hammered at one of the local watering holes and made a complete fool of himself?

Instead Theodosia said, "You're referring to Bob Basset?"

"The Basset Hound, yeah. What a colossal creep," Glass said. "I crossed paths with him at the police station this morning. He was sniffing around, asking questions nonstop. A total jerk." He smiled at her. "What do you know about him?"

"He was just here. Asking questions."

Glass's face twisted into an unhappy frown and he slammed a hand down on the counter, making the lid on a china teapot jump and clatter. "I hope you didn't tell him anything."

Theodosia just shrugged. Sometimes, with Glass, there were no words.

"You see what I mean!" Glass cried. "Coming in here, invading my turf, trying to obliterate it."

"Somehow I doubt that," Theodosia said coolly.

"Hey, it's your turf, too. A little bird told me you witnessed the murder last night. That you found the body."

"Only in an accidental sort of way."

"So what did you tell Basset? Concerning the murder?"

"Basically nothing," Theodosia said.

"Good girl. I *knew* you'd be loyal to me." Glass whipped a pen and paper from the pocket of his shabby photographer's vest. "So whatcha got? Gimme the scoop."

"I don't have anything and there is no scoop."

Glass looked supremely disappointed. "But you were *there*. As a prime *witness*. That's the grade A scuttlebutt I'm hearing all over town."

"I had the misfortune to come hurrying down a path and not quite interrupt a murder. But it was dark as pitch and pouring rain. I barely saw anything at all."

"Not even the killer?"

Theodosia thought of the faceless man with rain dripping off his hood. Yes, she had a general impression of him. But a detailed description? No way. She shook her head.

"So you got nothin'?" Glass asked.

"I'm afraid there's no more information to be had," Drayton said, stepping in. "So here's a cup of tea for you to drink on the go." He slid one of their take-out cups across the counter.

"Go? You want me to leave?" Glass asked.

Drayton's smile was almost imperceptible. "If you would. We're awfully busy."

"Now I'm really depressed," Glass said. "In fact, I've been worried lately that I might even be *clinically* depressed."

"You've been feeling down?" Theodosia asked. Maybe the man truly needed help.

"Yeah, 'cause there aren't any good stories. This murder—this is the first one in a long time."

Theodosia's sympathy drained away. "Brightened your day, did it?"

"You betcha," Glass said.

Drayton let loose a not-so-delicate snort.

Once Glass finally took off, Theodosia and Drayton tended to their afternoon customers. And as the day wore on, and Theodosia had a few free moments, she restocked the shelves of her two highboys with tins of tea, jars of Dubose Bees Honey, and some of her proprietary T-Bath products.

"I've decided to create a special tea blend," Drayton said when Theodosia wandered back to the counter. "I'm going to call it Hello Spring, as a kind of psychic inducement to hurry up what should be our lovely spring weather."

Theodosia glanced out the front window and saw rain still spattering down. "We could use a little positive juju. So tell me, what's your magic blend?"

"Green tea blended with hints of peach and ginger."

"Sounds yummy. But maybe you should call it Hurry Up Spring."

Drayton nodded. "Good one. Oh, and I think we should package our Hello Spring tea in those pretty yellow tea tins we bought a while back but never used."

"So let's do it." Theodosia tilted her head to one side, trying to stretch out the tension in her neck. "You know, all that information you gave me this morning about the Fogheel Jack character of seven years ago has got me wondering."

"Indeed?" Drayton said.

"I've been spinning all sorts of what-if scenarios in my head."

"That doesn't sound good."

"Maybe not, but I'm ravenously curious. If you can handle things here, I'd like to run over to the library and see if I can dig up a little more background information."

Drayton pursed his lips. "You're trying to ascertain if it's really the same person who's come back to haunt us." It was a statement, not a question.

"I suppose I am."

"All I have to say is please be careful."

Theodosia shrugged. "It's a trip to the library, Drayton, not a ride along with a SWAT team."

Drayton cocked a knowing eye at her. "With you they could end up being one and the same."

7

Nobody had written a book about Fogheel Jack. And, in going
through the library's catalog files, Theodosia couldn't find any
mention of him in books that detailed strange crimes (there were
many!) that had taken place in and around Charleston.

But she did discover several old *Charleston Post and Courier*
articles available on microfiche.

Just as Drayton had said, a strange meteorological phenome-
non had occurred seven years ago. Fog had drifted in, practically
blotting out the sky, then stuck around for almost a week. That's
when the two murders—both strangulations—had taken place.
And that's when one of the newspaper's crime reporters had
dubbed the killer "Fogheel Jack." Because the murders had been
similar in nature, the police were convinced they'd been committed by the same man. Suspects were questioned, a multitude of
tips poured in, and the police followed up on hundreds of leads.
Yet no one was ever arrested and charged. Charleston residents
had waited with bated breath for a third murder to take place,
but it never happened.

Not until now, Theodosia thought. *Now this same killer could be back.*

She dug through the rest of the old articles.

One of the victims had worked at a bakery in North Charleston and was strangled in the back alley as she was leaving for the day, her bag of almond croissants left strewn on the ground. The other victim had been a commercial Realtor who'd been found strangled in an empty building over on Huger Street. Her body had been there for several days.

Had these women been watched? Stalked and then lured to their deaths? Was that what was happening now?

The notion gave her chills. It meant nobody was safe. That today's killer—possibly the same one from seven years ago—was back in Charleston, moving about freely, biding his own sweet time.

But if it was the same killer—the same Fogheel Jack—why had he stopped killing seven years ago? Where had he disappeared to? Did he simply vanish into thin air? Did he move away from Charleston and resume his demonic hobby in a different city? Or maybe he'd been doing a stint in prison for another crime he'd committed and had just been released.

In any case, he's back now, Theodosia thought as she left the library. *Now he's back and has already killed twice. And, doggone it, but this monster is good at it!*

Rain pattered down as Theodosia hurried down Meeting Street. Head hunched forward, walking at a fast clip, she almost missed the little shop that was the Spice Bin. She stopped, gazed in the front window at an enticing display of spices and olive oils. Thought about stopping in to buy some fresh-ground cinnamon. Haley always loved sprinkling plenty of cinnamon into her sweet roll dough.

That's when an evil crackle sounded and a bolt of lightning

shot across the leaden sky. Glancing up, Theodosia caught sight of the jagged lightning bolt as well as a large white sign hanging from the second story of the building. The sign featured an ornately designed *O* with an abundance of curlicues, and then blocky black type that said SKYLOFTS FROM THE LOW 600's. COMING SOON FROM ORLOCK DEVELOPMENT.

Orlock. Theodosia knew that was the name of the developer who'd been putting pressure on Lois's landlord. A developer who was probably quite unhappy about Lois being locked into a nice long lease.

But what if this developer—Orlock—wanted to move fast? What if he was willing to hurry things along?

What could possibly motivate Lois to have a change of heart? To close her bookshop for good and terminate the lease?

A death in the family?

Theodosia stared at her reflection in the window of the Spice Bin. Orlock was a faint possibility. Still, he was a possibility.

"Ho," Drayton said when Theodosia walked into the tea shop. "So you did come back. I was just about to lock up. Did you find what you were looking for at the library?"

"Did I ever." She waved a handful of paper. "I basically researched the two murders from seven years ago. Printed out as many of the old articles as I could find."

His right hand crept up to his bow tie. "So gruesome."

"No kidding. Drayton . . ." Theodosia was so excited she was practically breathless. "From what I could tell, the murders are almost identical."

"You mean the two from seven years ago and the two that just occurred?"

"Yes!"

"Well, that's not good." Drayton studied her carefully, as if she were a museum object. "Why don't you look scared? Why aren't you locking the doors and pulling down the shades?"

"I am. I will."

"No, you're into this. I can tell."

"Maybe."

He let loose a sigh. "There's no 'maybe' about it."

Theodosia glanced around the tea shop. The tables had been wiped clean, the floors swept, all the dishes put away. Nothing for her to do. Except keep investigating. She'd found some basic information, she'd been an eyewitness last night, so . . .

"Where's Haley?" she asked.

Drayton jerked his head. "Upstairs. Hunkered in with Teacake. I think she's feeling nervous."

"That's understandable. We should all be a little wary. When disaster strikes this close to home it's unsettling. Sends a message that none of us are truly safe."

"I hope you don't really believe that," Drayton said. He reached out, grabbed the phone after one single, loud ring. Listened carefully for a moment, then handed it to Theodosia. *"Pour vous."*

"Hello?" she said.

It was Pete Riley. "Good," he said. "Glad I caught you."

"Something wrong? You're still coming over for dinner tonight, aren't you?" Theodosia was anxious to pump him for details.

"Apologies, but there's been a change in plans. I can no longer grace your table with my presence because a special task force meeting has been called."

"There's a task force? You mean on this Fogheel Jack thing?"

"Yes. Though I wish people would stop calling him that."

A task force struck Theodosia as a good thing. It meant the

police were treating these Fogheel Jack murders with the utmost seriousness and dedication. Maybe, hopefully, even zeroing in on a suspect.

"Did something happen to warrant this special meeting? Has there been some kind of breakthrough?"

"No and no," Riley said. "We've got a few balls spinning in the air but nothing concrete and certainly nothing I can share with you. Concerning our dinner, I really am sorry."

"Shoot. And I was going to whip up that she-crab soup you like so much."

"And corn muffins to go along?"

"And your favorite wine. The Zinfandel from Sonoma. Yup, that would've been the package deal," Theodosia said.

"Oh man, disappointment strikes hard. Please tell me there lurks the possibility of a rain check?"

"Considering the weather, I'd say it's more than likely."

"Kisses, then; you're the absolute best."

"Take care. Hope something good comes out of your meeting."

"Fingers crossed always," Riley said.

Theodosia was about to hang up when she said, "Wait . . . Riley? You'd tell me, right? If there was something new on the Cara Chamberlain case?"

"Um . . . maybe. Why?"

"Because I've got a vested interest in this," Theodosia said. "Because I was *there*."

"But I thought you didn't actually *see* anything. That it was dark and the guy's face was hidden in shadows."

Yes, but I did get a general impression. So maybe if I saw the same . . .

"You're right," Theodosia said abruptly. "I didn't see anything. Talk soon, okay?"

"Okay."

Drayton gazed at Theodosia over the top of his tortoiseshell reading glasses. "Everything okay?" He'd been going over the day's receipts.

"Yes and no."

"You look like you're pondering something important."

"I've been thinking about Wyatt Orlock, the real estate developer. Wondering if he put pressure on Lois to get out of her lease."

"Pressure," Drayton said, as if he was testing the word. "What do you mean exactly?"

"If there was a death in the family . . ."

Drayton looked horrified. "That would be a hideous thing to do! To kill someone's child—or have them murdered—just so you could move ahead with a commercial real estate deal." He said the words *commercial real estate* like he was referring to donkey poop.

"Skylofts from the low six hundreds," Theodosia said. "Probably twenty units in the building. We're talking twelve million dollars right there. People have been killed for considerably less money than that."

"I suppose you're right."

"I know I'm right."

Drayton shook his head. "I don't know anything about the man except to occasionally see his name in the Business section."

"Wyatt Orlock also owns that new club called Sparks over on Market Street."

"A club?" A frown danced across Drayton's face. "I don't frequent clubs. They're noisy and I'm unfamiliar with today's music."

"It's not that kind of club," Theodosia said.

"What kind is it?"

"A poser club. More like a bistro with lots of drinking and occasional music events."

"That sounds awful, too," Drayton said.

"I know, but I'm curious about this Mr. Orlock. In fact, I'd like to know a bit more about him. So what I'm thinking is . . . why don't we stop by Sparks for a drink?"

"Now? Tonight?"

Theodosia grinned. "Think of it as your one big burst of spontaneity for the week."

8

They did stop at Sparks for a drink. Drayton was a tad reluctant, but after Theodosia promised him a ride home, he finally agreed. After all, it was still pouring rain.

Sparks turned out to be cute and funky with a Caribbean cottage vibe. The dining room was light and airy, with linen slipcovered chairs, lots of leafy green plants, overhead paddle fans, and white shutters. The bar was clubby and had an Old Havana atmosphere. Dark and moody with antique brick walls and heart pine floors. There were rum barrels scattered around, displays of cigar boxes, and straw fedoras and flamenco guitars hung on the walls. Instead of cocktail tables there were high tables with stools clustered around them. All very conducive for singles to mingle.

When Theodosia and Drayton sat down at the bar, the bartender, a cheerful round-faced man in his late twenties, set coasters in front of them and said, "It's happy hour, folks. Which means all well drinks are four dollars and tonight's special is a Drunken Monkey."

"Excuse me?" Drayton said.

"That's orange juice, pineapple juice, two kinds of rum, lime . . ."

Drayton held up a hand to stop the bartender's jovial soliloquy. "Perhaps you also have a wine list?"

The bartender fumbled around and produced a small laminated card. "Here you go, short and sweet."

"Hopefully that doesn't describe the wine as well," Drayton murmured under his breath. He scanned the list, frowned, finally said, "Under the circumstances, I'd say this Barolo might be acceptable."

So that's what they ordered.

"Not bad," Drayton said, once he'd tasted his wine. "Though it does need to breathe a bit more. Preferably until next Thursday."

"Drayton." There was a note of caution in Theodosia's voice.

"What?"

"Be nice. After all, we're here on a fact-finding mission."

"And I thought we were supposed to be having fun."

They settled in and talked for a while, munched some of the free fire-roasted peanuts that the bartender put out. Then, when the bar was filled and buzzing with a mostly after-work crowd, Theodosia lifted a hand and said, "Excuse me," to the bartender.

He raised his eyebrows. "Another bottle?"

"Actually, I was hoping to say hello to your owner," Theodosia said. "Wyatt Orlock?"

The bartender gazed around, nodded, and said, "You're in luck. He's actually here tonight. He's, um . . ." He looked past her shoulder. "Sitting right over there."

Theodosia turned to look.

"With those two young ladies." The bartender couldn't help but smirk.

"Thank you," Theodosia said.

They watched for a few minutes, saw the two young blond women shake their heads, then get up and leave.

"Timing?" Drayton said.

"Couldn't ask for better," Theodosia said.

They picked up their wineglasses and headed for Orlock's table. He was talking on his phone now, jabbering away to someone named Ollie who was supposed to have supervised the installation of some drywall but hadn't. Orlock carped for a few more minutes, then hung up.

"Hello," Theodosia said pleasantly. Drayton, standing behind her, nodded.

Orlock stared at her as if trying to place her. He was in his mid-fifties and skinny, a brooding type with a slight comb-over of his dark hair. His suit was a Canali sharkskin and he wore a gold Rolex the size of an alarm clock on his left wrist.

"Hi," Orlock said finally. Not friendly, but not unfriendly, either. Cautious.

Theodosia sat down on the stool that had been vacated by one of the blondes. "My friend and I . . ." She indicated Drayton, who remained standing. "We wanted to meet you and tell you how much we enjoy your new club."

"Thank you," Orlock said. He was drinking a martini, straight up, with two olives floating in it like specimens in a jar.

"We also noticed that you're developing some condos in the area," Drayton pitched in helpfully.

"The skylofts, yeah," Orlock said, suddenly brightening. "They're going to be super luxurious. Panoramic views of Charleston Harbor, a porte cochere into the garage, roof deck, concierge service, Botticino marble bathrooms, Miele appliances, plus a fitness center. First-class all the way."

"And your skylofts will be ready when?" Theodosia asked.

"We'll be opening our sales center next week," Orlock said.

"Do you have a move-in date?" Theodosia asked.

"Why?" Orlock asked. "Are you interested?"

Not one to let a good opening line go by, Theodosia said,

"Funny you should ask. I am interested. But not in the way you think."

Orlock leaned forward. "Excuse me?"

"I understand you're trying to buy a building on Church Street. To complete your real estate package."

"So?"

"My friend Lois Chamberlain has her bookstore in that building."

"And?" A touch of defiance now.

"I'd hate to think that anyone was trying to force her out of her lease."

"Lady, what I do or don't do is none of your business."

"Oh, but it is," Theodosia said. "Especially if you use any kind of force or scare tactics on her."

"You're barking up the wrong tree." Now Orlock's tone was brusque to the point of rudeness. "I have people, accountants and lawyers, who deal with those types of details." He gripped the table and stood up so quickly his knees popped. "I'm the money guy, the big-picture guy. I don't worry about . . . what was your friend's name again?"

"Lois Chamberlain."

"Like I was saying, I don't worry about Miss Nobody Bookseller interfering in my business." And with that he turned and walked out of the bar.

They watched him go.

"I'd say Orlock's got about as much charm as a puff adder," Drayton said.

"The kind of guy you'd characterize as slippery when dry," Theodosia said.

"Shall we pay the tab and take off? If you were looking for a personality assessment, short of coercing Orlock into taking an MMPI test, I'm guessing you found what you came for."

"Sure. But I want to ask the bartender something."

As Theodosia was signing her credit card slip, she said, "How is Orlock to work for?"

The bartender stared at her. "You really want to know?"

"Please," Theodosia said.

"He's . . . wait a minute. He just walked back in."

Theodosia glanced over and saw Orlock talking to a tall, skinny guy in a black leather jacket. The man had a long face with high cheekbones and listened intently as Orlock gestured with his hands.

"Who's Orlock talking to?" she asked.

"That's Frank Lynch, head of security."

"You need security here?"

The bartender shrugged. "Orlock seems to think so. Anyway, you were asking about working conditions . . ."

Theodosia leaned forward, eager to hear what he had to say.

"It's sure no picnic. Orlock yells at the help, withholds tips, and harasses the female servers." The bartender shook his head. "That guy . . . he's a total jerk."

They drove down Archdale Street, the windshield wipers on Theodosia's Jeep beating time to the rain, tires hissing as they splashed through the occasional puddle.

"Heat," Theodosia said, fiddling with the dial. "We need heat."

"And the defroster," Drayton said. "We're fogging up."

"That's because we're talking."

"And breathing."

Drayton gazed out the front window. "Even though it's cool and rainy, this neighborhood's still lovely at night, don't you think? The rain makes everything appear soft-focus and ethereal."

"Makes all the big homes look cozy," Theodosia agreed. As they drove along they couldn't help but catch yellow glints of light through softly draped windows that revealed elegant dining rooms, libraries, and formal parlors.

"Orlock," Drayton said, tapping his fingers against the dashboard. "Where have I heard that name before? It sounds so familiar. I must look it up when I get home."

"Maybe the family is from Charleston?"

"No, I think it's something else. But darned if I can remember what."

"Here you go," Theodosia said, pulling to the curb in front of Drayton's house. Like Theodosia, he owned a small home in the Historic District, a 160-year-old brick stunner that had once belonged to a Civil War doctor. Now it had been updated, decorated to the nines with French and English antiques, and featured a Japanese garden out back where his bonsai collection resided.

"Door-to-door service," Drayton said. "Thank you kindly."

"And look there, I see that your faithful companion is peeking out the front window."

"Honey Bee," Drayton said, smiling at his Cavalier King Charles spaniel as she sat atop a plump sofa waiting for him.

"Does your dog realize that she won the golden ticket when you rescued her?" Theodosia asked. "That instead of living life as a stray and eating out of garbage pails, she's now snarfing down chopped tenderloin on Spode china plates?"

Drayton smiled as he pushed open the door and stepped out. "Don't you know it's impolite to talk about a lady's background?"

Since it was still early—well, eight thirty anyway—Theodosia decided to stop at Cara's apartment and grab the notebook Lois had mentioned.

She checked the address, figured she could find it with minimum effort, and drove down Wentworth to Ashley Avenue. Taking a guess, right or left, she headed left past Olive's Consignment

Shop, a martial arts studio, and Key Fitness, where people on stationary bikes were quickly going nowhere.

Theodosia found she'd guessed correctly. The block where Cara lived was a combination of Charleston single houses and small plantation-style homes. With few streetlamps and not many houses lit, it looked almost like a charcoal sketch.

Pulling up in front of Cara's apartment, she saw that it was an oversized single house that had been broken up into several small apartments.

So where is Cara's unit?

After checking apartment numbers and hunting around, Theodosia determined she had to follow a brick path that ran alongside the building, then step into a small screened porch at the very back.

Okay, here we go.

Theodosia stuck her key in the door, pushed it open, and fumbled for the light switch.

The place wasn't just small; it was minuscule, a studio apartment in the strictest sense of the word. The bed doubled as a sofa by virtue of a blue-and-green-plaid coverlet and a half dozen square plush pillows. A small kitchenette was set against the far wall with a two-burner stove, mini fridge, and small sink. The rest of the place was minimally furnished with a small metal desk and jumbled bookcase crammed in next to it.

Closing the door behind her, Theodosia took the grand tour even though there wasn't much to see. The hand-me-down furnishings, two director's chairs folded and stashed in a corner, and just off the kitchenette, a bathroom (shower but no tub) and small closet jammed with clothing. Definitely student-type digs.

Theodosia headed for the desk and sat down in a wobbly gray task chair. A laptop sat on top of the desk along with a pile of unopened mail, a scatter of take-out menus, and a flyer advertising an upcoming amateur production of *Cats* at the State Theater.

She pawed around and found Cara's notebook sitting beneath all the papers.

So far, so good.

And then, because Theodosia was definitely a curious sort, she decided to thumb through the notebook right then and there.

It wasn't so much a notebook as a kind of scrapbook. There were clippings, magazine articles, photos, computer printouts, handwritten jottings, and note cards.

Cara, bless her soul, had been both creative and imaginative. She'd made copious notes on news stories that she wanted to pitch. A planned artificial reef to help curb shoreline erosion. A story about a new Black theater company that would be performing at this year's Spoleto. A piece about medical marijuana possibly being legalized in South Carolina. Even notes on a new microbrewery called Taylor's Twist.

Theodosia skimmed the two cards that had slid out of the notebook when she first picked it up. One from Mazie Barnard, her roommate at the University of North Carolina, another from a guy named Tim Holt with the message *See you soon!* and an old *Far Side* cartoon enclosed.

Ten pages into the notebook, Theodosia hit pay dirt. Here were Cara's notes on Fogheel Jack. Much as she herself had done, Cara had researched the two killings from seven years ago. And had also amassed newspaper articles that detailed last week's university murder. She'd scribbled her thoughts and ideas as well. *Local? Single? Meets women in bars?* Then the note *Check local online dating sites* caught her eye.

Theodosia desperately hoped that Cara hadn't done exactly that.

But what if she had? What if Cara had accidentally-on-purpose made contact with a man who'd been actively hunting for his next victim?

Theodosia set the book down, put both hands to her face, and rubbed her eyes. No, she wouldn't let herself conjure such a ghastly scenario. She couldn't.

Closing the book, she spun around in the chair. And that's when she saw the bouquet of half-wilted flowers sitting on the kitchen counter next to a yellow dish drainer.

Theodosia had seen the flowers before and dismissed them. This time she walked over and stared at them. Dark red roses, almost burgundy in color, which were now drooping and tinged with black. The water in the glass vase was green and gloppy, and a small white envelope lay next to it on the ugly pink Formica counter. The envelope was half-open, with a card inside.

Holding her breath, Theodosia pulled out the card and read it. It said, *From your secret admirer.*

Theodosia's blood ran cold as she dropped the card. The tiny hairs on the back of her neck prickled and stood straight up.

Oh no!

9

※

Theodosia's brain was spinning like a centrifuge. Had Cara actually made contact with Fogheel Jack? Had they somehow connected online and then communicated back and forth? And met in person? And, dear Lord, who had initiated that first contact? Cara or Fogheel Jack?

This was big. Big like she had to tell the police. So big that they had to get a Crime Scene team over to this apartment immediately!

Theodosia pulled out her phone to call Riley. He'd know what to do, how to handle what had gone from doing a simple favor for Lois to an unsettling and bizarre situation.

She was about to dial when a faint noise caught her attention. She hesitated.

What was it? Something at the window? A *tick-tick-tick* like a branch rubbing against it?

Or was someone trying to jimmy the screen off with a screwdriver? Hoping to worm their way in.

Heart pounding out of her chest, Theodosia scurried around like a crazed banshee, turning on every light she could find in the apartment. Then she ran outside, probably besting the time of an Olympic sprinter. Once she was safely sitting inside her Jeep, doors locked and engine running, she made her call.

Thank goodness Riley picked up on the third ring.

"Hey," he said. "Didn't I tell you not to call me at the office?"

"Riley! This is important!"

"I'm kidding. We just broke for a fast fifteen and I'm standing in the hallway feeding quarters into our department's demonic coffee machine. Wondering what level of heartburn I can tolerate this time of night."

"Riley, I found something." Theodosia's voice was almost but not quite shaking.

"What?" he said quietly. "Tell me."

So Theodosia quickly told him. About getting the key from Lois, stopping by Cara's apartment, looking around, reading her notebook, and finding the flowers and the note.

"You said you're sitting in your car right now. Do you feel safe?" Riley asked.

Theodosia squirmed in her seat, looking out at the dark street. Nobody there. No cars moving, no people out walking, not even a stray cat ambling down the sidewalk. Just a faint mist all around her. "I think so. I'm locked in my car and I don't see a single soul."

"That's good. Keep your engine running so you can make a fast getaway if you start to feel nervous. But if you can manage it, I'd like you to sit tight."

"Are you coming?"

"Running down the hallway even as we speak, sweetheart. Bringing reinforcements."

"Please hurry."

Riley did hurry. Showed up in under five minutes with an entire cadre of law enforcement. Theodosia ran through her story once

again for the entire group, then watched, half-amused, as they
scattered and rushed inside. Only Riley remained, standing in
the street as she sat in her Jeep.

"This journal you mentioned," Riley said.

"More like a scrapbook," Theodosia said.

"It's inside?"

"Sitting on the desk where I found it. And left it."

"But you touched it? Your prints are on it?" Riley asked.

"Probably."

"That's okay," Riley said. "You did good."

"You mean because I called you?"

"Because you stayed chill under duress."

"Tried to anyway."

"You've had a crazy couple of days."

"Tell me about it," Theodosia said.

"Why don't you take off now and let us handle things. Go
home and hang out with your pooch. Give him an ear tug for
me." Riley peered at her. "You're sure you're going to be okay?"

"I'm okay now," Theodosia said. She was feeling a little shaky,
but nothing she couldn't work herself out of. "Oh, and you're going to need this." She handed him the key on the pink ribbon.
"So you can lock up afterward."

"Thanks," Riley said. He leaned in the driver's side window
and gave her a gentle kiss on the lips. Said once again, "You did
good."

Theodosia had never been so happy in her life to be home. She
let herself into the kitchen through the back door, then spread
her arms wide as Earl Grey came hurtling toward her. He jumped
up, halfway knocking her down, and delivered a big slobbery
kiss.

My second kiss tonight. How lovely.

She rubbed Earl Grey's muzzle, worked her way back to his ears, then segued into a quick tummy rub as the dog slid down onto the floor and rolled over, paws in the air.

"You're a good guy. A good guard dog," she told him. "You keep me safe."

Earl Grey gave her an upside-down grin, then managed a fast barrel roll that landed him on all fours. He was a good-sized boy, a mix of dalmatian and Labrador, with a fine, aristocratic muzzle, expressive eyes, slightly mottled coat, and a clever dog's sense of humor.

"Long day, huh?" Theodosia said. "Good thing Mrs. Barry came by." Mrs. Barry was Earl Grey's nanny and dog walker, a retired schoolteacher who had a knack for handling the neighborhood dogs, sometimes walking them three and four at a time.

"Long day for me, too," she told him. Then gazed around her newly refurbished kitchen. It had finally come together with Carolina pine cabinets, a ceramic tile floor, and a new Wolf range that Haley had helped her pick out.

The rest of her home made Theodosia feel happy and welcome as well. A few years ago she'd bought this small, cozy cottage that bore the charming name of Hazelhurst. It was tucked between two much grander homes, mansions really, and was built in the Queen Anne tradition, also known as Hansel and Gretel style. Which meant the exterior brick and stucco walls featured an asymmetrical design, and cedar shingles replicated a thatched roof. There was also an arched front door, a blip of a two-story turret, and wooden cross gables. Curls of lush green ivy meandered up the sides of the house. The interior was just as lovely, with pegged wood floors, fireplace, leaded windows, and chintz-covered furniture.

"Rrowr?" Earl Grey was staring at her, anxiously wagging his tail.

"You want to go out for a quick spin?"

"Yowwr." He shook himself, nose to tail, everything in motion at once.

"Okay, why not." Theodosia ran upstairs, did a quick change into workout gear and tennis shoes, then grabbed a leash and was out the back door with Earl Grey beside her. They sped through her back garden, danced past a small pond where goldfish floated, and exited the back gate.

Yes, she'd been somewhat shaken up, but with every step she began to feel more relaxed and stronger. Matching her dog's long strides, Theodosia jogged two blocks, did two more blocks for good measure, turned down Longitude Lane, circled around Rainbow Row, and headed back in the direction of home.

That didn't mean Theodosia wasn't mindful of her surroundings. It was dark, so she knew that an alley, a shadow, even a parked car, could serve as a hiding place for the maniac known as Fogheel Jack. Or did the man only come out when the fog started rolling in?

She looked around as she ran almost soundlessly. It was misting lightly, but the atmosphere wasn't so dense that you'd call it fog. Not like last night. Besides, she was moving fast and had Earl Grey along to hopefully scare off any strangers. Of course, Riley's brain would probably explode if he knew she was out here running through the dark streets.

Finally slowing their pace, Theodosia and Earl Grey turned down their alley. Just ahead of them, parked behind the Granville Mansion, was a dark green Jaguar XJ. And a man was standing there unloading something—manuscript boxes?—out of the car's rear cargo hold.

"That's a pretty fancy car," Theodosia said as they drew closer.

The man whirled about, clearly startled to hear a voice behind him. Then, when he saw Theodosia and Earl Grey standing there, when he registered they were probably harmless, he broke into a relieved smile.

"I'm guessing you must be one of my neighbors," the man said. He was fairly tall with wide shoulders and slim hips. He had longish brown hair, dark eyebrows, and a slightly crooked nose. He wore blue jeans and a faded green University of Miami Hurricanes sweatshirt that was almost the same color as his car.

"I'm Theodosia Browning from next door, yes. And you must be the author who's renting from Robert Steele."

"That's me. Nicholas Prince. Nick to my friends and, I guess, neighbors, of which you are clearly one."

"It's nice to finally meet you."

Prince gazed at Earl Grey. "And this handsome fellow is . . . ?"

"Earl Grey," Theodosia said.

"He looks like a fine guard dog."

"He often is. So. I understand you're writing a book on true crime?"

"Is that the neighborhood scuttlebutt?" Prince asked.

"I'm afraid so."

Prince stepped around the back of his car and smiled at Theodosia. "All I can say is I certainly arrived at an opportune time."

"How so?" Theodosia asked. She was fairly sure of what he was referring to and suddenly felt uncomfortable.

"The murders. The two strangulations." Prince poked a finger at his neck. "They're perfect fodder for my new book."

"I knew that young woman who was killed last night," Theodosia said, her words turning crisp and a trifle chilly. "She was the daughter of a good friend of mine."

"The bookstore lady?"

"You know Lois?"

"I've been to her bookstore anyway," Prince said. Then, "Wow, I'm sorry." He spread his arms wide in a gesture of contrition. "I didn't realize you had a connection. You must think I'm incredibly . . . insensitive."

"That did cross my mind."

"Please." Prince's brows furrowed deeply and his face sagged. "Allow me to apologize. As a writer who delves into murder, mayhem, and unsolved cases, I sometimes get a little carried away."

"Well . . ."

Prince put a hand out and Earl Grey nosed forward to sniff it.

"See? Your dog forgives me."

"Then I suppose we're cool."

Prince smiled. "A neighbor told me that you own that cute little tea shop over on Church Street, right?"

Theodosia nodded. "That's me. Stop by sometime." She was being polite but didn't really want to encourage Nick Prince. He seemed a little . . . weird.

Prince eyed her. "Maybe I'll do that. Say, you guys were just out for a run?"

"How do you figure that?" Theodosia asked. She was suddenly picking up vibes, vibes she didn't like.

"I've seen you and your dog ghost by my house a couple of times now. My rented house. You know, as you jogged down the alley."

"Ah." Theodosia supposed that explained things and decided to be a little more friendly. "Okay, have a nice night."

"You, too," Prince said, but Theodosia had already turned and was hurrying through her back gate.

Once inside, she put a kettle on the stove and let her mind wander while waiting for the water to heat. Thought about Nick Prince, the new guy in town. He was young, maybe early thirties, fairly good-looking. He probably hadn't had a chance to meet anyone yet, so he wasn't dating. On the other hand, he seemed more interested in dead women.

Definitely a little creepy.

Theodosia grabbed a teapot and tossed in a couple of scoops of organic chamomile tea. It was always conducive to relaxation and a good night's sleep. A few minutes later the teakettle let off a pouf of steam, then a low whistle began to build. Time to brew her tea.

Upstairs, in what Theodosia thought of as her sanctuary, she settled into the easy chair in her turret room to sip her tea. Then immediately changed her mind. *No, I'm tired. I'm going to crawl into bed.*

Her four-poster bed was a thing of joy. Good mattress, poufy cream-colored down comforter, and one too many pillows. She eased herself in, leaned back, and sighed. Perfection.

Right after she'd moved in, Theodosia had converted the small upstairs into one master suite—a combination bedroom, walk-in closet, master bath, and tower reading room. It was decorated, as she liked to say, in Southern Glam. That is, Laura Ashley wallpaper, several Baroque mirrors, and her mother's old-fashioned vanity. With its desk and drawers and cushioned stool, the vanity took up one wall and was the perfect spot for Theodosia to sit and apply makeup or brush her hair. Scattered atop the vanity were Theodosia's collectibles—perfume bottles by Chanel and Dior, leather-covered journal, ceramic box decorated with two jaguars that held her good pearl earrings, a large white bowl with scalloped edges that corralled her bracelets, cuffs, and a strand of pearls, and a Jo Malone candle.

Earl Grey settled into his dog bed and rested his head against one of the built-in bolsters. Theodosia sipped her tea, thought about the day, and slowly got drowsier.

Good. The chamomile's doing its thing.

She set her teacup on the nightstand, turned off the lamp, and closed her eyes. She was drifting off to sleep, floating happily, when a sudden brainstorm jolted her back to consciousness. Her eyes flew open and she sat straight up in bed.

Theodosia realized she knew the name of Cara's mystery boyfriend, the one Lois had known about but never met. It was Tim Holt. The guy who'd sent the card with the *Far Side* cartoon.

10

~✽~

"*You look like* the cat who swallowed the canary," Drayton said to Theodosia as he poured a cup of Fujian white tea for her.

It was Wednesday morning at the Indigo Tea Shop and they were gearing up for what was to be a particularly busy day. Their Rhapsody in Blue Tea was scheduled for noon; their afternoon catering gig at the Heritage Society started at three.

"That's because I have a secret," Theodosia said as she slipped a long black Parisian waiter's apron over her head and snugged the ties around her waist.

Drayton looked interested. "Please don't hold back."

"Actually two secrets."

Drayton studied her. "Okay."

"Turns out Cara Chamberlain might have had a previous connection to her killer."

"Whaaat?" Drayton's eyes bugged slightly and his voice rose a couple of octaves.

Theodosia explained how she'd gone to Cara's apartment last night, looking for the notebook Lois had told her about, then discovered all the background notes on Fogheel Jack. With the coup de grâce being the flowers and note from her secret admirer.

"The secret admirer being Fogheel Jack?" Drayton tugged at his bright-blue bow tie, almost whispering now.

"That's what I think and it's what the police think, too."

"So you *did* alert them?"

"I called Riley right away. Pretty much had to. He and his thundering herd came rushing over to take charge."

"So they're looking at Cara's notebook, the note from the secret admirer, and anything else that might turn up."

"Jumped right on it."

"Good. Now you don't have to be involved."

"Oh, but I do."

"No," Drayton said.

Theodosia stared at him. *Of course* she'd stay involved.

"Be honest," Drayton said. "Do you think what you did last night was smart? Tiptoeing into Cara's apartment all by your lonesome?"

Theodosia thought about the scratching she'd heard at the window. Just branches moving in the wind? Or someone trying to get in? Well, too late now. She'd rolled the dice and it had paid off. Maybe the note or the source of the flowers would lead to the killer.

"I probably should have asked you to go with me, but stopping at Cara's apartment seemed like a quickie errand I could handle on my way home."

"Mmn." Drayton thought for a few moments. "You mentioned two secrets. What's the other one?"

"I think I figured out who Cara's boyfriend was. A guy named Tim Holt."

"However did you discern that? Did the gods descend from Mount Olympus and whisper his name in your ear?"

"There was a card from him stuck in Cara's notebook."

"Of course there was." Drayton gave an expectant look. "So.

This boyfriend. Do you think he's the one who murdered her? Do you think this Holt fellow and Fogheel Jack are one and the same?"

Theodosia was taken aback by the directness of his question.

"No," she said. Then thought again. "Well, I don't *think* so. I mean, if they knew each other and had a *relationship*, why would Holt send flowers and claim to be a secret admirer?"

"A little game they played?" Drayton said.

"I suppose it's possible. Which is all the more reason for me to talk to this guy Holt. Get a read on him, see if he knew what Cara was up to."

"You think Holt will talk to you? I imagine the police are questioning him right about now."

Theodosia thought about the Crime Scene team going over Cara's apartment with a fine-tooth comb. Yes, they would undoubtedly make the connection and question Tim Holt. So . . . that was probably a good thing.

"I don't know if Holt will talk to me, Drayton," Theodosia said. "But I have to try. If only for Lois's sake."

The morning flew by then, with Drayton brewing tea, Theodosia waiting tables, and Haley fixing her usual adorable cream tea plates. This morning's special was an apricot scone served with Devonshire cream. Of course Haley had also baked cranberry scones and gingerbread muffins.

At ten thirty, an anxious-looking Miss Dimple flew through the front door. As their crackerjack bookkeeper for the last several years, Miss Dimple was often asked to help out at event teas. Today was one of those days.

"Good morning, good morning," Miss Dimple purred as she shrugged out of her cherry red raincoat and hung it on the brass coatrack in the entry. "It's still cats and dogs out there, though my darling Siamese babies probably wouldn't appreciate that particular metaphor."

"Top of the morning to you, dear lady," Drayton called to her.

"We appreciate your helping out," was Theodosia's greeting. "Because we're going to be super busy."

"Music to my ears," Miss Dimple said. She was an apple-cheeked eighty-something with a mop of pinkish hair and the disposition of a benevolent grandmother. "What would you like me to tackle first?"

"You can grab that pot of Indian spice tea off the counter and deliver it to table four," Theodosia said. "Then grab some more of Haley's apricot and cranberry scones to stick in the pie saver on the counter. After that we'll figure things out as we go."

"Works for me."

With Miss Dimple taking orders and pouring tea, Theodosia's stress level dropped a good twenty points. So she was able to chat with customers, hang her new grapevine wreaths (these were decorated with pink and green teacups and threaded with the same color ribbons), and restock her shelves with tins of Drayton's newly created house blends. He'd also made a Farmers Market Hibiscus, a hibiscus tea flavored with bits of lemon and apple, and one called Spring Grove Green, a green tea with notes of cherry and vanilla.

When Theodosia walked back to the front counter, Drayton glanced at her with a faraway gaze on his face.

"What?" she said. "Something wrong?"

Drayton touched an index finger to his temple and said, "I just remembered where I heard that name before."

"Which name?"

"Orlock."

"Where'd you hear it?" Theodosia was half listening to Drayton as she straightened a stack of indigo blue take-out bags.

"Do you remember that old black-and-white movie *Nosferatu?* Count Orlok was the name of the vampire."

"You're kidding. You think they're any relation?"

Drayton stared at her for a few seconds, then broke into a slow smile. "You think this is funny?"

"A little bit, sure."

"I find it eerie."

"You sound like Haley. She's always going on about ghosts and haunts."

"Probably because there's such a plethora of documented accounts concerning low-country hauntings."

"Trust me, there are no ghosts. Only enterprising guides who take willing tourists around our fair city on so-called ghost tours."

Theodosia was in her office, scanning the Internet to see if anything new had popped up about Fogheel Jack, when Monica Garber stormed into her office like an F5 tornado.

"The-o-*do*-sia!" Monica cried, as if they were long-lost friends, instead of a TV reporter sniffing around a potential source for a story.

Theodosia glanced up. "Hi, Monica." Today Garber wore a caramel-colored leather jacket snugged over shredded blue jeans and super-high snakeskin stilettos. "Where's the rest of your intrepid crew?"

"Sitting outside in the van, taking a much-needed break. We've been running ourselves ragged, following leads and working nonstop on this Fogheel Jack story." Garber paused to take a breath. "Guess who the number one person of interest is right now."

Theodosia blinked. Maybe Garber was more enterprising than she'd first suspected.

"The boyfriend?" Theodosia said, trying to keep her expression as neutral as possible.

Garber pointed a pink-lacquered index fingernail at Theodosia and nodded her approval.

"You are one smart girl. Oh yes, you are," she said in a staccato burst. "It's a guy named Tim Holt."

Theodosia was curious about Garber's source. "My guess was based on a few random rumors," she fibbed. "But how exactly did *you* figure this out?"

Garber preened. "I'd love to brag and say it's all smart investigative journalism on my part, but the fact of the matter is I found myself an inside man down at police headquarters." She dropped her voice to a stage whisper. "And he gave me the complete scoop!"

"Wow," Theodosia said, wondering who the leak was. One of Tidwell's men? Someone on the Crime Scene team? She hoped not.

"Anyway," Garber continued, "this Tim Holt is apparently an up-and-coming photographer. Does commercial work for local real estate companies, handles corporate projects and some weddings, too. He's not half-bad. In fact, Holt has a few of his photos in an exhibition that opens Friday at the Imago Gallery over on Queen Street."

"And your intentions are what?" Theodosia asked. "Interview Tim Holt or accuse him of murder?"

"Hah! If I can get him to go on camera with me—do a sort of impromptu interview—maybe I could accomplish both." Garber chortled at the idea.

"Maybe." But Theodosia figured that anyone who was savvy enough to commit two murders, maybe even four, was not about to blurt out a televised confession to help boost Monica's ratings.

Monica Garber's excitement continued to build. "I have to say, this Fogheel Jack thing is the biggest story I've ever covered. Do you know what this could mean for me? If I can get close to this story—I mean really close, maybe even help break it wide open—I'd garner serious national recognition. Then I could write my own ticket. I could even be a hop, skip, and a jump away from Fox News!"

Whoopee, was Theodosia's thought on that.

At eleven fifteen, with just two tables of morning guests lingering, Theodosia flew into event mode and began readying her tea shop for their Rhapsody in Blue luncheon tea.

"So we should use the white linen tablecloths?" Miss Dimple asked. She'd already pulled a stack from the highboy they used for storing linens.

"Topped with bright blue table runners," Theodosia told her.

Miss Dimple slid open the next drawer. "Got 'em."

"Then we'll set all the tables with blue-and-white china."

"The Blue Garland by Haviland or the Blue Fluted by Royal Copenhagen?" Miss Dimple had helped out so often she practically knew the patterns by heart.

"Let's go with the Blue Garland," Theodosia said. "And there are delphiniums and blue hydrangeas that Floradora dropped off this morning. They're sitting in pails of water back in my office, so we need to arrange those blooms in crystal vases for centerpieces."

"Pretty. What else do you have up your sleeve?" Miss Dimple grinned because she knew Theodosia was relentlessly creative when it came to her themed teas.

"I made photocopies of Gershwin's 'Rhapsody in Blue' sheet music, smudged the edges with gold paint, then rolled the pages up and tied them with pieces of blue velvet ribbon."

Miss Dimple clapped her hands together. "Perfection. Now, what about favors for the guests?"

"We've got sprigs of blue lavender compliments of Susan Monday, the Lavender Lady. I thought we'd wrap them with straw flowers and tie them on the back of each chair. And there are also little white soaps in blue net bags."

Miss Dimple eyed a few more pieces from Theodosia's china collection.

"What would you think about using the cobalt blue Depression glass butter dishes?"

"Go for it," Theodosia urged. She noticed Drayton answering a phone call and then nodding solemnly. He'd been humming along, brewing tea; now suddenly his demeanor had changed. He seemed thoughtful.

"What's wrong?" Theodosia asked as she wandered over.

"That was . . . Well, Cara's funeral has been scheduled for this Friday."

"We knew it was going to happen sooner or later. Where's the funeral going to be held?"

Drayton pursed his lips. "I don't know if this is serendipitous or a horrible coincidence."

"What are you talking about?"

"Her funeral's going to be just down the block from us at St. Philip's Church."

"Even though Cara was killed in the graveyard behind the church?" Theodosia touched a hand to her heart. "That's kind of weird."

"Tell me about it," Drayton said. He gazed out into the tea room, then shook his head as if to clear it. "Looks as if you've got everything shipshape."

"I think so."

"Blue," he said. "All blue. To complement a blue mood."

"Buck up, Drayton," Theodosia said. "We're going to figure out Cara's murder yet. We're going to track down the killer and hang a witch's hat around his neck."

Drayton gazed at her. "I have no idea what that means, but I think I like it."

11

Gershwin's "Rhapsody in Blue" played seductively over the sound system as the first luncheon guests arrived. Theodosia greeted them warmly, hung up their damp raincoats and umbrellas, and had Miss Dimple guide them to their seats.

As more guests arrived, more greetings and air-kisses ensued. Finally, Delaine Dish came flouncing in with her niece Bettina in tow.

Delaine claimed to be one of Theodosia's dearest friends, though she never missed a chance to correct or one-up her. On the plus side, Delaine was a consummate animal lover who raised copious amounts of money for Big Paws Service Dogs (of which Earl Grey was a card-carrying therapy dog member) and the Loving Paws Animal Shelter. Beneath Delaine's crusty, lusty exterior, she did possess a kind heart.

Today, her crusty outer shell was slathered in hot pink silk. As proprietor of Cotton Duck, one of Charleston's most upscale boutiques, Delaine never failed to indulge her love of fashion. Her pink jacket was nipped in at her tiny, almost nonexistent waist to accentuate her barely there hips. The skirt was daredevil short. And she wore pink silk heels (probably custom-dyed to match) and carried a trendy designer bag scattered with pink Gs.

"What do you think of my new outfit?" Delaine asked as she gave a little twirl. "*Très chic?*" Delaine's dark eyes glinted, her heart-shaped face suddenly crinkled into a smile.

"Very chic indeed," Theodosia agreed. It was always easier to see things Delaine's way.

"If you're interested, I have this exact same skirt suit in a gorgeous emerald green in a slightly larger size."

Theodosia smiled at the subtle dig.

"The green would be lovely with your auburn hair," Delaine purred as her eyes roved the tea room to see who'd taken notice of her theatrical entrance.

"I'm sure it would," Theodosia said. *Even though the outfit probably costs upwards of a thousand dollars. To pay for that I'd have to sell a truckload of scones.*

"Ooh," Delaine said, grabbing Theodosia's arm, "I have news. You remember my dear sister, Nadine? Bettina's mother?"

"Of course." How could she forget Nadine? She'd once tried to walk off with a handbag full of silverware.

"Nadine has a new business venture," Delaine said. "She's created her own line of athleisure clothing called Lemon Squeeze Couture. And it's going to debut in my store!"

"Actually, Mom is just one of a number of partners," Bettina said.

"Still, that's wonderful news," Theodosia said as she aimed a smile at Bettina, who was blond, adorable, and slim-hipped.

Even though Bettina was a recent graduate of New York's Fashion Institute of Technology, Delaine basically used her as slave labor in her shop.

"Are you going to be part of this new venture, too, Bettina?" Theodosia asked.

"I wish. But I'm still learning the ins and outs of retail marketing from Aunt Delaine," Bettina said.

"Dear," Delaine said. "Haven't I explained this ad nauseum? Calling me *aunt* sounds so fusty and arthritic."

Delaine turned to Theodosia and said, "Will you be coming to the vigil tomorrow night?"

"Vigil?" Theodosia said. This was the first she'd heard of any vigil.

"To honor and pray for the two women who've been murdered," Delaine said. "Cara and"—she shook her head—"that other one. I can't remember her name. Anyway, I helped organize the event."

Bettina coughed and poked an elbow into Delaine's ribs.

"Well, I *sort of* helped organize it," Delaine amended. "I put up a poster at Cotton Duck. I would have done more, but you know how terribly *busy* I am, what with all the new shipments of spring clothes." She rolled her eyes. "If spring ever arrives at all!"

When all the guests were seated, Theodosia took a deep breath and walked to the center of the room. This was her moment to shine, to bid everyone . . .

"Welcome to the Indigo Tea Shop," Theodosia said with great enthusiasm. "We're thrilled that you dodged your way through puddles and raindrops to attend our first ever Rhapsody in Blue Tea. In keeping with this blue-tinged theme, our first course will be blueberry scones served with Devonshire cream."

There was a spatter of applause, then Theodosia continued.

"Then we have three tea sandwiches du jour, which will be brought to your tables on lovely three-tiered stands. The first tea sandwich is blue cheese and organic honey on French bread, the second one is shrimp salad with tarragon on brioche, and our third tea sandwich is honeyed ham slathered with country mustard on rustic peasant bread. Your dessert—should you still be hungry—will be blueberry crumble with whipped cream."

"We'll still be hungry!" one woman called out.

"And what about the tea?" Delaine piped up.

"I was just getting to that," Theodosia said. "Better yet, I'll let Drayton, our tea sommelier, tell you all about it."

With that, Drayton stepped to the center of the tea room and executed a smart half bow. Everyone seemed to hush and listen closely as he projected his benevolent authority and tea know-how.

"Today's special tea blend will be our proprietary Earl Blue blend," Drayton said. "Which is to say a rich, fulsome Earl Grey tea, known for its robust flavor, and accented with delicate lavender blossoms."

"Sounds delightful!" a customer cried.

Drayton gave a quick smile. "Should anyone prefer a different blend of tea, be sure to let us know. As you can see by our ample assortment"—he waved a hand in the direction of his tea-laden shelves—"we can probably fulfill any tea fantasy you might have."

Theodosia and Drayton poured tea as Haley and Miss Dimple served the blueberry scones along with Devonshire cream.

"How do I slice my scone?" a woman whispered to Theodosia. She held her butter knife perpendicular to her scone.

"We recommend you slice it horizontally," Theodosia said in a soft voice. "That's the English tradition."

"Then what? Jam first or Devonshire cream?"

"That's strictly a matter of personal choice."

Conversation rose in a buzz along with clouds of aromatic steam. Then, when cups were refilled and scone plates cleared away, Theodosia, Haley, and Miss Dimple made their grand entrance, each of them carrying an elegant three-tiered stand that was practically overflowing with tea sandwiches.

And as additional trays were brought out, they proved to be quite the hit!

"Delicious," one guest proclaimed. "I know I shouldn't talk while I'm eating, but yum!"

"And there are so many different kinds of tea sandwiches to choose from," another guest cried.

"Don't you just love a tea party?" another woman chimed in.

"We're a smash," Drayton whispered to Theodosia at the counter. "They love everything."

"And we were worried our guests might be scared off by the rain," Theodosia said.

"Proved wrong again, and happily so."

If the scones were adored and the tea sandwiches a smash, then the blueberry crumble was the pièce de résistance. Especially when Miss Dimple went around to each table and plunked giant dollops of whipped cream atop everyone's still-warm crumble.

"Haley," Theodosia said when she ducked into the kitchen. "Where on earth did you find fresh blueberries in season?"

"Believe me, it wasn't easy." Haley chuckled, then said, under her breath, "Besides, who says they're in season?"

"They're frozen?"

Haley put a finger to her mouth. "Shhh."

By one thirty the tea party had pretty much come to its natural conclusion. Most of the guests had dashed off, with only a few hanging around to shop and pick up tea cozies, jars of jam, tins of tea, and T-Bath products.

Theodosia glanced at her watch, knowing the schedule was tight. They were supposed to be at the Heritage Society in about an hour. That would give them a half hour to set up their tea table before the Maritime History Seminar broke for afternoon refreshments. Before they were mobbed by a gang of hungry scholars and academics.

Theodosia checked with Haley, who was slathering an assort-

ment of toppings onto different breads and slapping them together into delicious tea sandwiches like a crazy, one-woman
production line.

"Do you want Miss Dimple to come in and help you?" she
asked.

Haley didn't even look up. "Nope. Not right now anyway.
Maybe in half an hour when I have to pack everything up."

"Okay, got it."

Theodosia walked out into the tea room just as Detective
Tidwell churned through the front door like an ATV in low gear.

Oh no, what does he want?

Theodosia hurried over to greet him, but Tidwell had already
executed a fast turn and was heading for the table by the fireplace.
The best seat in the house, of course.

"Aren't you just the little Nancy Drew amateur detective,"
Tidwell murmured to Theodosia as he shifted his bulk and sat
down heavily in a captain's chair.

Theodosia held her breath as the old wood creaked and
groaned. Would it stand up to him? Yes, at least for now the chair
remained intact.

"I assume you're referring to the events of last night?"

"At least you had the presence of mind to phone Detective
Riley. And thank goodness he wasn't so besotted by your beauty
and charm that he neglected to bring along a Crime Scene team."

"Excuse me," Theodosia said. "Why are you here? Is this the
harassment du jour or are you sniffing around for free scones?"

"A little of both. And I thought perhaps I'd dial in on today's
gossip." His eyes roved about the shop. "Since you own a tea shop,
you're privy to interesting rumors and rub shoulders with a great
many people."

"But not killer-type people," Theodosia said.

Tidwell leaned back in his chair and studied her. "I can think
of a few instances where you have."

He had her there. "Touché," she said. "Now I have a question for you."

Tidwell gave a disinterested "Hmm."

"The red roses from last night, with the secret admirer card. Do you know where the flowers came from?"

"We're still investigating. Calling florist shops, getting copies of all their orders for rose bouquets."

"Were they any sort of specialty rose?" Theodosia asked.

"Funny you should ask. Our lab rats analyzed what remained of them and believe they may be a variety called Dark Night. It's basically a hybrid tea rose, hence the extremely dark red, bordering on black, color of the petals."

"An order like that shouldn't be difficult to track down."

"Unless they were grown privately," Tidwell said. "Or shipped in from somewhere else. Remember, this man is a planner of the first magnitude."

"You're talking about Fogheel Jack. You think *he* might have sent them?"

"It would be a long shot, but perhaps."

Theodosia thought about the possibility that Fogheel Jack didn't actually live in Charleston. Maybe he dropped in to create his mayhem, then snuck away. That would make it much more difficult to get a bead on him.

"So . . . a scone and some tea?" she said in a distracted tone.

Tidwell smiled, pleased by her offer. "That would be lovely."

Theodosia ran into the kitchen, grabbed a blueberry scone and a chicken salad with chutney sandwich, and arranged them on a plate with a small bowl of Devonshire cream.

"Easy on those tea sandwiches," Haley cautioned. "Most of them are earmarked for the Heritage Society. I'm just about ready to pack the scones and sandwiches into baskets for you and Drayton to trundle over there."

"I only took the one sandwich. For Tidwell."

"*He's* out there? Holy Hannah, please don't let the man con you into seconds."

"I won't."

Theodosia carried the food out to the tea room, grabbed a pot of Madoorie Tea Estate tea that Drayton had wisely brewed, and set it all in front of Tidwell.

Tidwell leaned forward, barely able to stifle a satisfied smile. He had an appetite and a sweet tooth that wouldn't quit.

"I know you love our scones," Theodosia said. "But why are you here—really?" She knew Tidwell hadn't just shown up on a whim. He was far more methodical than that. Cagey.

"I wanted to issue a warning for you to be on your best behavior." Tidwell cut his scone in half and slathered it with jam.

Theodosia sat down across from him. "What are you talking about? Best behavior for what?"

"That tea you're catering later today? At the Heritage Society?"

"Yes, yes." Theodosia was starting to tire of his cat-and-mouse game. "What about it?"

"The ex-boyfriend is going to be there." Tidwell's beady eyes focused on her without blinking. "Serendipitous, no?"

"Wait, what exactly are you saying?"

"Tim Holt, Cara Chamberlain's ex-boyfriend, has been hired as the photographer for today's event." Tidwell still hadn't blinked.

Theodosia, on the other hand, was pretty much rocked back on her heels by the news. "Why him?" she sputtered.

"Don't read too much into this. Holt is simply the photographer that the Heritage Society hired a few weeks ago to take publicity photos." Tidwell's focus was back on his food as he took a bite of scone, then a larger bite.

"If you say it's no big deal, then why are you here? What do you want from me?" Theodosia said. Her brain was starting to leap ahead. This would present the perfect opportunity to pepper

Tim Holt with a few hard-edged questions. And hopefully get some answers.

Tidwell offered a maddening half smile. "I'm here because I want you to leave the man alone. I want to enforce a hands-off, no-questions-asked policy." Tidwell talked with his mouth full, chewing with relish.

"Sure," Theodosia said, smiling and trying to fake being agreeable. "Whatever you say."

Tidwell saw right through her little white lie. "No, I mean it," he said. "Consider this a request, an order, and a personal favor to me."

"I hear you," Theodosia said. But as she continued to digest Tidwell's news, she was really thinking, *No way, José. This is my big chance. I'm gonna grill Tim Holt like he's a two-inch-thick porterhouse steak.*

12

❧

The Heritage Society was Drayton's pride and joy. He'd served on the board of directors of this cherished museum for almost a dozen years now. And under his stewardship—and that of Timothy Neville, the executive director—the Heritage Society had amassed an amazing collection of historical paintings, books, objects, furniture, drawings, antique linens, important documents, and even antique weapons and firearms.

Theodosia loved the Heritage Society, too. Not just because Drayton served on its board, but because it stirred the romance and fantasy within her. Tucked inside this marble edifice was a library filled with leather chairs, floor-to-ceiling cases of leather-bound books, and brass lamps with emerald green shades. A half dozen period rooms were furnished with English and French furniture, priceless silver, and faded (but still glorious) oil paintings. With its high ceilings, manor house interior, and tucked-away rooms, the place reminded her of a castle, where tapestries dampened sound, contented hounds could stretch out in front of an oversized fireplace, and a girl could curl up and read to her heart's content.

All of that and they had a kitchen, too. Imagine that.

"Let's get our tea sandwiches and scones set up first," Drayton said. "Then I'll brew my tea."

They carried the baskets filled with scones and tea sandwiches across the hallway to the Palmetto Room. It was adjacent to the large meeting hall where the seminar was being held. In fact, they could hear one of the speakers going on about the *Queen of France*, the first US Navy ship that was sunk to block British ships from entering the harbor.

"How are we doing on time?" Theodosia asked.

Drayton crooked an arm and looked at his ancient Patek Philippe. "Allowing for the five-minute delay this watch is famous for, I'd say we've got half an hour. So we're right on schedule." He opened one of the baskets and said, "Mmn, what do we have here?"

"Lemon cream scones," Theodosia said. "And the other basket is stuffed full of tea sandwiches."

"Several kinds, I hope."

"Haley pretty much outdid herself. We've got chicken salad with chutney, crab salad with Bibb lettuce, smoked salmon, and mango-tomato salsa on crostini."

"Tasty," Drayton said. "Aren't we lucky the Heritage Society is loaning us all these lovely silver trays so we can arrange our goodies? And I see that plates, cups, and saucers are already stacked here alongside my tea urn. Efficiency, that's what I like. The world could use more efficiency."

Once they'd laid out the scones and tea sandwiches, Theodosia slipped down the hallway, found a bouquet of yellow and white daisies on one of the curators' desks, and added it to their tea table.

"Lovely," Drayton said, standing back to admire their handiwork. "Where'd the flowers come from?"

"Borrowed them. A kind of lateral transfer thing."

"I see."

"What tea did you finally decide on?" Theodosia asked as they
walked back across the hall, Drayton carrying the serving urn
with him.

"I'm going to brew Simpson & Vail's China Red Oolong. As
you know, the dark, twisted leaves yield a toasty, woodsy nectar
that's sure to please."

"I was hoping Timothy would give us an intern to help out,"
Theodosia said. "When I met with the staff on Monday they said
it might be a possibility."

Drayton measured tea into a small bowl as he began heating
his water. "You see anyone helping us?"

"Nope."

"Then it looks like it's just you and me."

Twenty minutes later, the doors to the great hall opened and the
seminar guests spilled out. June Winthrop, Timothy's super-
efficient admin assistant, quickly ushered the guests into the Palmetto Room and afternoon teatime, such as it was, began in
earnest.

Theodosia decided it was far more expedient to use a pair of
tongs to serve scones and tea sandwiches to their guests, while, at
the far end of the table, Drayton poured cups of tea.

There was an initial rush, of course, with everyone eager to
grab some food. And then, some fifteen minutes later, things
began to settle down. That's when Timothy Neville sauntered up
to their table.

"Timothy!" Drayton was delighted to see his friend. "How's
the seminar going?"

"Wonderful. A real success," Timothy said. "We have over a hundred and twenty attendees." As the octogenarian head of the Heritage Society, Timothy was an energetic gnome of a man who was always immaculately dressed and groomed. Today, he wore a camel blazer and gray slacks, with a starched white shirt and rep tie setting off his simian face and thin cap of silver-gray hair.

"I'm thrilled your seminar is going so well," Theodosia said as she attempted to place a scone on Timothy's plate.

But Timothy held up a hand and said, "No, just two sandwiches please. Chicken salad if you have it." Then he said to a man standing behind him, "Perhaps you could take a few shots of our refreshment table as well." Timothy turned back and gave Theodosia a slow wink. "Potential donors always like to know they'll be well fed."

That's Tim Holt, Theodosia suddenly realized. He was the photographer Tidwell had warned her not to talk to.

So of course she immediately spoke to him.

"Mr. Holt? Would you care for some refreshments?"

Tim Holt was in his early thirties, medium height, with warm amber eyes and a shock of dark blond hair. He had wisps of blond facial hair that weren't quite a beard but were probably supposed to look sort of hip and *GQ*. Only they mostly looked scruffy. He held a Nikon in his hands and had a large brown leather camera bag slung over one shoulder.

Holt peered at Theodosia. "Have we met before?" He was wondering how she knew his name.

"You're the boyfriend," Theodosia said.

Holt stared at her, a little bug-eyed now. Then he recovered from his surprise and said, "*Used* to be, as in past tense. But . . . how did you know? Or should I say *what* do you know?"

"I'm Theodosia Browning," she said.

Understanding dawned. "You're the one who . . ."

"Found Cara, that's right," Theodosia said.

"And the police undoubtedly mentioned my name to you as well," Holt said.

"Something like that."

"As did Cara's mother?"

"Yes, but in a roundabout way," Theodosia said.

"I can't say I'm surprised," Holt said. "Since the police found my name scribbled in Cara's notebook, *everybody's* been asking questions and pointing fingers." He sighed. "For the record, Cara and I had already broken up."

"So you *weren't* her boyfriend?"

"Not since a week ago Saturday night."

"What happened a week ago Saturday night?" Theodosia asked. "If you don't mind my asking."

"I do mind." Holt gazed at her, then his reserve seemed to slip and he said, "Hey, everybody else has tried to break me down, why not you?"

"The police don't believe your story?"

"Not really, since they've questioned me every which way to Sunday. The truth of the matter is, Cara and I were having drinks at Poogan's Porch and I decided—spur of the moment, stupid me—to have a heart-to-heart talk with her. I took her hand in mine and told her, quite seriously I might add, that I wanted to spend more time with her. Cara hemmed and hawed and finally said that wasn't possible because she was far too involved in her job. Actually, the word she used was *committed.*"

"Committed to her internship at Channel Eight?"

Holt shrugged. "To her unpaid internship, but not to me."

"What was your response?"

"We didn't have a knock-down, drag-out fight if that's what you're asking." Holt peered at her. "Is that where you were going?"

"I suppose I was heading in that direction," Theodosia said.

Holt looked defeated. "Cara and I talked some more—

actually, she did most of the talking, slipping in a short apology along the way. I made a final, impassioned plea, and then we shook hands and told each other to 'have a nice life.' She walked out the door and I paid the bar bill." Holt blew out a long breath. "But the police have been browbeating me like crazy about this breakup. When, really, it was just a normal thing."

"I'm not sure there's anything normal about a woman you care for telling you she doesn't want to see you anymore," Theodosia said. "There had to be hurt feelings on your part."

"There were a few. But by *normal* I meant we were, like, 'Okay, good luck. Take care.'"

"A friendly breakup."

"Under the circumstances it was. Besides . . ." Holt seemed to consider something, then stopped. Clammed up completely.

Theodosia peered at him. "You were about to say something else."

"Not really."

"Sure you were. Come on, what was it?"

"It was just a sneaking feeling I had. About the breakup."

"Which was?"

"That maybe Cara was seeing somebody else."

"This is going to sound a bit preposterous," Theodosia said. "But do you think Cara had somehow gotten a line on Fogheel Jack?"

Holt frowned at that but took a long time to answer. "Interesting question. Nobody's asked me that quite so pointedly, so I'd have to give it some serious consideration." He looked thoughtful for a few moments, seemed to be weighing his words, then said, "I think . . . it's *possible* she had."

"Talk to me. Tell me what you know."

"For one thing, Cara was completely addicted to any and all stories about Fogheel Jack. Even before the first murder a week ago, she'd been doing tons of research."

"You mean researching the two earlier murders, the ones from seven years ago?"

"Right. Cara was hot to pitch them as a cold case story. An unsolved crime. She figured the publicity might help shake something loose."

"It might have," Theodosia said. She knew that law enforcement agencies often planted stories with the media on the anniversaries of particularly heinous crimes. To try to do exactly that . . . shake something loose. To bring the crime back into the public eye and maybe dredge up a witness or some new information.

"What else?" Theodosia asked.

"Cara was acting very secretive, more so than usual," Holt said.

"And you think it had to do with Fogheel Jack?" Theodosia said.

"I think . . ." Holt stopped abruptly. "I don't know. Same thing I told the police, I don't really know." He looked around, realized he had a job to do, and said, "It feels weird being here like this, right on the heels of Cara's murder. But I was offered this job well over a month ago." He lifted his camera and added, "Who would've guessed . . . ?"

Theodosia found Drayton out in the hallway, where a collection of maritime maps and paintings was on display. Drayton was studying the map of Charleston Harbor with great intensity.

When he saw her he said, "Look at this. It's absolutely incredible. Do you know there are almost a dozen major shipwrecks still in the harbor? Well, at the bottom of the harbor anyway. And that some date as far back as the American Revolution."

"It's like an underwater theme park," Theodosia said. "I'm surprised some enterprising dive shop hasn't organized tours."

"Don't even breathe that idea into the ozone," Drayton warned. "Or someone will actually do it."

Theodosia wandered down the hallway, looking at the art, surreptitiously watching Tim Holt as he moved about and took photos of the guests. He struck her as a fairly competent photographer who did his job with little or no wasted effort. She knew from her previous stint in marketing that some photographers required lots of direction. They wanted to be told what shots to take, how many, and what angle. Holt, on the other hand, seemed to know instinctively what was important, what shots could be used for publicity stills.

At one point, Holt seemed to feel Theodosia's eyes trained on him and he turned to look at her. His brows shot up as if to ask, *What are you doing?*

Theodosia's thought-answer was, *I'm surveying my quarry.*

Holt shrugged and went back to snapping photos. Until he was interrupted by an uninvited guest Theodosia recognized immediately.

Bob Basset? What's he doing here?

It seemed Basset wanted to question Holt just as much as she did.

"Hey, you're Tim Holt, aren't you?" Basset said in a booming, faux-friendly voice.

Holt seemed to freeze.

"Mind if I ask you a few questions?" Basset asked, ignoring Holt's discomfort.

"I do mind," Holt said as he focused his lens on a ship model. "Because I'm busy."

"Come on," Basset said in an urgent I'm-talking-to-a-fellow-journalist voice. "Like it or not, you're a big part of the Fogheel Jack story."

Holt shook his head. "I'm *no* part of it."

"Look, man," Basset said. "You knew the victim; you *dated*

her, for crying out loud. So why don't you gimme something I can use?"

"I'm sorry," Holt said, "but I really don't know anything."

Basset continued to pressure Holt and ask such creepy questions that Theodosia began to wonder about him.

Why was Basset here, really? What kind of story did he want to write for the sleazy news outlets he worked for? A tragedy about star-crossed lovers or something else? What was his angle? Was he trying to get inside the mind of a serial killer or, heaven forbid, did he already know something?

Theodosia started for the two men, determined to ask Basset a few questions of her own. But when Basset saw her coming, he turned and moved away, disappeared into the crowd that milled about in the hallway, eager to return to the symposium.

"Don't let him bug you," Theodosia said to Holt.

Holt eyed her carefully. "You know Bob Basset?"

"Met him."

"Then you know he's a jerk," Holt said.

"Noted, yes."

"And FYI, this isn't the first time he's taken a run at me."

"He came into my tea shop yesterday and threw a million questions at me as well," Theodosia said.

Holt stood there for a few moments, then said, "You know, setting aside these bizarre circumstances, and the fact that you view me as a suspect, I'm actually a nice guy."

"So you say."

"Seriously, I wouldn't hurt a fly. That's why accusations that I had anything to do with Cara's death are preposterous."

"Okay," Theodosia said. "Sure." She was being amenable, but still reserving judgment.

"And while we're at it, I'm a pretty decent photographer as well." Holt pulled a postcard from his camera bag and handed it to Theodosia. "See? I'm even represented by an honest-to-goodness gallery."

Theodosia scanned the card. It was from the Imago Gallery and featured a montage of photos—two of them by Holt, a slightly out-of-focus landscape and a crisp black-and-white shot of Charleston Harbor. The gallery's address and time and date for the event were printed across the bottom of the card.

"Come to the opening Friday night," Holt said. "Bring your friends for appetizers and the de rigueur cheap white wine. It'll give you a chance to see my photographs and maybe get to know me better. Maybe even come to trust me."

Theodosia favored him with a cool smile. "Maybe."

13

How did it go at the Heritage Society?" Haley asked as Theodosia and Drayton trooped in through the back door. She stood in the hallway outside Theodosia's office, arms crossed, wearing a towering white chef's hat. A petite but formidable vision of culinary authority.

"The tea went very well," Drayton said. "Everyone adored your sandwiches."

"But not the scones?" Haley asked.

"They loved those, too," Theodosia said. She tilted one of the baskets so Haley could peer in. "See? Nothing left. Barely a few crumbs." She gazed down the hallway into the tea room. "Is Miss Dimple still here?"

"She's straightening up," Haley said. "Putting everything right."

"Hey," Miss Dimple called out when Theodosia and Drayton walked into the tea room. "How'd it go?"

"A major success," Drayton said. "And thank you so much for taking care of everything here."

"My heavens, it was a pleasure," Miss Dimple said.

She was prone to good old-fashioned expressions like that. *My heavens, good gravy, holy cow.* The expressions, and her exuberance, were part of her innate charm.

"Oh, and we had a customer who requested a tea that was warming and aromatic. I was a bit flummoxed at first, but then, thank goodness I remembered you telling me that Twinings Prince of Wales tea is the perfect warm-up for a cool day. Was that right?"

"A perfect choice," Drayton said. "Masterful, in fact."

"Thank you," Miss Dimple said. "It's good to know this old gal still has all her buttons." She shrugged into her raincoat, waved goodbye to everyone, and headed for the back door. At that exact moment a knock sounded at the front door. Drayton turned and rolled his eyes, ready to tell whoever it was that the tea shop was closed for the day.

Then the door opened and Nick Prince walked in, his hair looking damp and his jacket slightly soggy from the rain.

He stared at Drayton, a serious look on his face. "Is Theodosia here?"

Drayton peered at him over his half-glasses. "And you are?"

"Nick Prince, her neighbor."

"And author in residence," Theodosia said as she strolled into the tea room. She aimed a distracted smile at Prince and said, "Hello, what are you doing here?"

"You invited me, remember?" Prince said.

"We were about to lock up for the day," Drayton said. He took a step forward, edging into protective mode.

Prince cast a hopeful glance at Theodosia. "Please, do you have a moment to talk?"

Theodosia looked around the tea shop, searching for some kind of excuse, something to do. Only there wasn't a doggone thing. Miss Dimple had been a little too efficient.

"I suppose," Theodosia said. "Why don't you, uh, come back to my office." She shrugged at Drayton, whose jaw knotted in response.

Prince followed Theodosia down the hallway to her small office, where an overflow of teapots, trivets, stacks of red hats, boxes of tea cozies, tea magazines, and grapevine wreaths made it seem even more crowded.

"Cute," he said, looking around.

"Have a seat." Theodosia sat behind her desk while Prince settled into an oversized upholstered chair they called *the tuffet*. He gave her a solemn look, as if he were about to deliver a criticism. Which he pretty much did.

"A little bird told me you were in the graveyard the night Cara Chamberlain was murdered." Prince shook his finger at her in a mock scold. "Something you failed to mention last night."

"Why would I bring up something like that?"

"Because I was quite candid when I told you my newest project was a book on true crime. And since I plan to include the two recent murders as part of the subject matter, telling me that *you* were the one who discovered Cara's body would've been the neighborly thing to do."

"Who told you I discovered her body?"

"I prefer to keep that confidential. I have to protect my sources."

"You'll have to do better than that, neighbor," Theodosia said, putting a knife's edge on her words.

Prince looked glum, then, a few seconds later, folded like a cheap card table. "Okay, okay, I'll tell you. It was a guy by the name of Bill Glass. Claims he's a big buddy of yours."

Theodosia ground her teeth together. *That stupid Glass. Probably caught something over his police scanner and passed my name on to Prince. I'd like to wring Glass's scrawny neck next time I see him.*

"Glass is no friend of mine. Fact is, he's a certified muckraker.

If I were you I'd watch out for him. The only reason he's talking to you is because he's trying to pick your brain for a good story angle."

"An ugly image to be sure," Prince said.

"You really intend to write about these murders?" Theodosia asked.

"Are you kidding?" Prince looked taken aback. "Fogheel Jack has the potential to be a *huge* deal. He could be right up there with the Zodiac Killer and Hillside Strangler."

Theodosia found his words both repulsive and ridiculous. "The serial killers' hall of fame?"

"Something like that," Prince said. "Especially since our boy is developing such a tried-and-true MO."

Our boy? What a strange thing to say. As if Prince is almost a collaborator.

"The MO being death by strangulation?" Theodosia said. The words tasted terrible in her mouth.

"That and if Fogheel Jack decides to adopt a kind of signature, as many serial killers do."

"What do you mean by *signature?*" Theodosia had a good inkling of what he was referring to but wanted to hear it from Prince himself.

"Oh, some killers steal a piece of their victims' jewelry, a lock of their hair, or even an article of clothing."

"Interesting." *I will definitely need to take a shower after this conversation.*

"And then there's the reverse," Prince said. "Sometimes the killer *leaves* a piece of himself. His calling card, if you will."

"Like a note?" Theodosia said.

"That's happened in a few cases, sure. Killers have also been known to leave flowers, letters, even small trinkets behind. The Zodiac Killer penned weird symbols, the Night Stalker painted pentagrams. Some killers are obsessed with posing their victims."

"Explain, please," Theodosia said, even though she knew something about posing. Probably gleaned it from Serial Killer Week on TV.

"Posing is a common fetish," Prince said. "Once the actual killing has taken place, many killers arrange their victims, and their victims' clothes, according to their whim. Jack the Ripper did it. So did BTK."

Theodosia stared across her desk at Nick Prince, realizing what a terrible conversation they were having, feeling slightly fascinated but repulsed at the same time.

"Do you think today's Fogheel Jack was responsible for those killings seven years ago?" she asked.

"Could have been. A serial killer that the LA cops dubbed 'the Grim Sleeper' had a fourteen-year hiatus between killing sprees. But when he came back, he returned with a vengeance. Pretty grisly, huh?"

"Do you think the Grim Sleeper was in jail during his fourteen-year hiatus?" Theodosia asked.

"Maybe. Or he could have simply pooped out for a while. Hit his limit. His tank was full. Then, after a few years, the old hunger came roaring back. The bloodlust."

Theodosia turned away. She didn't like the way Prince had smiled when he said *bloodlust*. Nope, she didn't care for that at all.

"Everything okay?" Drayton poked his head into Theodosia's office once Prince had gone. When he saw her thoughtful expression, he said, "Oh my, it looks as if you're puzzling over something."

"Just random thoughts," Theodosia said. Then, "You didn't care for him, did you?"

"Your new neighbor the Crown Prince?" Drayton said. "It was that obvious?"

"From forty paces. What set you off?"

"He's far too forward for my liking. Plus, he has a weird smile. Like he's privy to some bit of knowledge that we aren't." He peered at her. "Do you like him?"

"Can't say as I do."

"Okay, then."

"C'mon," Theodosia said, getting up. "Let's get your teapots rinsed out and put away. Then I'll drive you home."

"I can walk, it's no problem."

"No. It's late. And dark. And . . ."

Drayton shrugged. "And you never know what's out there. Okay, I'll gladly accept a ride."

A half hour later, driving down Church Street, Theodosia said, "I did learn one weird thing from Nick Prince."

"What's that?"

She hesitated as rain pattered gently on the roof of her Jeep and slid down the windshield. "He talked about posing. How murderers sometimes arrange their victim's body in a certain way."

Drayton shuddered. "Good grief. What an awful conversation you two must have had. Gives me goose bumps just thinking about it."

They drove along, the dashboard the only illumination inside Theodosia's dark car.

"So you have some concern about this posing thing?" Drayton asked.

Theodosia clutched the steering wheel a little tighter. "Kind of."

"Why?"

"Because now that I think back on it and form an image of what Cara's body looked like lying on that grave, it *did* look somewhat posed."

"Go on," Drayton said.

"As if her body had been arranged just so. A human still life. Like something an artist or photographer might do."

Drayton almost choked. "A photographer like Tim Holt?"

"There's a terrifying thought."

"Is it possible we rubbed shoulders with Cara's killer this afternoon?" Drayton asked. "Do you think you ought to talk to Tidwell about this posing thing? Better yet, tell him about Tim Holt?"

"Holt's already one of his prime suspects."

"Well . . . that's good, I suppose."

"We really should stop obsessing about this murder," Theodosia said. "*I* should stop anyway."

"Change of subject, then. You see that lovely home over there?" They'd turned down Legare Street, one of the Historic District's most elegant streets.

Theodosia gave a quick glance out the passenger side window. "Uh-huh."

"It's just been put on the National Register of Historic Places."

"How many homes in Charleston have that designation?" As a self-described history fiend, Drayton kept track of things like that.

"I'd say close to four dozen. Of course we also have churches, monuments, alleys, lighthouses, plantations, and parks on that list as well. And just outside Charleston are . . ."

"Holy smokes!" Theodosia shouted as a police car suddenly rounded the corner up ahead, swerved crazily, and came screaming toward her right down the middle of the street. The siren whooped and blatted as light bars pulsed red and blue.

"Watch it, watch it!" Drayton shouted.

Theodosia cranked the steering wheel hard as adrenaline shot through her like white lightning, and pulled to the curb just as the cruiser roared past her.

"Whoa," she said as she tried to catch her breath and get her blood pressure back to normal.

No dice. Ten seconds later another cruiser screamed by them. WHOOP, WHOOP, SCREECH!

And then a third rocketed by them, siren blaring, also going full tilt. The racket was deafening.

"Something big is happening," Drayton said as they squirmed around in their seats trying to see where the cruisers were headed.

"You don't suppose . . ." Theodosia threw Drayton a worried look, a look that said, *Has there been another murder?*

Drayton grimaced, immediately reading her thoughts.

"Could there have been another murder? I sincerely hope not."

"There's only one way to find out." Theodosia was already making a tight, hurried U-turn in the middle of the block.

"How are we going to . . . oh, we'll follow the sirens," Drayton said.

Theodosia floored it, sent her Jeep rocketing back down Legare, got to the end of the block, and spun left, picking up speed as she did so.

Three blocks down East Battery it looked like a cop convention. Lights, sirens, black-and-white cruisers, and a few slickbacks (unmarked but with city plates) thrown in for good measure.

"Dear Lord," Drayton said. "There must have been another murder!"

"Right here in White Point Gardens," Theodosia said. "Maybe we should . . ." Her words were interrupted by a tinkle from her cell phone. She pawed in her bag, pulled it out, and said, "This is Theodosia."

"Stay where you are!" a voice shouted.

"Riley?" Theodosia recognized his voice immediately. At first she didn't understand why he was yelling at her, telling her to sit tight. "Why are you . . . ?"

Seconds later, she put it all together. Something *had* happened right here in White Point Gardens. And Riley was babbling at her, warning her to stay away.

Nope, that's not going to happen.

"I can hardly hear you," Theodosia said. "I'm afraid we have a terrible connection."

"Theo!"

But she'd already clicked off her phone and dropped it in her bag.

14

White Point Gardens was normally the picture of serenity. A spacious park at the tip of the peninsula where magnolias bloomed, fountains pattered, and the views of Charleston Harbor and Fort Sumter were postcard perfect. Newlyweds traditionally came here to pose for pictures, kids loved to climb on antique cannons, and tourists photographed the countless historic statues and monuments.

Not tonight.

On this rainy, overcast Wednesday evening, White Point Gardens swarmed with first responders. Police cruisers, ambulances, and even fire department vehicles had gotten the call and come pouring in.

Theodosia and Drayton stepped out of the Jeep and stood on the curb watching the melee. Besides law enforcement there were dozens of curiosity seekers as well, no doubt drawn by the sound and fury.

"Where do you think . . . ?" Drayton began.

But Theodosia was already scanning the area and zeroing in

on the small white gazebo-like bandstand that sat almost in the middle of the park.

"There," she said. "The police are converging on the bandstand. I need to . . ."

"What? Take a look?" Drayton said. "I can't imagine we can get within fifty feet of that bandstand."

But Theodosia's curiosity was piqued. "C'mon," she nudged him. "Let's give it a try."

They walked across wet grass, dodging historic cannons and monuments, and made a beeline for the bandstand. Out in Charleston Harbor, boats bobbed like corks, their wavering reflections glinting off restless water. Across the way the lighthouse at Patriots Point shone its familiar beacon. Swollen clouds hung overhead.

Ten feet from the open-air bandstand, a police officer stepped into their path and held up a hand.

"Sorry," he said. "This area's restricted. You'll have to stay back."

"Sure," Theodosia said as she backed up a few feet and watched the officer fumble with a roll of yellow-and-black tape with the words POLICE LINE DO NOT CROSS. Once he'd finished stringing it from tree to tree, she pushed forward again, straining against the plastic boundary. Drayton was right beside her.

In the bandstand, things were heating up. Detectives wandered around, grim-faced, their collars turned up and their hands shoved deep into pockets. Two officers hastily set up lights, and when a portable generator began to hum, the area was aglow. Theodosia stood on tiptoes and kinked her neck, trying to see who the poor victim might be. But she was still too far away and bits of mist and fog obscured her view.

"Can you make out a body?" Drayton asked in hushed tones. "Because I cannot."

"Still trying," Theodosia said. By now a small group of curious onlookers had gathered around them. "I think we have to get closer."

They pressed closer, straining the yellow tape, and the crowd, which was growing larger by the minute, followed them.

Behind Theodosia, a man suddenly brayed, "Whadya see? Anything?"

She whirled around to find Bill Glass staring at her. He was dressed in his usual baggy cargo slacks and shabby photographer's vest, the cap sleeves sticking out like wings. A rumpled scarf and two cameras were slung casually around his neck.

"Mind if I borrow one of these?" Without waiting for an answer, Theodosia reached a hand out and lifted one of the cameras up and over his head.

"Pushy, ain't ya?" Glass chuckled. Then added, "Here, maybe this'll help grease the skids." He handed her a brown plastic lanyard with a white card dangling from it that said PRESS. And underneath it in smaller type SHOOTING STAR MAGAZINE.

"Thanks," Theodosia said. She hung the lanyard around her neck, ducked under the crime scene tape, and walked slowly toward the bandstand. At the last minute, she remembered to lift the camera on the pretext of snapping photos.

"No press," one of the officers up on the bandstand said when he saw her. But his words were half-hearted and he didn't make a move to enforce them.

Theodosia crept closer.

The scene was beyond eerie. Lots of law enforcement mumbling to one another, milling around in the glow of too-bright portable lamps.

But the victim. What about the victim?

Taking a deep breath, wiping rain from her eyes, Theodosia stepped sideways into a shadow. And finally got a good view. What a professional photographer would call *the money shot*.

What she saw stunned her. Dark hair, leather jacket, frayed jeans.

Monica Garber!

Theodosia's heart thumped like a rabbit chased to ground by snarling dogs.

Is it really her? Yes, I'm pretty sure it is!

She spun in her tracks and rushed back to Drayton. Grabbing the sleeve of his jacket, she said, "You're not going to believe this!"

"What? What!" Drayton said. "Did you get a look at the victim?"

"I . . . Yes . . . It's Monica Garber!"

Drayton touched a hand to his forehead as if he'd just developed the worst migraine ever. "The TV reporter?"

"What?" Glass said, perking up. "The TV lady? I gotta get a closer look."

"It's Monica. I'm positive," Theodosia said as they watched Glass pick his way forward. "I recognized her clothes from when she stopped by the tea shop this morning."

"But why would she be . . . ?" Drayton looked sick at heart as he tried to wrap his brain around Monica's murder. "Why would she be *here?*"

"Think!" Theodosia cried. "Monica must have made contact with him!"

"Him?"

"Fogheel Jack!"

Now Drayton's shoulders caved. "How would she have done that?"

"I don't know."

Theodosia felt like an anvil was being pounded between her eardrums. She stared at Drayton as her brain fought to process this horrific turn of events. And, finally, the answer came to her in the form of a comic strip balloon. One word inside a bubble that seemed to form in the air above them.

"Cara."

Drayton looked confused. "What?"

"Monica could have figured out that Cara made contact with Fogheel Jack. So she followed some sort of clue, got in touch with him, and—"

"Got killed for her efforts," Drayton said.

He glanced past Theodosia to a parking lot where additional law enforcement and newly arriving media were congregating.

"Things just got more complicated," he said.

"What?"

"A Channel Eight van just pulled in."

Theodosia looked across the park and saw a shiny white van rock to a stop. It had the words CHANNEL EIGHT and NEWS ON THE GO emblazoned on its side.

"Oh dear," she said.

Bobby the cameraman came stumbling toward them. His eyes were glazed, a shock of dark hair dangled in his eyes, and his brown leather jacket hung off one shoulder.

"The cops are saying . . ." Bobby said to Theodosia. Then, "Tell me it isn't her." His words came out in a pleading gasp.

"I'm afraid it is Monica," Theodosia said in a soft voice.

Bobby shook his head. "No. Uh-uh." He was clutching a video camera that was attached via a thick black cable to equipment his sound and lighting guy, Trevor, was carrying. Trevor, who was probably twenty-four but looked like a teenager, seemed devastated as well. His eyes darted back and forth and his mouth worked soundlessly.

"I'm so sorry," Theodosia said, her heart going out to them.

"How can I shoot footage of this!" Bobby shrilled. "We were partners! Monica and Trevor and I are a team!"

"*Were* a team," Trevor whispered.

They looked so desolate, so shaken, that Theodosia decided to try to prop them up.

"You can do it because it's your job," Theodosia said. "Your TV station depends on you for news stories. Charleston needs you to cover this and help spread the word—warn people about this dangerous killer."

Bobby's face had turned a sickly green. "Oh man." He staggered a few feet away, cords trailing him, then turned back. "I warned her not to go."

Theodosia caught up with Bobby, grabbed his arm, and hung on. "Warned her not to go where?"

"Monica got this goofy e-mail from some guy who claimed he had important information for her."

"Information about Fogheel Jack?"

"I guess so," Bobby said.

Theodosia continued to press him. "Do you think Fogheel Jack was the one who sent Monica the e-mail?"

"Maybe." Bobby looked like he was ready to cry. "I don't know." He shook his head. "She wouldn't tell me."

"Why would you let Monica go somewhere alone?" Theodosia asked. "Especially after all that's happened. Knowing she might be walking into a trap."

Bobby shook his head slowly. "You don't know Monica. Once she got an idea in her head, there was no stopping her."

"But somebody did stop her," Drayton said. "Permanently."

"Oh man." Bobby fumbled with his video camera.

"Come on," Theodosia said, taking charge. She lifted her press pass to show Bobby. "I'll go with you, help you get your story."

"You will?" Bobby looked skeptical.

"As much as I can anyway," Theodosia said.

Bobby and Trevor adjusted their gear, handed Theodosia a microphone, and the three of them walked slowly toward the bandstand.

They got within five feet of the actual murder scene before anybody noticed. And as luck would have it, the one guy who recognized Theodosia turned out to be Jesse Trumbull, the department's public information officer.

Trumbull peered at her. "Theodosia? What are *you* doing here?"

Theodosia lifted her press pass in reply.

"Seriously?" Trumbull offered a weak smile. "So you've enlisted with the people who enjoy making my life miserable? By that I'm talking about the media."

Theodosia touched an index finger to her lips.

"Please don't tell anybody that I'm just a temp. It was the only way I could get close enough to see what happened."

"She's a friend of yours?" Trumbull asked.

Theodosia nodded. "And she worked with these guys."

"Oh man." Trumbull seemed genuinely concerned for Bobby and Trevor.

Theodosia looked across the park and saw a man with a shaggy black-and-white dog straining at its leash. The man wore a dark green windbreaker over his jeans and looked upset as he gestured and talked to a command officer.

"Is that the guy who found her?" she asked.

Trumbull looked over at the man with the dog and nodded. "Yup, he was out walking Fido there and they stumbled upon her. Dog started barking and whining. Good thing the guy had the presence of mind to call it in. That was around seven fifteen. His call started ringing the bells and whistles, then Tidwell got wind of the murder and sent everyone he could round up over here."

"This has to be a nightmare for the department."

"It's pretty awful, yeah."

"So Monica was strangled?" Theodosia asked.

Trumbull nodded. "Yes, but this time the guy also used a knife on her."

Fighting down her revulsion, Theodosia decided to push Trumbull a little harder. "And you're thinking it was Fogheel Jack?"

"Look around," Trumbull said. "You see that ground mist rolling in?"

As if on cue, tendrils of diaphanous white fog crawled across the grass in their direction, almost like a living, breathing thing.

"That's what brings him out. The fog." Trumbull shifted his gaze to the microphone in Theodosia's hand. "Say now, did you want to actually do an interview?"

"With you?" All at once it struck Theodosia as a good idea. She glanced at Bobby. "Bobby?"

Bobby nodded in agreement.

"Sure. That would be terrific," Theodosia said.

Bobby moved in closer to start filming as Trevor adjusted lights and sound. Then Theodosia held up the microphone and said, "Mr. Trumbull, as public information officer for the Charleston Police Department, could you tell us what happened here tonight?"

Trumbull stared into the camera for a few seconds, then began. "I'm sad to report that the Charleston police believe the man known as Fogheel Jack has struck again, right here in White Point Gardens."

Trumbull went on for another minute and a half, leaving enough pauses so the editor back at the station would be able to cut or splice the report any number of ways.

"That was great," Theodosia said when Trumbull had finished. "Thank you so much."

"Thank you, guys," Bobby said, aiming a weak smile at Theodosia and then at Trumbull. "You pulled our fat outa the fryer, both of you. This was tough duty for me and Trevor."

Theodosia bade goodbye to the two news guys, then headed back to meet up with Drayton. Where, surprise, surprise, she found him in conversation with Bob Basset. Well, not exactly polite conversation. Drayton had his arms folded tightly across his chest and was shaking his head no.

"No?" Basset said as Theodosia walked up. "You really don't know any details?"

"Afraid not," Drayton said.

Basset saw Theodosia and said, "How 'bout you? You seem to be Little Miss Information Central. Care to fill me in?"

"Not really," Theodosia said, when what she really meant was *Track down your own story.*

Basset stomped away from them, only to be replaced by a note-taking Nick Price.

"Good Lord," Drayton hissed when he saw Price. "Will it never end?"

"Working on your book?" Theodosia asked Price. "Looks like there's plenty of fodder for a new chapter." She said the words facetiously, but Prince took her literally.

"Is there ever! Moving back to Charleston was the smartest thing I ever did."

At that, Drayton turned his back on Prince.

Prince stuck a pencil behind his ear and said to Theodosia, "What's with your friend anyway? He doesn't seem to like me."

"Drayton's upset," Theodosia said. "We all are. Not only has another murder taken place, but it's someone we know."

"Yeah," Prince said. "I heard. Monica Garber, TV personality and would-be journalist."

Theodosia narrowed her eyes. "How did you know to come here tonight?"

"Hmm?" Prince was busy scribbling a few more notes.

"I said, how did you know there'd been another murder?"

The pupils in Prince's eyes seemed to contract. "I don't know. Just lucky, I guess."

Theodosia studied Prince. He always seemed a little on edge and she wondered if he took Ritalin.

Drayton tapped Theodosia on the shoulder. "Time to go."

"Gotcha," she said.

As they turned to leave, Prince called after them, "Was it something I said?"

They walked a good ten yards and then Drayton said, "Jackass."

"Drayton!" Theodosia was shocked. Drayton was normally reserved and able to hold his temper in check.

"Well, he is. Your Mr. Prince Uncharming."

"You know what? You're right," Theodosia said. She turned and her eyes followed a black van. It was the Crime Scene guys. She shivered as she watched them roll across the grass and pull up beside the bandstand. She knew they'd be doing all the CSI things that Crime Scene people do. Take scrapings from under Monica's fingernails, search the area for trace evidence like hairs or fabric, look for blood.

Drayton gazed at her, then his eyes drifted off to the left and behind her. "Oh my."

"What?"

"You, my dear, are about to be plunged into hot water. And not the kind we use for tea."

Theodosia whirled around. "Huh?"

15

Looking across a bed of waterlogged cordgrass, Theodosia saw a
determined Pete Riley striding toward her. His mouth was set in
a grim line and he was closing in fast. Coming in hot.

"I told you not to come here tonight," were Riley's first words.
He sounded angry, determined.

"You did?" Theodosia's response was innocence personified.
Drayton just looked embarrassed.

"I called you, remember?" Riley said. He wore a navy windbreaker that said CPD on the front and had his gold shield strung
around his neck.

"I think something's wrong with my phone," Theodosia said.
"Or maybe it's my carrier's fault. Lately, calls have been dropping
left and right."

"Uh-huh." Riley said it as though he didn't quite believe her.
He thrust his hands deep into his jacket pockets, looked around,
and said, "So Monica Garber is our latest victim. But I'm guessing you've got the full story by now?"

"Almost the full story," Theodosia said. Then, "Why? Is there something else I should know?"

"Doubtful. Even though everyone's beating their brains out, trying to make sense of these cases."

"These cases being the Fogheel Jack murders?" Drayton asked.

Riley gave a tight nod.

"So you're definitely attributing Monica Garber's murder to Fogheel Jack?" Theodosia asked.

"I wish you wouldn't call him that," Riley said. "It gives him too much credence."

"He's the unsub?" Theodosia asked. "The unknown suspect, like they always say on cop TV shows?"

Riley shrugged. "Whatever." Then he peered carefully at Theodosia. "Theo, do *you* know something?"

"Well, I . . . maybe I do. It's kind of weird and could be nothing, but Monica mentioned that she had someone feeding her inside information," Theodosia said.

"That so?" Riley frowned. "When did she tell you this?"

"Today. This morning," Theodosia said.

"Who was her informant? Did she say?"

Theodosia shook her head. "Monica wouldn't tell me. But I assumed it was someone connected with the investigation."

"Ah jeez, I hope it's not one of my guys," Riley said. "We've got enough problems keeping a lid on things."

"And then Monica received a weird e-mail . . ."

Riley gave Theodosia a sharp look. "What e-mail? What are you talking about?"

"According to Bobby, Monica's cameraman, she received an e-mail and—"

Riley interrupted her. "An e-mail from Fogheel Jack?"

"I thought we weren't supposed to call him that," Drayton said.

Riley ignored him and focused on Theodosia. "Well?"

"That's what Bobby assumed," Theodosia said slowly.

"Doggone, I've got to talk to this guy Bobby," Riley said. "I mean two murders, both women working at Channel Eight? What are the odds? This has to be associated with the TV station, right?"

"It sure looks that way," Theodosia said, while Drayton nodded in agreement.

"Okay," Riley said. "I've got to huddle with Tidwell since this e-mail thing is brand-new information that could possibly knock something loose. Which means we also need to have our tech guys crawl through Monica's computer. Probably check Cara Chamberlain's computer, too."

"Maybe Drayton and I should stick around for a while," Theodosia said. "We won't interfere or anything, but we might—"

Riley grabbed her by the shoulders and said in a low, urgent voice, "Are you crazy? What if Fogheel Jack is still here?"

Theodosia gazed at him, a little nervous, more than a little rattled. She'd never seen Riley quite this upset. "What do you mean?"

"You see the big crowd that's gathered here? All the lookyloos that are acting as if it's a big fat carnival? What if the killer's among them? What if he's hanging around and watching us right now? Gloating over his kill and enjoying his impromptu moment of semi-celebrity?"

"I don't think he—"

"Sweetheart, this guy is an apex predator. He gets his jollies by killing people. Do you not get that?"

"Yes, I get that," Theodosia said. She was starting to feel more and more uneasy. Could Fogheel Jack be ghosting around White Point Gardens exactly as Riley had said? Had she rubbed shoulders with him? Had she talked to him or brushed past him? The idea made her skin crawl.

Drayton stepped in. "We were just on our way home. In fact, we're leaving this very minute," he said. "Aren't we, Theodosia?"

Theodosia glanced over at the crowd again, saw only a blur of faces. Then the crowd shifted and she noticed a face that looked slightly familiar.

No, it's not his face; it's his jacket. His black leather jacket.

She watched as Frank Lynch, Wyatt Orlock's head of security, slid deftly through the crowd. And wondered—*Why is he here? Just passing through or is there another reason?* She looked for Lynch again, but he was gone. Disappeared like a shark slicing under a dark wave.

Drayton was talking to her again, saying something about leaving.

Theodosia looked out over Charleston Harbor, where a police helicopter flitted through the dark sky like a firefly. Looking for someone? Assuming Monica's killer had escaped by boat? Then she shook her head, looked at Drayton, and said, "What were you saying?"

"That we were just leaving," Drayton said. He and Riley stared at her, as if waiting to hear the correct answer.

"Right," she said finally.

Theodosia's head was still spinning when she arrived home. There were too many dead women, too many coincidences, too many questions, and no discernible answers to anything. She'd made a promise to Lois that now seemed almost impossible to keep. If the Charleston police couldn't figure out who was committing these murders, how could she?

Which was why Theodosia changed into her running gear and decided to take Earl Grey for a quick jog. She simply had to clear her head.

It was misting but not raining, and they started out slow. Did three blocks through the Historic District at a warm-up pace, coasting along fairly easily. Interestingly enough, they didn't see another soul on the sidewalks. People were either scared to death of Fogheel Jack or they'd caught a TV news flash about tonight's murder and were staying in. Or both.

When Theodosia and Earl Grey hit Ladson Street, they upped their speed, accelerated to a full-out muscle-strumming sprint that, after six blocks, left them both winded and gasping for air. Still, the exercise—and the endorphins that were subsequently released—felt awfully good. Enough to blow out the carbon and reboot Theodosia's thinking.

Turning down her back alley, Theodosia made up her mind to get in touch with Bobby the cameraman first thing tomorrow. Maybe he could shine some—

A GURGLE and a loud THUMP stopped Theodosia dead in her tracks. Made Earl Grey pause as well.

Strange noises were emanating from inside the carriage house that belonged to the mansion Nick Prince was renting.

But what was she hearing? Certainly not car sounds.

Theodosia tiptoed to one of the sliding garage doors and wedged her fingers into a crack. Slowly, carefully, she pushed the door open along its metal track. Then she peeked inside and in the dim light saw . . . a washing machine. And heard . . . something sloshing around inside. And wondered . . .

What's Nick Price washing this time of night?

The question rattled around inside her brain for a few seconds; then the answer came rushing at her like a runaway freight train.

Bloody clothes?

That was enough to scare the living hell out of Theodosia. She ran to her house, slammed the door behind her, and threw the dead bolt. Unclipped the leash from Earl Grey's collar and said, "I sure hope that's not what he's doing."

Standing in the kitchen, Theodosia tried to sort out her thoughts. Drayton thought Nick Prince was creepy, while she had found him mostly annoying. But were those first impressions, that little tickle of her brain's spider sense, a kind of early warning system that not everything was on the up-and-up with Prince? That he was, in reality, a sinister character to be wary of?

If so, where did she take it from here? Call Riley and tell him her deep, dark suspicions? No, he'd tell her there was no concrete evidence and decide she was a raving maniac. Maybe not the girl for him. So what else could she do? Theodosia stood in her kitchen wondering.

Well, for one thing, the Internet being what it was, nobody's life was completely private anymore. So that might be a dandy place to start.

Theodosia brewed a cup of orchid plum tea and carried it upstairs along with a peanut butter dog cookie for Earl Grey. Grabbing her laptop, she curled up in the easy chair in her tower room.

While rain gurgled and sloshed down her drain spouts, and Earl Grey got crumbs on the carpet, Theodosia looked up Nick Prince's books on Amazon. There were two books, both published by Peakskill Press, an imprint she'd never heard of.

Maybe that means he's self-published?

One book was titled *The True Case of the Maryland Slasher*, the other *Secrets of the Sorority Row Strangler*.

Theodosia was struck by the ominous words *slasher, secrets,* and *strangler* in Prince's book titles.

So he likes killers. Or at least men who kill women.

There were only two reviews for each book, but both were glowing and filled with high praise. Nice testimonials, but she knew they could have easily been posted by friends or relatives.

Next, Theodosia checked Prince's website, which turned out to be not much of anything. A plug-and-play template with a photo that must have been taken five years ago, a short bio that was coy and woefully short on detail, and links to purchasing his books.

Come on, girl, you gotta keep trying.

Theodosia yawned as she clicked over to Nick Prince's Linked-In profile.

Fortunately, that site proved to be somewhat more informative. The dates were interesting, too.

Prince had been working as the assistant manager at the Barnes & Noble in North Charleston when the two murders had occurred seven years ago. Then he moved to Atlanta, where he worked as a writer-producer at Sloan & Associates Advertising. After that, he listed four years in which time he authored his two books. Now Prince was back in Charleston writing another book and the murders had started up again.

Coincidence? Theodosia's heart gave a little blip. Or could Nick Prince be Fogheel Jack? The dates certainly worked out. And what if these most recent murders were committed as fodder for his new book?

The idea stunned Theodosia as she sipped her tea. But the more she thought about it, the more plausible it sounded.

Yes, what if he's writing his own script? What if he's creating his own characters and story line?

Another thought banged its way into her brain. If Prince was actually the killer, wouldn't he try to hang the murder on someone else? After all, every book, even a true crime book, creepy as it might be, needed an ending. Not necessarily a happy one, but an exciting wrap-it-up conclusion all the same.

If Nick Prince *was* Fogheel Jack, who would he pick to be his patsy? What innocent man would he try to hang the Fogheel Jack murders on?

Could Prince be trying to set up Tim Holt, Cara's ex-boyfriend? Maybe Prince was the one who'd sent the flowers to Cara, assuming the police would track down Holt.

Or had Prince figured out that Wyatt Orlock was interested in Lois's building and would make a dandy suspect? Then there was Frank Lynch, Orlock's head of security. Though she wasn't sure how Prince could cause Lynch to fall under suspicion.

On the other hand, Prince might have known that Bob Basset was a murder aficionado and also a bit of a bumbler—and could somehow be fed to the police.

Theodosia stood up, stretched, and padded into her bathroom to take a hot shower.

Later, feeling more relaxed, she crawled into bed and turned on her small TV. She caught the tail end of an old movie—*The Ghost and Mrs. Muir*—once again loving the magical, romantic ending. Then she changed channels to catch the late news. There was a swoosh of red-and-blue graphics and the words CHANNEL EIGHT—NEWS ON THE GO burst onto the screen. The two anchors, a man and a woman, looked as if they'd been carved out of cream cheese. Perfect hair, glowing smiles, no-wrinkle navy blue poly jackets. The female anchor assumed a serious gaze as she faced the camera and announced a breaking news story.

Theodosia watched as they switched to footage of White Point Gardens. There were the police milling around in the gazebo, the scene silhouetted by a nightmarish glow, and Jesse Trumbull giving his account. Her heart pounded inside her chest at seeing it, at reliving the tragedy. She sank back against her pillows and watched the rest of the news without really absorbing it. When the weather report came on and the cheery weatherman in the ugly windowpane suit predicted another strong line of showers and storms, she turned off the TV.

Once again, Theodosia's brain hummed with ideas and suspects. Nick Prince, Bob Basset, Wyatt Orlock, Frank Lynch, or Tim Holt? Any one of them could be guilty. Or none of them.

A lot to ponder. Except now, as Theodosia snuggled down beneath the covers, she knew she had to get some sleep.

Try to anyway.

16

❧

Theodosia waited until she was alone with Drayton. Until Miss Dimple was busy setting tables for their Thursday morning tea and Haley had scurried back to the kitchen to check on her raspberry scones, benne wafers, and banana cake.

When they were finally alone, Theodosia said, "I think my neighbor could be the killer."

Drayton had been carefully measuring Pu-erh tea into a yellow teapot. When he heard Theodosia's words his hand jerked and he promptly set down his scoop. He turned to face her. "Your neighbor, the true crime writer? The one who visited the tea shop yesterday and last night came screaming in to take copious amounts of notes?"

"That's the guy."

"Well now." Drayton resumed measuring out his tea with a slightly steadier hand. "Tell me why you think an infamous killer is living next door to you and masquerading as a writer."

"Because I went to his LinkedIn page . . . You know what that is, don't you?"

"Somewhat, yes. Go on."

"Anyway, I searched the dates that Nick Prince lived and worked in Charleston."

"And?"

"Prince was living here in Charleston seven years ago when the first two murders took place. He was gone for a few years, presumably writing his two books, but now he's back. It looks to me as if his movements coincide perfectly with the timing of the murders."

Drayton looked interested. "The killings from seven years ago and the current murders?"

"That's right. Problem is, I don't have any solid evidence that links Prince to these recent murders. Or to any of the women."

"So this is all grand supposition on your part," Drayton said.

"Call it a hunch."

Drayton gave a small smile. "I have to admit, you're often blessed with excellent hunches."

"There's more, Drayton. When Earl Grey and I were walking down the alley last night, coming back from our run, I peeked into Prince's garage." Theodosia hesitated. "His washing machine was working overtime."

"Doing what?"

"Washing bloody clothes?"

"Goodness, if you're sneaking around, peering into his garage like that, you really do see him as a prime suspect," Drayton said.

"Unfortunately, I also like Bob Basset because he's kind of a nutcase outsider, Tim Holt because he's Cara's ex-boyfriend, and Wyatt Orlock the hot-shot real estate guy because he's after Lois's building. Oh, and do you know who else I saw last night?"

"Who?"

"Frank Lynch."

"Remind me again who Frank Lynch is?"

"He's the guy who works for Wyatt Orlock. He's head of security or something like that."

"Orlock is in need of security?"

"Apparently so."

"And you saw this Lynch guy in White Point Gardens last night?"

"Just for an instant."

"Interesting."

"Maybe. Maybe not."

"Tell me again why you suspect Orlock? Aside from the fact that he's a nightclub impresario."

"Because there's big money involved."

"You mean his real estate? The condo sales?" Drayton said.

"Right. We know Orlock is hot to buy the building that Antiquarian Books now occupies. Except Lois has a good long lease. So what better way to exert unbearable pressure on her than to kill her daughter?"

"Yes, you mentioned that before. Send Lois into a tailspin so she's amenable—maybe even relieved—to shut down her bookshop for good," Drayton said.

"That's my general thinking at this point."

"Attacking Lois would be outrageous," Drayton said as he lifted a teakettle and poured hot water into his teapot. "But your accusation is basically unfounded."

"It sort of works except for . . ."

"What?"

"I keep thinking about the weird duo that showed up last night," Theodosia said.

"Meaning?"

"The minute Monica Garber's body was discovered, both Bob Basset and Nick Prince were Johnny-on-the-spot, ready to soak up the drama and take notes. Prince for his book, and Basset for a feature article in one of his scandal rags. I mean, how did they *know?* Unless maybe one of them was involved?"

"You make another semi-valid point," Drayton said.

"Again, my problem is I don't have any concrete evidence of wrongdoing," Theodosia said. "In order to get the police to sit up and take notice, there has to be actual evidence."

"Then we need to work that much harder," Drayton said.

"You're still willing to help me investigate?" Theodosia paused. "Actually, it's more of a shadow investigation. Riley knows some of it, but he doesn't know the whole story."

"Call it what you wish, but haven't I been there for you thus far?"

"You have. And thank you for being my partner in crime. Or partner in trying to *solve* crime anyway." Theodosia was happy to know she wasn't in this all by her lonesome.

The next hour was frantically busy at the Indigo Tea Shop. At least two dozen customers showed up, happy to escape the rain that still plagued the area, happy to indulge in a nice hot cup of tea and a scone to go along with it. Theodosia and Miss Dimple worked side by side taking and delivering orders until around eleven fifteen, when the rush finally ended.

"Whew," Theodosia said when she had a moment to relax and talk to Drayton again. "Busy morning."

"You'll never guess who just called," Drayton said as he lined up a row of teapots, looking pleased.

"Please tell me it was the police. With news they've apprehended Fogheel Jack."

"Noooo." Drayton adjusted his bow tie—today it was yellow polka dots—and said, "It was a lovely call from the editor at *Southern Gourmet Magazine*. You know that fancy Primavera Tea we're planning for next month?"

"Sure, the one we listed in their magazine's 'Upcoming Teas' section," Theodosia said.

"*Southern Gourmet* is sending one of their food critics to cover it."

"Seriously? To do a story?"

"More of a review," Drayton said.

"Just for our event?"

"Not exactly. Per the editor, their food critic will also be reviewing several new Charleston restaurants."

"Did you ask what was on their list?"

"I did. Since I knew your curiosity gene would be working overtime."

"Was one of them Sparks? The place Wyatt Orlock owns?"

"Unfortunately, that *is* one of the restaurants," Drayton said.

"I wonder if Sparks's food is notable enough to even warrant a review."

Drayton shrugged. "These days, if a restaurant has the right buzz and craft bartenders, it doesn't seem to matter."

"Buzz?" Theodosia was amused. This was a departure from Drayton's usual formality. "Where did you learn about buzz?"

Drayton smiled. "From Haley, where else?"

"So some of her youthful exuberance has rubbed off on you?"

"Only some of it."

With a quick glance at the tea room, Theodosia hurried into her office. She grabbed her phone, dialed Channel Eight, and asked to be put through to Bobby (she didn't know his last name) the cameraman.

Apparently, *Bobby the cameraman* was enough because two minutes later he was on the line.

"Yello," he said.

"Bobby? It's Theodosia. Remember me? The lady from the tea shop who helped you do the interview with Jesse Trumbull last night?"

"Oh yeah," Bobby said. "Hi. Thanks again for doing that."

"How are you holding up? You and Trevor?"

"Hanging in there," Bobby said. "But it's not easy. Monica was a good team leader and we all got along great." His voice caught in this throat, then he added, "It's gonna be tough to replace her."

"I'll bet. Say, did the police show up at the studio to check out Monica's e-mail?"

"Yup, a squad of techs showed up first thing this morning."

"They find anything?"

"I think it's too early to tell. They had to get a bunch of warrants or subpoenas or something to go into all the various computers, e-mail accounts, service providers, networks, servers, and routers . . . you know how it is."

Actually, I don't, Theodosia thought. *That's the one good thing about being an amateur snoop. No pesky protocols to hold me back.*

"I do," Theodosia said. "And it probably won't be easy."

"What?" Bobby said.

"I said it probably . . ."

"Sorry," Bobby said. "I was talking to dispatch. We just got a call that there's a big spinout on the Ravenel Bridge. Eighteen-wheeler. We have to cover it. Gotta run."

And he was gone.

Business at the Indigo Tea Shop picked up speed the closer they got to lunch. That's when guests began pouring in. Including Tim Holt.

"Hey," Holt called to Theodosia. "Have you got a minute?"

Theodosia really didn't, but decided she'd make time for him. *You never know*, she thought. She might pick up some new information.

"Let me seat these guests and I'll get right back to you," Theodosia told him.

She led two parties of guests to their tables, gave them a quick rundown on the menu, told them about Hello Spring, Drayton's new house-blended tea, then ran back to greet Holt.

"What's up?" Theodosia asked.

"I heard about what happened last night," he said. "Weird."

"More like terrifying."

"I hope you don't think I was involved," Holt said.

"That's why you stopped in? To try and convince me of your innocence?"

"Not exactly. But it couldn't hurt, right? I mean, even now you seem a little skeptical."

"Probably because I am. Right now I'm a firm believer in Napoleonic law. Guilty until proven innocent."

"Aw, come on," Holt said. "The police have badgered and bugged me for the past three days—and found nada." He opened his arms wide, as if pleading his case. "I'm a good guy, an innocent guy."

"Yet you're following these murders closely," Theodosia said.

"So are you."

"Because Cara's mother is a dear friend of mine."

"Look." Holt leaned in and his voice turned serious. "I really liked Cara. She was special to me. Yeah, she broke my heart. But, believe me, what happened to her, getting murdered by that maniac, broke my heart all over again. If you're investigating, and I'm fairly sure you are, I hope you're able to dig in hard where the police can't." His eyes burned with intensity. "And if I can help—in any way—just let me know. Okay?"

"Okay."

As Theodosia watched Tim Holt walk out the door, she felt strangely mollified. Maybe Tim Holt was an innocent bystander after all.

Or maybe not.

A strange thought buzzed through Theodosia's brain. *Does Fogheel Jack date his women before he kills them?*

Then she remembered the black roses at Cara's apartment. Someone had sent them.

*Someone who wanted to get close to Cara? Or did get close to her?
Conned her into meeting him in St. Philip's Graveyard and then
killed her?*

Theodosia shuddered. No, she didn't really want to go there.
The idea was too twisted for words.

With every table but one filled, Theodosia watched as Delaine
came swirling into the tea shop like a grand duchess. And who
should she have in tow but Lois Chamberlain!

Theodosia hurried over to greet them. Delaine was dressed in
a fire-engine red skirt suit with tons of gold jewelry—necklaces,
pins, bracelets—while Lois wore an olive drab raincoat over her
navy crew-neck sweater, khaki pants, and sensible shoes.

Delaine, being Delaine, immediately began talking in her
loudest, most authoritative voice.

"You see this dear lady here?" Delaine brayed, three charm
bracelets rattling on her wrist as she gestured at Lois. "She was
just in my shop—"

"Looking for an appropriate funeral dress," Lois said quietly.
"For tomorrow's service."

"Oh no," Theodosia said. For some reason this struck her as
being terribly sad.

"I said don't give it another thought," Delaine interrupted. "I
told Lois that I'd deliver a few dresses to her home so she can
choose what she wants in privacy—and then send the rest back."

"That's very kind of you," Theodosia said.

"Nonsense," Delaine said. "You know I always go the extra
mile."

Actually, Theodosia knew firsthand that Delaine was spiteful,
erratic, and self-centered, existing only in her little Delaine bubble. Today, however, she was brimming with the milk of human
kindness. Interesting. She must be up to something.

"Anyway," Delaine said. "I decided to invite our dear Lois to
lunch. Well, more like *drag* her since she did put up a pro forma

protest. But here we are anyway." Delaine favored Theodosia with a brilliant smile, then looked past her into the tea room. "So you have a table for us? A good one I hope?"

"Absolutely." Theodosia led Delaine and Lois to a small table by the window that Miss Dimple had hastily set up. With candles glowing and teacups sparkling, it looked cozy and inviting.

Delaine made a big show of setting her Gucci bag on the table, then said in a stage whisper, "Can you believe there was *another* murder last night?"

"Tragic," Theodosia said, hoping Delaine wouldn't natter on about it.

But she did.

"I figure it had to be the same maniac who killed Cara," Delaine said. "Our resident strangler."

The color drained from Lois's face and her hands clutched into fists. She looked, at that moment, as if she wanted to jump up and flee the tea shop. Fortunately, she didn't.

"Let's leave that sort of speculation to the authorities, shall we?" Theodosia said. "In the meantime, I'm delighted you both dropped in for lunch because Haley whipped up her special lobster Benedict with grilled asparagus."

Delaine, who was easily distracted, said, "Ooh, sounds delish." She smiled across the table at Lois. "Don't you think, dear?"

Lois nodded, as if in a trance. "Sure."

Delaine turned her attention back to Theodosia. "Did you remember the vigil was tonight? I assume you're coming, correct?"

"I suppose so," Theodosia said. "But . . ."

Delaine cocked her head like an inquisitive magpie. "Hmm?"

"Is the vigil still going to be held in White Point Gardens?"

"Of course," Delaine said as she studied her French manicure. "That's what's printed on all the posters, so that's where it will be."

"Even after last night's murder?" Theodosia said.

"Especially after last night's murder," Delaine replied curtly.

"We'll certainly include that poor lady reporter in our thoughts." She nodded as if making a note to herself. "Anyway, after the candle lighting and prayers, we're having a choir perform. They're going to sing two of my very favorites—'Wind Beneath My Wings' and 'Tears in Heaven.'"

Lois gazed at Theodosia with slightly lowered lids. "As you can see, Delaine enjoys taking charge. My dress, tonight's vigil . . ."

"I've noticed that about her," Theodosia said in a commiserating tone.

"Because I'm *good* at it," Delaine shot back. "Honestly, people, *someone* has to show a bit of can-do spirit and gumption." When she saw Theodosia and Lois cringe, she said, "I didn't mean *you two* weren't doing your part, I just meant I'm always happy to step in and take the lead. Help organize things."

"Of course," Theodosia said. Better to drop that particular hot potato. Just let it sit there and hopefully cool down.

Theodosia took their orders—both women opted for the lobster Benedict—then ran them in to Haley. In the kitchen she picked up four just-completed luncheon orders and delivered them to tables four and six. When Delaine's and Lois's lunches were ready, she ran them out, only to find Delaine prodding Lois about suspects.

"Surely you must be suspicious of the boyfriend," Delaine was saying. "What's his name? Tim something?"

"I'm suspicious, yes, though I never did get around to meeting him in person," Lois said.

"How strange," Delaine said.

Lois shook her head. "They weren't together that long and you don't know Cara. She could be . . . secretive."

Delaine frowned. "That's unfortunate."

Theodosia made a big show of setting down their plates and explaining that the lobster was fresh from Phil's Fish Market and how Haley's sauce was actually a lovely Mornay sauce.

"This luncheon looks delicious, dear," Delaine said. Then a smile exploded on her face as if she'd just been struck by a magic thunderbolt filled with stars and unicorns. "Ladies." Delaine fluttered her hands. "I just had the most *brilliant* idea."

"What?" Theodosia asked.

"Again?" Lois said.

"Why don't we have an après funeral reception tomorrow?" Delaine squealed. "Do it right here at the Indigo Tea Shop. You know, invite a few close friends and relatives?"

"Are you sure about this? It's awfully spur-of-the-moment." Theodosia noticed that Lois looked beyond uncomfortable at Delaine's suggestion.

"I think it's a *fantastic* idea, a way to gain closure." When Theodosia and Lois looked puzzled, Delaine added, "I meant closure on the service itself." She aimed a dazzling smile at Theodosia. "You can be a dear and handle a teeny-tiny reception, can't you, Theo?"

"I'd be happy to. As long as Lois is on board with it."

"Well, maybe," Lois said. She seemed to weigh the idea, then said, "Actually, it does sound lovely. And I think Cara would approve."

Theodosia nodded. "That's all I need to know."

17

❧

Delaine ate sparingly, talked incessantly, then threw down a handful of money on the table, apologizing for the fact that she needed to rush back to her shop to supervise a fitting for an important client.

Lois lingered over her second—and then third—cup of tea as Drayton fussed over her with refills and soothing words. By the time one thirty rolled around, Miss Dimple was handling all the remaining customers with ease. So when Lois stood up to leave, Theodosia slipped on her raincoat and walked with her back to Antiquarian Books.

As they strolled through the rain, Lois said, "When you went to Cara's apartment everything was okay, wasn't it?"

"Aside from the mysterious bouquet of roses, which the police are still investigating, everything looked fine," Theodosia said. Truth be told, the place had felt lonely to her, the way any home feels when you know the owner isn't coming back.

"I stopped by this morning and Cara's place looked as if someone had ripped it apart. Books were scattered all over the floor, desk drawers pulled out, the clothes in her closet shoved aside."

"I didn't do any of that," Theodosia said. "It had to be the police. I'm sure when they came to collect the roses, they searched the place top to bottom for clues."

Lois sighed. "I suppose."

Theodosia thought about the scratching sound she'd heard the night she was there.

"On the other hand, it's entirely possible that someone broke in and went through Cara's stuff. Or maybe the manager moved things around, deciding if the place needed any repairs before he rented it again. Or the ex-boyfriend slipped in?"

Lois shook her head. "No idea."

When they reached the front door of Antiquarian Books, Lois pulled out a ring of keys.

"How long do you think you'll stay closed?" Theodosia asked.

Lois turned the key in the lock and pushed open the door so they could step inside, out of the rain. The interior was dim, with just a faint light in the back office, and smelled heavily of old leather and paper. But in a pleasant way.

"I haven't given it much thought," Lois said. "Maybe a week?"

"This means you *will* keep the bookshop going?"

"Haven't you heard?" Lois said in a voice tinged with irony. "I have a nice long lease."

Back at the Indigo Tea Shop, Theodosia and Drayton huddled together at the front counter. They were staging their Murder at Chillingham Manor Mystery Tea this coming Saturday and Theodosia wanted to review the plans.

"So you've hired two actors?" she asked.

"Both hot off the stage from our very own Dock Street Theatre," Drayton said as he opened his spiral notebook. "The female actor, Maria, will be playing the Duchess of Lennox, and the male actor, John, will be Viscount Ragley."

"And they have the script you wrote?"

"Yes, but remember, we're all characters in the mystery play as well."

"I remembered. I just haven't had a chance to memorize my lines," Theodosia said.

"Maybe you need cue cards."

"Maybe I should write my lines in the palm of my hand."

"No," Drayton said. "Probably not. But while we're on the subject of event teas, I think we should go over some of our ideas and firm them up." He spread out several loose calendar pages. "Remember, spring is our busiest season, what with the Spoleto Festival, our Easter Tea, and our Garden Party Tea. To say nothing of Bridal Shower Teas, and Mother's Day Teas."

"I hear you," Theodosia said as she studied the calendar pages. "And we've tentatively scheduled a Primavera Tea, Limón Tea, and Great Gatsby Tea."

"I think we should heavy up even more. Add a Bird Tea or Butterfly Tea."

"I love both those ideas."

"Bridal Shower Teas . . ." Drayton tapped a pencil against his notebook. "Those can pop up anytime. There's no dearth of women getting married, and brides do love their tea parties."

"I've been thinking, when we do our Limón Tea it would be great to stage it outside in a lemon grove."

Drayton looked pleasantly startled. "Here I've been dreaming of glass bowls heaped with fresh lemons on each table, but you're talking about tea tables set in an actual lemon grove? Where would we find that sort of location?"

"There was a recent article in the *Post and Courier* about a lemon grove nearby that's thriving. It's actually part of a citrus hobby farm at a place called Brittlebank Manor just south of here."

"So we'd set up our tea on-site?"

"If they'll have us, why not?"

"Actually, it's a marvelous idea. Gives us a chance to stretch our creative wings. We could also—" The phone rang, interrupting their conversation. Drayton answered it, gave a silent nod, and passed it to Theodosia.

"Hello?" she said.

"Theo." It was Riley and he sounded beat.

"How's your day going?" she asked, hoping for a break in the case. "Got any new information?"

"Nada."

"Seriously? Nothing at all?"

"We're still waiting for the techies to tell us what they found on the computers over at Channel Eight, and about e-mails on their server. Unfortunately, it's slow going."

"Okay. Gee, it's good to hear your voice."

"Likewise, sweetheart."

"Do you have any interest in cashing that rain check tonight?" Theodosia asked. Her mind was running ahead to she-crab soup, biscuits, and . . .

Then she remembered.

"Oh, wait, Drayton and I have tentative plans for dinner tonight . . ." She looked over at Drayton, saw him nod in the affirmative. "So there's that. Then I was going to hit the candlelight vigil."

"Please don't tell me the vigil's going to be held in White Point Gardens," Riley said.

"It's going to be held in White Point Gardens."

"Doggone, that means there'll be a whole bunch of women milling around over there, potentially vulnerable women."

"What about safety in numbers?"

"That only works until your event breaks up. Then it's everyone for themselves."

"You make it sound like nobody should leave their house."

"If I had my way, they wouldn't," Riley said. "Not until this maniac is apprehended and put under lock and key." Then, "Sorry, Theo, I don't mean to be so grumbly."

"That's okay, I know you're under all kinds of pressure."

"Wish I could stop by tonight, but it looks like I'm out of luck. More meetings."

"Soon," Theodosia promised. "Real soon."

"Problem?" Drayton asked when she hung up.

"Just the usual. The wheels of justice turning slowly."

"Huh. In my life I view slow as a good thing, something to be appreciated."

"What's a good thing?" Haley asked as she strolled up to the counter.

"Your baking skills," Drayton said. Then, "You look like you're about to run out somewhere. Are you?"

"I thought I'd dash over to Perry's Restaurant Supply on Market Street. Pick up a new garlic press and a couple of strainers." Haley gazed at Theodosia. "If that's okay with you."

"Sure thing," Theodosia said. "Just charge them to our account."

"You know it's still drizzling outside," Drayton said. His eyes flicked to the front window. "And it's getting dark."

Haley shrugged. "I guess."

"Do you have a raincoat? An umbrella?" Drayton asked.

"I think I have an umbrella upstairs somewhere," Haley said.

"Grab my raincoat," Theodosia said. "It's hanging on the coat rack in my office."

"Don't you need it?" Haley asked.

"Not for a while. I'm going to stick around and do some more event planning with Drayton. Probably still be here by the time you get back."

"Okay, thanks. See you guys later," Haley said as she headed for the back door.

"So this magical lemon grove," Drayton said. "You think we can reserve a Saturday afternoon there?"

"I'll give them a call tomorrow, see if we can set something up."

"Excellent. And then we talked about having a Jane Austen Tea."

"I love that idea. I think there's even a Jane Austen Society here in Charleston. Maybe we could hook up with them—they could do some sort of reading or presentation."

Drayton made a note. "Works for me."

They worked for another ten minutes or so, kicking around ideas, deciding to try to shoehorn in a British-themed tea as well.

"Maybe call it Tea in the Cotswolds," Drayton said.

"Or even a Charles Dickens Tea," Theodosia said. "Although that might work better for Christmas."

"That's it, then," Drayton declared as he set down his pen. "My brain is starting to feel fried. Or at least gently sautéed."

"If you're tired, maybe we should do dinner another time?"

Drayton waved a hand as he stood up and stretched. "Nonsense, I still want you to come tonight. Please. I was planning to whip up something fast. No big deal. I already bought groceries."

"Okay, that'd be great." Theodosia checked her watch. "Maybe leave in a half hour or so?"

"Mmn." Drayton had wandered back to the counter and was stacking tea tins on his shelves.

Theodosia closed her notebook and went into her office, anxious to check her e-mail. Maybe something new? She clicked through the list quickly. Most concerned upcoming tea reservations, so she tippy-typed confirmations back to them. But as she was typing, she thought she heard a strange noise.

Looking up from her keyboard, she said, "What?" to nobody in particular. A few seconds later, when she didn't hear it again, she returned to her e-mails.

Then . . . THUMP.

Another noise, louder this time, as if somebody was outside banging on a metal trash can.

The guys in the garden apartment across the alley? A stray cat? A really big stray cat?

Sighing, Theodosia threaded her way through the boxes piled in her office, pulled open the back door, and peered out into semidarkness.

It took a few seconds for her to realize that Haley lay sprawled on the ground some fifteen feet away from her.

"Help!" Haley cried in a faint voice when she saw Theodosia framed in the doorway. "Help me!"

Heart in her throat, Theodosia sprinted to where Haley was lying and dropped to her hands and knees. Never mind the rain and the puddles.

"Haley, what happened?" Theodosia figured Haley must have slipped on the wet cobblestones and taken a tumble. But then she'd lain there for . . . what? Ten minutes? Who knew how long?

"I think I'm . . ." Haley groaned as she rolled over and fought to sit up.

"Haley, you're hurt!" Terrible scenarios suddenly capered through Theodosia's brain.

Haley blinked, tried to focus, and groaned again.

"What happened, Haley?" Maybe this wasn't just an awkward tumble. Had Haley been pushed or stabbed or shot? Theodosia quickly checked her over. There wasn't any bleeding; no bones seemed to be broken. Still, she probably needed medical attention.

"My head," Haley said in a piteous whisper. "Somebody hit me." She reached up, touched a spot above her right ear, and said, "I can feel something wet and warm trickling down. I think maybe I'm . . . bleeding." Now a thin note of hysteria entered her voice.

Suddenly, the back door flew open, a black rectangle oozing yellow light. Drayton walked out and shouted, "Theo, where did you . . . ?" He cast his eyes up and down the alley, then did a kind of double take when he spotted the two of them on the ground. "What are you two doing down there?"

"Haley's hurt!" Theodosia cried. "Somebody hit her on the head and shoved her down. We have to call 911."

"No," Haley said, lifting her head and squinting at them. "It's not like I'm *dying* or anything. But, um, maybe you guys could help me up?"

Theodosia and Drayton got on either side of Haley and lifted her gently. She proved to be light as a feather.

"Easy now," Drayton cautioned once Haley was standing upright on wobbly legs. "You can never be too careful with head injuries."

"You think she's concussed?" Theodosia asked.

"I do feel like cussing!" Haley blurted out. "Because it hurts like crazy!"

Theodosia and Drayton exchanged glances. Even though Haley was back on her feet, she seemed a little out of it.

"Haley, what happened?" Theodosia asked.

"Huh?" Haley's eyes were glazed. She really was having trouble following the conversation.

"What happened?" Drayton said. "Was someone lurking in the shadows when you came out or—"

"It was like a drive-by," Haley said, her arms starting to flail.

"How so?" This from Theodosia now.

"A car came whipping down the alley the minute I stepped out the back door."

"Like they'd been waiting for you?" Theodosia asked.

"Now that you mention it, yeah," Haley said. "Kind of."

"And then what?" Theodosia said.

"The car roared down the alley and swerved at me, like they were trying to run me down."

"Did they actually *hit* you?" Drayton asked.

"Lucky for me I jumped out of the way, but the car came so close that the side mirror whacked me in the head. Spun me around and dropped me like a sack of potatoes," Haley said. Her lower lip trembled. "Cut me."

"Let's get you inside and take a look at that cut," Theodosia said.

They helped Haley inside and sat her down in Theodosia's desk chair. Theodosia brushed Haley's hair aside while Drayton took a look at her scalp wound.

"Hmm. I'd say you need stitches, my dear," Drayton said.

"Maybe you could stick a Band-Aid on it?" Haley asked.

"And gum up your hair?" Drayton said.

"Hold everything, this cut looks fairly deep," Theodosia said. She moved her Tensor lamp closer to Haley's head and saw that the jagged wound was still seeping fresh blood.

"Oh yeah, stitches for sure," Theodosia said.

"I hate hospitals," Haley said.

"No hospital," Drayton said. "Just a simple trip to the emergency room."

"Drayton's right," Theodosia said. "We need to get you to the emergency room. Once they patch you up, we'll bring you right back here."

"You guys promise?" Haley reached for Theodosia's hand and clutched it tightly.

"We promise," Theodosia said.

* * *

Haley was lucky. The ER wasn't one bit busy this Thursday night, so a young resident by the name of Dr. Tony Wieks was able to see her right away.

"That's quite a cut you have," Dr. Wieks said to Haley. "You want to tell me how you got it?"

"I fell down," Haley said.

"Somebody shoved her down," Drayton said. He seemed more nervous than Haley at being in the ER.

"Am I telling this or are you?" Haley grumped at him.

"Judging by the tone of your voice, you seem to be feeling better," Drayton said. "Feisty."

"She's going to be fine," Dr. Wieks said. He gazed intently at Haley. "Five stitches should do the trick. But first I'm going to numb you up."

Haley groaned. "With a needle?"

"No," Drayton said. "He's going to hit you over the head with a tire iron."

"You guys," Dr. Wieks laughed. "You all work together?"

"If you could call it that," Drayton said.

"This has been kind of a crazy week for us," Haley said as Dr. Wieks picked up a syringe and injected lidocaine into Haley's cut.

"Ouch!" she cried. "That hurt more than getting knocked down."

While Haley got her stitches, gripping Drayton's hand like a vise, Theodosia walked out into the hallway and called Riley.

"Theo?" he said. "I thought you had to—"

"Haley just got assaulted," Theodosia said.

"What!"

"Right outside our back door."

"At the tea shop? What happened? Is she all right?"

"We're at the ER now; she needed a couple of stitches on the side of her head."

"Holy crap."

"I know," Theodosia said. "Somebody drove their car down our alley and tried to run her down. It's weird."

"It's more than that."

"Do you think you could send a patrol car over to search the Church Street area? I mean, I'm sure whoever went after Haley is gone now. But you never know."

"I'll send a cruiser right away," Riley said. "Don't . . . are you going back there?"

"Haley wants to go back to her apartment, yes."

"Do you think she'll let you stay with her?"

"No," Theodosia said. "Knowing Haley, she's going to want to curl up with her cat, drink some hot cocoa, and watch TV. Something mindless on Bravo."

"So you're still having dinner at Drayton's place?"

Theodosia looked down the hallway to where Drayton was standing, chatting with one of the nurses now.

"That's the plan," she said.

"So Haley's okay, but what about you?"

"Oh, you know me. When I get to the end of my rope I just tie a knot and hang on."

That brought a chuckle from Riley.

Then Theodosia turned serious. "There's something I need to tell you."

"What's that?"

"It might be nothing, but . . ."

"Spit it out."

"Haley was wearing my raincoat. So maybe . . ."

"Maybe her assailant was really after you?" Riley said.

"The thought had crossed my mind."

"You'd better go straight home," Riley said.

"No, I'm going to stick to my original plan. Dinner at Drayton's, then the vigil."

"Don't be out alone. Please don't be alone."

"I won't."

"Promise?"

"I promise."

Once Haley was pronounced good to go, they drove her home and walked her upstairs to her apartment.

"Teacake," Haley said happily when she spotted her little orange-and-brown cat.

The cat immediately jumped into Haley's arms, snuggled against her, and purred.

"I'll be okay now," Haley said. Teacake was purring as if there were an electric motor inside his fuzzy little body.

"Are you sure?" Theodosia asked. "Because you could always pack a few things and come home with me." She gazed at Teacake, who looked at her and stretched out a paw. "You'd both be welcome."

Haley shook her head. "No, you guys go on, have your dinner. We'll be okay. I plan to flake out in front of the TV with his nibs here and then hit the sack early."

"Lock the door behind us," Drayton said. "And we'll check both doors downstairs to make sure they're latched tight. And if you need anything . . ."

"Just call." Haley nodded. "I know the drill."

"We hope you do," Drayton muttered as he and Theodosia stumped down the back stairs.

"She'll be fine," Theodosia said as they double-checked the locks on both doors. "As for you, if you're not in the mood . . ."

"My dear," Drayton drawled. "I'm always in the mood for a well-cooked dinner. I just hope you are, too."

18

◈

As Drayton sizzled a half dozen pieces of free-range chicken, Theodosia decided she was definitely in the mood. Dinner at Drayton's was always an event, and not just because he was a superb chef—he'd taught at Johnson & Wales culinary school for several years—but because he made everything special. Food, wine, table setting, conversation. Right now he was adding chopped onions and garlic to his pan. A bottle of white wine was standing by.

"So what exactly are you making here?" Theodosia asked.

"I call it Drunken Southern Chicken," Drayton said. "It's an old family recipe."

"Uh-huh."

"Or maybe I found it in a magazine, I can't quite recall. Anyway . . ." He lifted his hands to show his ingredients. "I have my mise en place ready to go. Or, in this case, my mess in place."

Theodosia giggled.

"You think I'm not serious?" Drayton lifted one eyebrow, then turned, saw that Honey Bee had finished her food, and said,

"What would you think about taking the little princess out for a romp?"

"Happy to."

Theodosia was always delighted to hang out with a dog, especially when it was in Drayton's carefully curated backyard. Besides a brick patio and ribbon of green lawn, the yard consisted of a small Japanese pavilion, curved fishpond with Taihu rocks, groves of tall bamboo, winding gravel paths, and all manner of benches and pedestals where his prize Japanese bonsai were on display.

When Theodosia finally took Honey Bee back inside, the kitchen was even more fragrant with cooking aromas.

"It smells fantastic in here," Theodosia said. Bubbling away in a rich golden sauce, the chicken looked plump and enticing and she was suddenly feeling ravenous. It had been a tough day— actually, a tough week.

"Almost done. The chicken's coming along nicely and I've got a pot of rice going as well."

"Carolina gold?"

"Is there anything else?"

"Be still my heart," Theodosia said as she gazed about Drayton's elegant kitchen. The stove he was working on was a six-burner Wolf gas range, the sink was custom-hammered copper, and the cupboards were Carolina pine faced with glass. The better to show off his collection of antique teapots and Chinese blue-and-white vases.

"Is that a new teapot?" Theodosia pointed to an ornate blue-and-gold teapot that sat in one of the cupboards. "I thought you said you'd hit your limit, that you'd declared a moratorium on buying any more teapots."

"Did I say that?" Drayton's response was pure innocence.

"Yes. And yet . . ."

"I couldn't help myself. There it was in full glorious color in the auction catalog, just staring straight out at me. Hard to resist an antique Gaudy Welsh teapot."

"So you put in a bid and won," Theodosia said. "Probably made sure it was the high bid."

"You know I have a passion for English soft-paste porcelain," Drayton said as he opened the cupboard door, took it out, and handed it to Theodosia. "What do you think? Do you like it?"

"Are you kidding?" Theodosia turned the teapot one way, then another, savoring the heft of it and the hand-painted design. "It's drop-dead gorgeous."

"I thought for fun I'd bring it to the tea shop and use it. And by the way, Miss Theodosia, have you counted the number of teapots in *your* personal collection?"

"Never mind that."

Drayton pursed his lips. "Right."

Theodosia decided to change the subject. "Anything I can do to help?"

"Actually, yes. Since this is about ready to serve, you can grab a spoon and ladle rice from that cooker into those two Chinese blue-and-white bowls sitting on the counter. It'll just take me a sec to taste and finish off my sauce." He dipped a spoon in and said, "Much like a pinch for the pot, I think this could use a tad more paprika."

Theodosia set the teapot down and got to work. She grabbed a clean spoon and scooped steaming mounds of rice into the two bowls.

"Now what?"

"You've done a masterful job, but I'll take it from here," Drayton said. "Do you prefer your *poulette* white or dark?"

"Dark, please."

Drayton placed a plump golden-brown thigh atop one of the mounds of rice, then poured a generous amount of cream sauce over it. He fixed a bowl for himself, then they carried their dinners on trays into the adjoining dining room. Here candles flickered, silverware gleamed, a bottle of Chablis sat chilling in a wine bucket, and warm, crusty poppy seed rolls nestled in a traditional South Carolina sweetgrass basket.

"I love that your dining room is so formal," Theodosia said as she pulled out her chair and sat down.

"As opposed to mindlessly gulping dinner in front of a TV set?"

Theodosia chuckled. "Do you even own a TV?"

"Well, yes," Drayton said. "As an accommodation to modernity and the fact that I like my news on demand, I do have a small one. But really, Theo, formal dining is a good thing. Most people today are too *in*formal. They've forgotten many of the niceties, especially when it comes to an evening meal."

"That's why people come to the Indigo Tea Shop. Because we offer a gracious, semiformal experience."

Drayton's face expressed contentment. "Almost a ritual, isn't it? The steeping of the tea leaves, a table set with glowing candles, white linen tablecloths, polished silver, genuine bone china teacups . . ."

"To say nothing of our food," Theodosia said, thinking about Haley and what an amazing chef she was.

"And our tea," Drayton added. "No other coffee or tea shop in Charleston rivals our array of fresh, whole-leaf teas."

"Or your curated house blends. Your China Black Orchid, Sweet Lady Grey, and Chamomile Crush are always popular."

Drayton poured out glasses of wine and they enjoyed their chicken and rice, talking easily, chatting about friends and about the upcoming tea parties they'd begun to plan. They didn't mention the dead, strangled women, nor did they talk about possible suspects. For now, it was enough to sit on velvet-tufted chairs and enjoy fine food and wine in Drayton's Southern-style dining room with its crystal chandelier, damask draperies, and Sheraton sideboard.

"Excuse me," Theodosia said, "but your drunken chicken is so delicious I'm practically scraping the bottom of my bowl."

"Tonight it's allowed," Drayton said.

"Do you think we should call Haley and check on her?"

"Make sure she didn't pass out from post-concussion complications? I think calling her is probably a smart idea."

"Even if I make the call while sitting at the table?"

"With such extenuating circumstances, I think we can skip protocol."

Haley answered on the third ring, sounding a little sleepy.

"How are you feeling?" Theodosia asked.

"Kinda tired," Haley said. "And bruised. My left shoulder hurts where I landed on it."

"She should turn in early," Drayton said.

"Did you hear that?" Theodosia asked. "Drayton says you should turn in early."

"I will," Haley said. "Hey, thank you, guys. If you hadn't come along when you did and peeled me off the pavement like a piece of roadkill, I'd still be lying there."

"That's what we do," Theodosia said, a smile in her voice. "Rescue each other as needed."

"Okay, I appreciate your checking on me," Haley said. "Thank Drayton for me, too, will you?"

"Will do," Theodosia said as she clicked off. She turned to Drayton. "Haley's doing okay. She sounded bone weary but doesn't seem to be suffering any major ill effects."

"Good. Who do you think . . . ?"

"Who do I think came after Haley?" Theodosia said. "I honestly don't know."

"Haley was wearing your raincoat, you realize. Which means you could have been the intended target."

"A case of mistaken identity. I thought about that."

"Maybe we should put our heads together and talk about this," Drayton said.

"See what we can come up with," Theodosia said. Suddenly, the events of the past four days came flooding back to her, making her feel tired and a little overwhelmed. "I think that's a good idea."

"With all the terrible goings-on lately, it's like Charleston is having a grand mal seizure."

"I hear you."

"Let me clear the table first," Drayton said. "Then we can enjoy cookies and a dessert tea in the library."

Theodosia was late getting to the vigil. She and Drayton had talked for almost an hour. Going over their suspect list, ticking off reasons why each person might be guilty. They came to the conclusion that *someone* had realized Theodosia was investigating and they'd come after her, only to get Haley by mistake.

Still, when all was said and done, they were left without any real answers.

Feeling frustrated, mumbling to herself about not finding a parking space, Theodosia circled White Point Gardens until she finally found a spot she could squeeze into. As she sat there, letting her engine tick down, she gazed across the lawn, where at least a hundred women had gathered together in a group. They'd just finished lighting their candles, and as the flames bobbed and shifted, the effect was like an undulating carpet of light.

Theodosia strode toward the group. There was a faint mist in the air, but it didn't seem to deter the women who'd shown up. She saw a few friends, waved at them and whispered hellos. When she finally located Delaine and Lois, the group was being led in prayer by a female deacon from St. Steven's Church.

Delaine spotted Theodosia immediately and toddled over, trying to keep her balance as the heels of her black stilettos sank into the damp turf.

"The-o-*do*-sia," Delaine hissed. "Where have you *been*?" Delaine was dressed in a black wool jacket and black leather slacks and sporting a huge button that said SISTERHOOD.

"Sorry, I got tied up," Theodosia said as the large group of women suddenly dissolved into smaller groups. Some bowed their heads and offered prayers; others sang and talked softly among themselves. "But it looks as if your vigil is a rousing success."

Looking suddenly pleased, Delaine said, "It is, isn't it? So many people showed up to pay tribute." She grabbed Theodosia's hand and squeezed it. "Luckily, you came just in time to hear the choir." She pointed at a group of two dozen women dressed in long white robes. "See? They're just warming up."

"How wonderful," Theodosia said as the choir leader stepped forward, raised both arms, and brought them down fast, signaling the group to begin a rousing version of "Wind Beneath My Wings."

"Gives me shivers," Delaine whispered, though she was generally short on sympathy and wasn't particularly religious.

Theodosia glanced around the park. She had shivers, too, but of a different sort. From where she stood, everything was quite solemn and lovely. It spoke of female solidarity and determination. But darkness was all around them. Shapes, wind-whipped trees, fog rolling in from Charleston Harbor. A strange vibe hung in the air and seemed to signal that anything could happen. That a killer could be lurking close by, like a wolf sniffing at the edge of an unsuspecting herd, ready to pounce on one of the weak ones and make a fresh kill.

The vigil went on for another fifteen minutes, with the choir singing "Tears in Heaven," a woman from a Take Back the Night organization giving a short speech, and Delaine thanking everyone for showing up.

When Theodosia finally arrived home at nine o'clock, Earl Grey thrust his muzzle at her and his limpid brown eyes cast a pleading look.

"Let me guess, Mrs. Barry stopped by to feed you and let you outside, but she didn't take you for a run."

"Rowr."

"Well, she is getting up there in age."

It was late, but Theodosia felt antsy and restless, her mind still working nonstop, turning things over and over.

"I've got monkey brain," Theodosia said to Earl Grey. "So let me change out of these clothes and we'll do a quick spin down the block. Okay?"

"Row-rahr."

Ten minutes later, Earl Grey bounded alongside Theodosia as they ran out the back door and headed down the alley. Head held high, he was happy to be out with his beloved human, delighted to be stretching his legs. Theodosia was also enjoying herself. The rain had finally backed off, leaving the night air thick with moisture. It was as if you could reach out and squeeze it like a sponge. But even with the ever-present dampness, the evening felt refreshing and cool, with a tuxedo-black sky overhead and the faint scent of jasmine on the wind.

They loped down Atlantic Street, then crossed over to Church Street, running past the Indigo Tea Shop, White Rabbit Children's Shop, Cabbage Patch Gift Shop, Antiquarian Books, and Bill Boyet's Camera Shop. As Theodosia crossed Water Street she hung a right and decided to take a quick detour down Stoll's Alley.

This hidden lane was one of Charleston's architectural treasures. A narrow, brick-paved passageway that was so narrow it couldn't even accommodate a small car. A centuries-old brick wall ran along one side of the alley, with Colonial-designed homes scrunched up together on the other side. Most sported latticed windows, brass door knockers, and faint porch lights. Stoll's Alley was definitely a fabulous amalgam of historic homes, moss-covered bricks, and overgrown greenery and flowers. Plus, you pretty much had to be a Charleston insider to find its quasi-secret entrance.

Halfway down Stoll's Alley, swallowed by darkness, Theodosia and Earl Grey breezed past the infamous devil with a violin statue. And that's when a SLAP-SLAP suddenly sounded behind them.

Theodosia turned to see what other soul was taking a nightly sprint, but it was nearly impossible to tell.

Feeling nervous, a sense of danger suddenly prickling inside her, she picked up her pace.

SLAP-SLAP-SLAP. So did the runner behind her.

Theodosia glanced over her shoulder, but with a single, faintly lit wrought-iron lantern illuminating the alley and casting a complex of shadows, it was impossible to see who was behind her.

Maybe not just behind me, maybe chasing me? The same person who went after Haley?

That thought exploded in her brain, compelling her to run faster.

Theodosia flew down the alley, came out on Bay Street, and hooked a right. Maybe if she ran back toward Church Street she could lose this bozo?

Not quite. Whoever was behind her continued to trail her.

"C'mon, boy." Theodosia shortened up on Earl Grey's leash, ran pell-mell down Church Street, turned down Lamboll, and headed for home.

She didn't have to look back because she could still hear footsteps and harsh breathing from the runner behind her.

Turning down her alley, closing in on home base, Theodosia put her head down and gave it everything she had. She was winded and the muscles in her legs were starting to burn, but she knew she was finally putting some distance between them.

Then everything went KA-BOOM as a shadowy figure materialized directly in front of her!

Whuh?

Theodosia tried to put on the brakes—too late!—and instead skittered crazily right into the arms of . . .

"You!" Theodosia shouted as she fought to turn sideways at the very last second, tried desperately to get away.

But Nick Prince had opened his arms wide, ready to embrace Theodosia as she careened into him.

"Let me go!" she shouted. She'd slammed into Prince so hard the impact made her teeth rattle. Tangled together in a macabre dance, they stumbled, sidestepped, practically collapsed together in a heap, but somehow managed to maintain their balance.

"Then go!" Prince shouted as he released her and spun away. "Hey." He looked angry and bewildered. "*You're* the one who crashed into *me*. You and that stupid dog of yours."

Theodosia retreated backward, bent over, and fought to catch her breath. Once she made sure Earl Grey was okay, she said, "Sorry. I didn't mean to run smack-dab into you like that."

"Apology accepted."

"And my dog's not stupid."

"Okay, I'm sorry about that. Now. Why were you running so hard? Are you training for a triathlon or one of those marathon endurance races?"

Theodosia shook her head. "Somebody was chasing me."

Prince eyed her warily, then looked down the dark alley. "I don't see anybody. Are you sure about that?"

"Pretty sure. Yeah, there was someone running behind me."

"Did you ever think that maybe they were just running? Like you do most nights?"

"It didn't feel that way," Theodosia said.

Prince took a step closer, looking interested. "What *did* it feel like?"

Theodosia took a step backward, pulled Earl Grey next to her, and said, "Danger."

19

Safe in her own kitchen, Theodosia grabbed a bottle of Fiji water from her fridge and gulped it down voraciously. Earl Grey went to his water dish and did the same.

She tried to tell herself she was okay, but her mind kept circling back to what had just happened.

I was out running and somebody followed me. Like, five hours after Haley got assaulted. So . . . am I a target?

The idea unnerved her because it was totally within the realm of possibility. She'd been investigating, asking questions, and . . . what? Getting too close to the truth? Now she had someone worried?

Who's worried? Is it Fogheel Jack?

Theodosia shuddered at the idea, knowing she'd probably stepped out of bounds and put herself in danger—definitely put Haley in danger. Maybe even Drayton if they continued to poke around. She drew a deep cleansing breath like she'd been taught in yoga class, blew it out, then gazed at Earl Grey and said, "We have to be a lot more careful, right, fella?"

Earl Grey glanced at her, a solemn look on his face. Then his ears suddenly flicked forward as if he'd suddenly gone on full alert, and his eyes locked on the back door. A low, menacing growl erupted from deep in his throat.

"What's wrong?" Theodosia said at the exact moment she heard footsteps scrape hard against patio bricks. Then, horror of horrors, the brass doorknob turned and the door began to creak open slowly—the door she'd forgotten to lock! It felt like a scene right out of a scary movie. *The Last House on the Left* or something like that.

Thinking fast, glancing around her kitchen for a weapon, any kind of weapon, Theodosia grabbed the first thing she saw. A copper fry pan. Hefting it high above her head, she stood poised and quivering, ready to clobber her intruder.

That's when Riley poked his head around the door.

"Hello? Anybody home?"

Theodosia, who was wound up like a Major League hitter fresh from the dugout, caught herself mid-swing.

"What are *you* doing here!" she screamed. She'd come within inches of bashing in Riley's skull.

Riley turned his head, blinked, and fought to focus in the darkness. "Theo? I came to see you?" His answer sounded like a question. Then he did a double take as he spotted the fry pan in Theodosia's hand. "Wow, were you about to crack my skull open with that thing? Did I come at a bad time?" His head swiveled in the direction of the dining room. "Is someone . . . here?"

"No!" Theodosia cried. "It's just that you scared me to death!" She sounded angry but was actually relieved.

Riley appraised her with a crooked grin. "I'm intrigued. You don't frighten all that easily."

"I'm sorry, somebody was following a little too closely when Earl Grey and I were out jogging and . . ." She grabbed a quick breath. "And this Fogheel Jack thing has me totally on edge."

"Sweetheart, it's got everybody on edge." Riley pried the fry pan out of Theodosia's hand and set it on the counter. "Somebody was chasing you?"

"I *thought* they were."

Riley put his arms around Theodosia and pulled her close.

Theodosia snuggled against him, feeling safe and comforted, enjoying the strength of his body. Knowing that Riley was armed with a Browning Hi-Power 9mm pistol also gave her a nice warm feeling.

They kissed, hugged some more, kissed again, then finally relaxed.

"What are you doing here?" Theodosia asked.

"I wanted to see you," Riley said. "Took a chance that you'd be home by now."

Theodosia smiled.

"How's Haley?" Riley asked.

"Five stitches at the ER, doesn't seem any worse for wear. I called her a while ago from Drayton's house and she said she was okay. Mostly just tired."

"I sent a cruiser to patrol your neighborhood just like you asked, but they didn't report anything out of the ordinary."

"I'm not surprised."

"And you went to the candlelight vigil?" Riley asked. "How was that?"

"Okay, I guess. I didn't stay long. The whole thing felt a little too formatted for my taste. Kind of like a bad infomercial." Theodosia looked up at him. "On the investigation front, is there anything new I should know about?"

"Kind of."

She was practically holding her breath. "What is it?"

"I've been temporarily reassigned."

"What? Why?" Theodosia was taken aback. "You've been investigating these Fogheel Jack cases from the get-go. Why would they take you off them now?"

Riley shrugged.

"Last month you were fast-tracked to Homicide-Special. Now you're reassigned? What do they want you to do? Write parking tickets? Round up stray cats? Or does this mean you've been busted down a few pegs and you're no longer a detective?"

"No such luck. I'm still a D2, but now I'm also working with the Open-Unsolved Unit."

"I've never heard you mention them before. Is it a large unit?"

"It's basically three guys and a goat."

"A goat?" Now Theodosia knew he was kidding.

"Okay then," Riley said. "How about three guys and a dog."

"Whose dog?"

Riley glanced down at Earl Grey. "Yours?"

"Uh-huh. And let me guess. You're one of the guys?"

"Yup. Part-time anyway."

Theodosia stared at him. "What's really going on?"

He stared back at her. "You can probably guess, can't you?"

"Let's see, Open-Unsolved." She tapped an index finger against her lower lip. "You've been tasked with analyzing the two Fogheel Jack murders from seven years ago?"

"Bingo."

"Sounds like Tidwell is clutching at straws, hoping you'll dig something up on those two unsolved cases that might shine a light on the current murders."

"Aren't you the clever one," Riley said. "Maybe *you* should be working in the Open-Unsolved Unit."

Theodosia flashed him a crooked smile. "I kind of am already."

"What do you mean?"

She took his hand. "Come with me, I want to show you something."

Riley followed her into the dining room, waited while she snapped on a light, then stared at the array of papers spread out across the table.

"What's this?" Riley asked. He picked up a couple of sheets and studied them. "You've been doing research. A good amount of research."

"Most of it is pretty basic stuff. Primary research, I guess you'd call it, not the deep-dive kind. Articles I discovered at the library, most of them culled from the *Charleston Post and Courier* and the *Goose Creek Gazette* from seven years ago. Anyway, I printed out everything I could find, hoping there might be some kind of clue or pattern. I haven't found anything yet . . . but maybe you could take a look. Oh, and I dug up some background stuff on Nick Prince as well."

"You've been a busy little detective." Even though Riley didn't approve of Theodosia's snooping, he sounded interested.

"You have no idea." Theodosia picked up a sheet and handed it to him. "Check this out; it's from Nick Prince's LinkedIn page."

Riley scanned the paper. "What am I supposed to be looking for?"

"You see the dates from when Prince lived in Charleston? They coincide with the murders."

"Okay, I see that now. Interesting, but still circumstantial."

"It could be a starting point," Theodosia said. "After all, he is writing a true crime book and could be looking for a story line."

"Maybe." Riley frowned, then said, "But seriously, this is good stuff. What else have you got?"

Theodosia showed him the rest of the news articles she'd made copies of and they sifted through those for a good half hour. Earl Grey, curled up on a rug nearby, snored a serenade.

Finally, Riley tipped his chair back onto two legs and said, "I don't know. This stuff is fascinating from a historical perspective, but I don't see anything that helps shine a light on current cases." He brought the chair back down with a thud. "I'm sorry, is this chair an antique?"

"I think it's got another ten years to go before it qualifies,"

Theodosia said. Then, "Have you developed any kind of profile on Fogheel Jack?"

"We have, but it's fairly basic."

"Try me."

"We think he's on the young side of middle-aged," Riley said. "Thirties to forties. Professional, probably decent-looking, not someone you'd be fearful of if you met him on the street. Let's see, what else? Intelligent, capable of planning, probably able to sling a good line of BS."

"Anything else?" Theodosia asked.

"Yeah, he enjoys killing women."

"Strangling them."

"Yes," Riley said.

"And now he's using a knife."

Riley sighed. "He is even though last night's scene was fairly ordered. This is a guy who doesn't allow himself to lose control."

Theodosia nodded as she scrounged through one of the piles of paper and pulled out a short news item that had run in the Business section.

"Here's what I wanted to show you," she said. "Orlock."

Riley offered a blank stare. "What's an Orlock?"

"You don't know?"

Riley shook his head.

"Wyatt Orlock is a big-time real estate developer here in Charleston. Don't you ever read the business section?"

"Most of the criminals I go after don't own property or head major corporations. They're petty thieves and garden-variety stickup guys who get busted because they dropped their gym membership card while knocking over a gas station for twenty-eight bucks and a twelve-pack of Budweiser. So what's the deal with Orlock?"

"He's trying to force Lois out of her lease."

"Wait, you mean he owns her building?"

"No, but he wants to. His plan is to buy Lois's building and combine it with the building it backs up to and create a bunch of luxury condos. Skylofts, they're called."

"Sounds fancy." Riley thought for a moment. "So you're saying this Orlock guy is the one who's been strangling women?" He sounded skeptical. "He's not even on our radar."

"I thought he might be a possibility because he's desperate to get hold of Lois's building. Then I dug around some more and found out that Orlock has a security guy by the name of Frank Lynch working for him." She paused. "I saw Frank Lynch skulking around at the murder scene last night."

"At White Point Gardens? Interesting. So Orlock is a big-time property owner who has his own private security guard?"

"Plus, Orlock just opened that new restaurant, Sparks, over on Market Street. Drayton and I stopped there Tuesday night to check it out. While we were there we managed to have a semi-friendly chat with him."

"Of course you did," Riley said. "For you that means poking your nose where it doesn't belong. That could be the reason Haley was targeted—they thought it was you in the alley."

"I know, I know."

Riley squinted one eye closed. "I suppose we should fire up your laptop and see exactly what this Orlock guy owns. See how far his real estate domain extends."

"I thought you'd never ask."

Theodosia grabbed her laptop, powered it up, and said, "You're the one who should be doing the search. I'm guessing there are all sorts of local and federal databases you can access with your magic police passwords." She slid the computer over to Riley.

"Sure, but let's check the basics first. The city's property tax rolls and all that good stuff."

"Works for me."

Riley got into the city system with a minimum of effort,

scrolled to the property tax department. "Say now, it looks like Orlock is the proud owner of a number of properties."

"Let me see."

Riley turned the laptop toward her.

Theodosia scanned a list of properties and said, "Holy cats, look at all the buildings this guy owns. It's like a megaton of real estate. Seems like most of them are duplexes and apartment buildings, too."

"Maybe the guy's a slum landlord. You know, buy 'em, rent 'em, never put a penny in to fix 'em."

Theodosia touched a finger to the computer screen and slowly traced down the list of properties. What she finally discovered stunned her.

"Riley, Orlock owns the apartment building Cara was living in!"

"You can't be serious."

"Look at the address."

Riley moved closer to her and peered intently at the screen. "That's it all right."

"As building owner, he might have had a key."

Riley made a face. "Crap."

"You know what else is weird?"

"No, but I bet you're gonna tell me."

Theodosia dug through the mound of papers, said, "No, no, no," as she pushed several aside, then finally found what she was looking for. "Here." She handed Riley one of the printouts. "See this article? It says one of the women who was murdered seven years ago worked as a commercial Realtor. You think that could mean something?"

"It might," Riley said slowly. "It just might."

"So what happens now?"

"I go back to Tidwell and strongly suggest we bring Orlock in for questioning. See if he can produce credible alibis for his whereabouts at the time of these last three murders."

"You think Orlock could be Fogheel Jack?"

"You say you've met the guy. What was your impression of him? What's he like?"

"Rather arrogant and caustic. And not exactly young anymore."

"In other words, Cara probably wouldn't have dated him."

"Doubtful, since he's twice her age. On the other hand, Orlock could have run into her at his restaurant, liked what he saw, and sent the roses."

"Then she rejected him," Riley said. "So he killed her?" He shook his head. "I don't know. That doesn't account for the woman last week or the killing of Monica Garber."

"You're not convinced."

Riley shook his head. "We can give Orlock a tentative sniff, but no, I'm not nearly convinced."

20

It was perfect weather for a funeral. Gloomy, a light sprinkle of rain, clouds swirling like bats in the sky.

Theodosia usually looked forward to Fridays, but this was one she dreaded as she hurried down Church Street toward St. Philip's Church. And couldn't help but think about the dreary cemetery behind the church. It was as if poor Cara had come full circle. She'd been murdered in that cemetery and now her funeral service was being held in the adjacent church. Somehow the connection felt creepy.

"You look lost in thought," came a familiar voice at her elbow.

Theodosia turned to find Drayton striding alongside her. He was dressed in a charcoal gray pinstripe suit, a light blue shirt, and a somber dove gray bow tie. In her black skirt suit and pale gray blouse, Theodosia decided they could pass for professional mourners.

"I was thinking about the cemetery out back," Theodosia said as the wind lifted her hair and fanned it out into streamers, giving her a moment of panic.

Drayton gave a knowing nod. "Ah."

Legend held that the cemetery was haunted, though Theodosia had never witnessed any ghostly presence. Drayton, on the other hand, had once claimed to have seen a glowing orb among the tombstones. Now Theodosia didn't know what to think. Not haunted, but maybe . . . a bad-luck place?

As they stepped into the quiet sanctity of St. Philip's Church, both Theodosia and Drayton glanced around. With its storied history, the church was both elegant and filled with majesty. Heads of state had worshipped here; so had schoolchildren. Tall windows flooded the interior with natural light. A barrel ceiling and tall interior pillars lent touches of architectural grace.

"There's Lois. Sitting in the first row," Theodosia said. "I hope she's able to stay strong and make it through this service."

"Looks like she has a number of relatives with her."

"That's a comfort and a blessing."

"But perhaps we should seat ourselves near the back of the church," Drayton suggested. "That way we can slip out . . ."

". . . early and make sure the food for the funeral reception is ready to serve," Theodosia finished for him. "I think that's a smart idea."

"Did you get a head count as to how many people are supposed to show up?"

"Last I heard from Delaine, the event was by invitation only. So she thought around twenty or twenty-five people."

"That's certainly manageable," Drayton said as they both sat down.

"As long as Haley's feeling up to it after last night."

"I just came from the tea shop. Haley seemed fine and Miss Dimple is coming in to help out." Drayton gazed at his Patek Philippe and added, "In fact, she should be arriving right about now."

Just as solemn organ music started up—Theodosia thought it

might be a piece by Bach—Jesse Trumbull slid into the pew alongside her. He wore a navy suit, light blue shirt, and striped tie, very corporate-looking as opposed to his usual casual attire of leather jacket and khakis.

"A sad day," Trumbull said to her. His youthful face was arranged in a solemn mask.

"Terrible," Theodosia said.

"Just FYI," Trumbull said, "I happen to know that Tidwell and his people followed up on your tip."

"Which tip was that?" Theodosia asked. She felt like she'd been crying wolf for the last five days but nobody had deigned to take her seriously.

"The one about Wyatt Orlock," Trumbull said. "I never heard the guy's name mentioned until this morning. Apparently no one in the department had. But now they're all scrambling."

"So Tidwell's going to interrogate him?"

"Question him anyway. Should be happening right now."

"I hope something comes out of it," Theodosia said.

Trumbull looked somber. "So do I. This Fogheel Jack character is about the worst thing that's ever happened to Charleston. This kind of crazed sociopath has to be stopped." He hesitated, then added, "Sociopath. That's what our consulting police psychologist called him. Though I'd say Jack presents more as a person consumed by psychopathic rage."

"Sounds like you've read up on the subject."

"I was a journalism major with a psych minor. Anyway, the pathology of a killer's brain is fairly interesting—that's if you're not too closely involved. I mean, nobody wants to get *that* close." He touched Theodosia's shoulder lightly, said, "Thanks again."

"You're not staying for the funeral?"

"Can't," Trumbull said as he slipped out of the pew. "I have to go liaison with the chief. See what kind of spin he wants me to put on this week's crime report."

Theodosia gave a little wave. "Take care."

"What was all that about?" Drayton whispered.

"Good news, actually. Tidwell's decided to question Wyatt Orlock. Turns out Orlock owns Cara's apartment building and one of the women murdered seven years ago was a commercial Realtor."

Drayton's brows shot up. "Indeed? Sounds like the pieces may be coming together."

"Let's hope so."

"I take it this was your doing?"

"Sort of."

"Good work," Drayton said.

They sat there together, listening to the organ music, watching the mourners file in.

"Look." Theodosia nudged Drayton in the ribs with an elbow. "There's Tim Holt, the boyfriend."

They watched as Holt walked woodenly down the center aisle, eyes downcast, looking fairly grim. He took a seat in the tenth row from the front.

"Did you expect to see him here?" Drayton asked.

"No, but I didn't not expect him, either."

And there were more surprise guests. Nick Prince arrived a few minutes later and took a seat in the aisle across from Theodosia and Drayton. He probably noticed them sitting there but chose to keep his eyes focused straight ahead.

"The Prince of Darkness just arrived," Drayton whispered to Theodosia.

Then, a minute later, Bob Basset walked in. Basset was dressed in his usual shabby clothes, and one of his jacket pockets bulged with what looked like a notebook and camera.

"That skunk," Theodosia whispered. "If a candid shot from this funeral ends up gracing the cover of *Star Tattler Magazine* I'm going to personally eviscerate him with a soup spoon."

"I'll lend a hand," Drayton whispered back.

There was a loud CLUNK as the church's double doors were pulled open, then a faint *squeak-squeak*, like metal wheels that needed oiling.

Theodosia turned to look, along with everyone else.

"Oh no," she said, tears forming in her eyes as a white coffin was slowly rolled in.

The small white coffin had an enormous spray of white lilies on top, and the sad image made Theodosia's heart lurch inside her chest. It felt doubly terrible that Cara had been murdered at such a young age. The poor girl hadn't even graduated from college. Hadn't begun to live a life filled with promise and potential.

As if reading her thoughts, Drayton leaned over and said, "This is beyond tragic."

Theodosia nodded. "Isn't it?"

"And such a small casket," he whispered as they watched it roll by on a metal dais covered with white velvet. A single black-suited man with a poker face—no doubt the funeral director—pushed the casket along slowly. Mourners touched hankies to eyes, cleared their throats, and a few people sobbed openly. When the casket reached the front of the church, the funeral director turned it and seesawed it into place so it was stretched horizontally across the sanctuary for all to see.

"Do you know when Monica Garber's funeral is going to be held?" Drayton whispered as the minister walked out and everyone rose to their feet.

"I heard next week."

"That should be a media circus."

Cara Chamberlain's funeral service was lovely as funeral services go. There was a solemn invocation, countless prayers, a tribute to Cara read by her cousin Naomi, bittersweet songs that everyone joined in on, and tears. So many tears.

Just as the minister concluded the service and the funeral

director strode to the altar to wheel back the casket, Theodosia and Drayton edged their way out of their pew. Then, as the final musical note seemed to shimmer in the air, high and silvery, they ducked out and ran back to the Indigo Tea Shop.

Miss Dimple looked up from the front counter, where she was brewing a pot of tea.

"You're here," she said. "How was the funeral?"

"Sad," said Theodosia.

"About as tragic as it gets," said Drayton. He pulled off his jacket, hung it on their brass coatrack, and draped a long black apron over his head. "Want me to take over?" he asked Miss Dimple.

"Please do," she said. "I love pretending that I know all the tricks of the trade when it comes to brewing tea, but the truth is I'm kind of a fumble-fingered amateur. And I'm still learning proper names for all your various teas."

"I'm sure you're doing just fine," Theodosia said as she eyed the tea room. Only three tables were occupied, which meant she could reserve the rest of the tables for the funeral guests. She'd be able to seat—she counted empty chairs at the already-set tables—twenty-four people. Just about right.

Haley came out of the kitchen, wiping her hands on her apron, her chef's hat cocked at a rakish angle.

"How was the funeral?" she asked.

"About as expected," Theodosia said. "Sad and depressing."

"For sure," Haley said. "And the guests are on their way?"

"Probably show up in about five minutes. Is everything okay on your end?"

"Oh yeah. I thought we'd serve orange scones with Devonshire cream as a first course and then a small plate of crab quiche and grilled asparagus, the asparagus being left over from yesterday. I didn't plan for any dessert."

"I don't think they'll be expecting it. We're really just serving a midmorning snack," Theodosia said. "But I'm more worried about you. How does your head feel today?"

"Okay. Better than last night. Here." Haley reached out and pressed a pink tube into Theodosia's hand. It was cute and plastic, the size of a lipstick.

"What's this?"

"Pepper spray. I picked some up for both of us. And I want you to carry it just to be on the safe side, okay?"

"Sure, why not. And, Haley, if you need help in the kitchen, please don't hesitate to ask." Theodosia stuck the tube in her pocket and began lighting the tea lights on each table.

"Will do," Haley said. She gazed at the flickering tea lights as they came to life and smiled, said, "Makes it kinda cheery in here." Then she headed back into the kitchen.

Once the candles were all lit, Theodosia double-checked to make sure the tables were set with matching cups and saucers, bowls of Devonshire cream, pitchers of cream, slices of lemon, and sugar cubes. Just to be safe she placed RESERVED signs on the tables and then ambled over to the front counter.

"Is there a special tea you're planning to serve?" she asked Drayton.

"I'm brewing a pot of orange pekoe as well as a pot of silver needle," Drayton said. "They're both nice hearty teas that should help fortify everyone after such a sad event."

"Tea and sympathy," Theodosia said.

"Something like that, yes."

The funeral guests arrived a few minutes later. Theodosia stood at the front door and greeted everyone warmly, then shepherded them to the reserved tables. All in all, eighteen people showed up. Most were Lois's relatives, whom Theodosia had never met before. A few, like Delaine, and Leigh Carroll from the Cabbage Patch Gift Shop, were friends.

Delaine pursed her lips, upset by the small turnout.

"I thought we'd get more takers," she said.

"Most of the people who attended the service are probably headed in to work," Theodosia said. "So this smaller group of close friends and relatives is fine. Easy to manage."

"Yes, but *you* weren't the one who planned it," Delaine huffed.

Just as Theodosia was about to bring out the scones, Detective Tidwell stomped in. He glanced around, looking bulky and unsure of what to do.

"Are you here for the funeral reception?" Theodosia asked.

Tidwell shrugged, then gave a quick nod. So Theodosia led him to one of the large round tables and seated him with the other guests. What could it hurt?

"I didn't see you at church," she said to him.

"Because I wasn't there," Tidwell mumbled.

"You've been busy interviewing your, um, most recent suspect?" Theodosia was careful not to say the name *Wyatt Orlock* or the words *murder* and *Fogheel Jack*. Figured they could trigger a negative reaction among the guests.

Tidwell shifted heavily in his chair and said, "I daresay we've managed to eliminate a few people that were deemed questionable."

"Care to share those names with me?" Theodosia asked.

"Not on your life."

As Drayton made the rounds, pouring tea, clucking sympathetically, and answering questions, Theodosia and Miss Dimple began running out food to the guests. First the orange scones, which were well received, then Haley's crab quiche. As Theodosia served Lois and Naomi, she said, "Excuse me, Naomi. I have to compliment you on your lovely tribute this morning. It felt very meaningful."

Lois put a hand on Naomi's shoulder. "This is the wonderful woman I've been telling you about, Naomi. Theodosia Browning. Or as we sometimes call her, the Tea Lady."

Naomi turned and smiled at Theodosia. She was young, maybe around Cara's age, and had long dark hair and luminous brown eyes.

"Nice to meet you," Naomi said. "And thank you for the compliment. It was easy writing about Cara, but difficult to deliver."

"I'm sure it was heartbreaking. I take it you two were close?"

"Like sisters," Naomi said. "We texted back and forth every day."

Theodosia decided to take a chance. "Did Cara ever say anything about a new man in her life?"

Naomi looked thoughtful. "She did mention that she'd ended a relationship and was surprised that she'd been kind of swept off her feet so soon by somebody new."

"Did Cara ever mention a name?" Theodosia asked.

"No, but she told me he wrote her a poem."

"So a writer?"

But Naomi's attention was suddenly somewhere else. She held up a finger and said, "Do you by any chance know who that man over there is? The one sitting at the next table?"

Theodosia looked over, assuming Naomi was referring to Tidwell. She wasn't. Instead she was staring at a middle-aged man with dark hair, curious white sideburns, and a pink, pinched face. He seemed focused on the last bite of his scone and wasn't talking to anyone else at the table.

"I have no idea who that is," Theodosia said. "I thought he was with your party."

"He's not," Naomi said.

Do I have a freeloader? Theodosia wondered. *Or one of those ghouls who get their jollies hanging out at visitations and funerals?*

Lois cleared her throat, then spoke in an almost robot-like cadence as she stared at the man. "I know him."

"Who is he?" Theodosia and Naomi asked at once.

"Gavin Goulding, the man who owns my building," Lois said.

"Your apartment building?" Naomi asked.

But Theodosia knew what Lois meant. "You mean the commercial building where your bookshop's located, don't you?" She let loose delicate snort. "He shouldn't be here." Then, "Was he at the funeral?"

Lois shook her head. "I have no idea. I kind of . . . hope not."

"I'm going to ask him to leave," Naomi said to Theodosia. "He's not welcome here and it's obvious his presence is upsetting Aunt Lois."

Theodosia held up a hand. "Let me deal with this. Why don't you two stay put and enjoy your lunch."

"Thank you," Lois said.

Theodosia walked over to the next table, where Gavin Goulding was sitting. He'd just dropped three sugar cubes (shudder) into his tea and was taking a taste.

"Excuse me," Theodosia said. "I need a word with you."

Goulding took a loud slurp of tea, looked up at her, and said, "Who, me?"

Theodosia crooked a finger and smiled. "In private, please?"

Goulding threw down his napkin, stood up, and followed her to the entryway. "What's this all about?" he asked. "Is something wrong?"

Theodosia had made up her mind to be pleasant but firm.

"Actually, yes," she said. "I'm afraid you'll have to leave immediately."

Goulding stared at her as blotches bloomed on already pink cheeks.

"You've got to be kidding,"

"Your uninvited presence here has upset a few guests."

"Oh really," he said, his voice suddenly strident, his manner bristling. "Which ones?"

"I think you know," Theodosia said.

Goulding stared angrily across the tea shop at Lois. "You

mean her? I went to the funeral 'cause I felt sorry for her. Now the old biddy wants me to *leave*?" Goulding's upper lip curled inward. "I'm even trying to do her a big favor by buying out her lease."

"So you can sell the building to Wyatt Orlock?" Theodosia said.

Goulding stared at her with beady, birdlike eyes that were filled with fury.

"What do you know about that?" he shouted.

As his voice rose steadily, heads turned and people began to stare. And listen in.

"I know enough to see where your plan is headed," Theodosia said. "You and Orlock have formed a cozy little cabal to try and force Lois out of a favorable and binding lease. Once you do that Orlock can build his condos and you'll both end up making a tidy profit."

Theodosia was wound up and ready for battle.

"For all I know, murdering Lois's daughter was part of your plan," she added.

"What!" Goulding shrieked.

"Maybe you wanted to defeat her emotionally so she'll give in and shutter her business."

"Are you insane?" Goulding shouted. "I'm a real estate guy, not a maniacal killer. How dare you accuse me of such a despicable act!" Now his face had turned the bright red of a Roma tomato and he was practically spitting venom.

"The thing is, you've seriously outstayed your welcome," Theodosia said.

"And if I don't leave? What are you going to *do*?" Goulding challenged. "Toss me out on the sidewalk?"

Theodosia saw the nasty smirk on Goulding's face. Did he really want to play it that way? Obviously he did. But he had no idea what she held in her arsenal.

"You see that man sitting over there?" Theodosia pointed at Tidwell, who was watching them closely and seemed more than a little interested in their conversation.

Goulding gave Tidwell a passing glance. "The fat guy? What about him?"

"That's Detective Burt Tidwell, who heads Charleston PD's Robbery and Homicide Division. He's a man you don't want to cross."

Goulding peered at Tidwell, saw the look of determination on Tidwell's face, and decided Theodosia wasn't kidding. He made a guttural sound and spun on his heels, couldn't get out of her tea shop fast enough.

Theodosia hunched her shoulders, then dropped them, forcing herself to relax and calm down. *Breathe, just breathe*, she told herself.

Did she really believe Gavin Goulding was some kind of mad-dog killer?

Probably not. But at this point pretty much anyone could turn out to be the much-feared Fogheel Jack.

21

The funeral reception had started at ten fifteen, with the last guests leaving the Indigo Tea Shop around eleven twenty. Now, after an abundance of hugs and thank-yous from Lois and Naomi, Theodosia and Miss Dimple were scrambling to set up for lunch.

"Who was that crabby guy you booted off the premises?" Miss Dimple said to Theodosia as she spread a pink linen tablecloth on one of the round tables and carefully smoothed it out.

"He's the man who owns the building where Lois's bookshop is located," Theodosia said. "He's angling to get her out of the building so he can sell it to a real estate developer."

"What does the developer want to do with it?"

"Turn it into condos."

"More condos? How awful," Miss Dimple said, giving a shudder. "Don't they know it's important to *preserve* our Historic District? I mean, how would they even get something like that past city officials?"

"I don't know," Theodosia said. "Bribe somebody, I guess." She dug in one of her cupboards and pulled out a square snack plate with a matching teacup. "Do you know what Haley's serving for lunch?"

"I think more quiche and asparagus. Only she's adding a side salad."

"This would make a perfect serving set, then."

"Do you have enough of them?" Miss Dimple asked.

"I think so. Let me look. Yup, I think we're set."

"Good, because that Rose Chintz Pink pattern is a fun matchy-matchy with the tablecloths."

"Looks like we've got it figured out."

Theodosia popped into the kitchen, where the aroma coming from Haley's bubbling pot of cioppino was practically aphrodisiacal.

"Your seafood stew smells amazing," Theodosia said.

"It should. I threw in enough seafood to make a pack of hungry seals scream for joy," said Haley. She grabbed a large spoon, dipped it in the stew, and tasted. "Yup, it's good."

"I know you're baking two more pans of quiche, but what else do you have on the menu to tempt our luncheon guests?"

Haley smiled as she began hollowing out the interiors of a half dozen rounds of sourdough bread. "Besides the quiche and my cioppino served in bread bowls, I've got rosemary scones, turkey and Gouda tea sandwiches, cream cheese with roasted red pepper sandwiches, and cinnamon swirl bread. Not a huge selection but a potent one."

"Agreed. And, Haley, I'll be needing that cioppino recipe," Theodosia called over her shoulder as she headed back out into the tea room.

The tables were set and looking lovely—actually gleaming. Miss Dimple was doing a last-minute polish of the silverware while Drayton was glued to the phone accepting take-out orders.

"Once again, we're heroically busy," he said as he hung up. "Not a lot of luncheon reservations came in—I suppose that's because of the rain—but we've been flooded with take-out orders from all our nearby B and Bs. It's sweet the innkeepers continue to recommend us."

"For one thing we're the only place in the neighborhood that serves decent food," Theodosia said.

Drayton touched a hand to his bow tie and said in a highbrow voice, "Oh, you don't *like* packaged sandwiches from the grocery store?"

"Gag me with a piece of cellophane," Theodosia said.

Which elicited laughter from both Drayton and Miss Dimple.

A few minutes before noon, with three tables of guests already seated, Bob Basset strolled through the front door. He saw Theodosia, shot her a mock salute, and said, "Howdy do." He'd changed into a tacky outfit that consisted of a gray-and-red-flecked tweed jacket with suede shoulder patches, saggy blue jeans, and desert boots.

She walked over to greet him. "Are you here for lunch, Mr. Basset?"

Basset's eyes swept the tea room, then focused back on her. "Why not? Any port in a storm, right?"

"I hope we're more than that," Theodosia said as she led him to a table. Then, while she waited for him to sit down and settle in, her curiosity got the best of her and she plopped down across from him.

"I saw you at the funeral this morning," she said.

"I thought it might be worthwhile to cover," Basset said. "Seeing as how the funeral was for one of the murdered women."

He said it so casually, Theodosia wanted to scream. Instead she said, "How goes your story?"

"Hoping for a good conclusion."

"And a good conclusion would entail what?" Theodosia asked. "Another murder?"

Basset's brows pinched together and he shook his head vigorously. "Ah jeez, no. That would be awful. No, I'm hoping that this Fogheel Jack character gets caught before any more killing takes place."

Still curious about Basset and his motives, Theodosia said, "You must have quite an interesting background. I mean in order to cover all these big stories." She'd made up her mind to remain pleasant to Basset if it killed her, knowing she'd catch more flies with honey than vinegar. At least that's what her aunt Libby had always preached.

"I've been writing about crime for over twenty years," Basset said. "Started out as a cub reporter covering the cop beat in Los Angeles. Did that gig for four years, worked for a true crime magazine that went belly-up, then struck out on my own. Between the supermarket tabloids, a few TV shows, and the Internet, there are plenty of outlets for my stories."

"That's pretty amazing." It wasn't really, but Theodosia wanted to keep Basset running his mouth. Maybe (hopefully) he'd spill something she could actually use.

"I never looked back, either," Basset said, flattered by her attention, puffing out his chest like a bantam rooster.

"So you've never settled down? You just keep moving from place to place?"

"I look at it as jumping from one barn burner of a story to another."

"Where are you staying while you're in Charleston?" Theodosia asked.

"A cute little guesthouse called the Featherbed House."

"Oh, my friend Angie owns that B and B," Theodosia said. "It's a wonderful place."

Basset's eyes crinkled as he smiled at her. "Small world."

"So I take it this is your first time in Charleston?"

Basset leaned back. "Actually, I covered a murder over in Goose Creek a half dozen years or so ago. Spent a little time in Charleston as well. Nice city, friendly people, good food." His face lit up. "Great food. I'm addicted to the she-crab soup at Poogan's Porch and the lobster and grits at the Charleston Grill."

"Theo?"

Theodosia snapped her head to the right. Drayton was calling. She looked at him, saw him give a curt nod, then turned her attention to the party of three that was waiting in the front hallway, expectant looks on their faces.

She rapped her knuckles against the table. "Gotta go," she told Basset. "Nice talking to you. Miss Dimple here will take your order. My personal recommendation? The cioppino."

Theodosia seated the party of three, took orders from two other tables, then delivered those orders to Haley.

"How goes it out there?" Haley asked as she ladled cioppino into two sourdough bread bowls.

"A little slow."

"That might be a good thing since Drayton just brought me a dozen take-out orders. And they're good-sized orders, too. Each one is for, like, five or six people."

"From the B and Bs?"

"Mostly, yeah."

"When it rains it pours," Theodosia said.

Back out in the tea room, Theodosia greeted two more customers, seated them, then swung back to take another order. As she ferried it in to Haley, she thought about her conversation with Bob Basset. He mentioned that he'd covered a murder in Goose Creek some six or seven years ago. That piece of information niggled at her brain for a few moments, then it came to her. Wouldn't that be around the same time Fogheel Jack had first hit Charleston? Yes, it would indeed.

Theodosia was antsy all through lunch service, thinking about Basset and his zest for murder, thanking him as he left. And wondering—could a stone-cold killer be lurking inside his irksome, semi-bumbling reporter facade? Was that his cover? Was that how Basset got close to his victims? He bored them into complacency? Or was she completely and totally off base?

Cashing out one table, Theodosia returned the change to her customer, thanked them, then wandered back to the counter.

Only one way to find out, she decided.

"Drayton, I need to run out on a short errand," Theodosia said. "Will you keep an eye on things?"

"Absolutely," Drayton said. "But first . . ." He grabbed a teapot, poured a stream of amber liquid into a floral teacup, and handed it to her. "I want you to try this new estate Darjeeling I just sourced."

Theodosia took a sip. When Drayton spoke, she listened. If he thought a new tea was worth tasting and maybe putting on the roster at the Indigo Tea Shop, then she would certainly give it careful consideration.

One sip and she knew Drayton was spot-on. Then again, he always was.

"Okay, this is amazingly complex," Theodosia said. "It starts out flavorful and slightly brisk, then finishes dry."

"Like a good champagne," Drayton said. "Effervescent to light up the taste buds, but with a dry finish."

"So dry it rolls up your tongue like a window shade." Theodosia laughed.

Drayton's brows shot up. "Well, not quite *that* dry."

The Featherbed House was located two blocks from the Indigo Tea Shop and was always a charming oasis to visit. The enormous old inn had a wide front porch complete with porch swings, a balcony on the second floor, and a riot of decorative turrets, finials, and balustrades.

Inside was a cozy lobby filled with chintz sofas and chairs, woven rag rugs, and a redbrick fireplace. Geese, Angie Congdon's signature image, were everywhere. Geese were embroidered on the sofa cushions, geese photos and paintings hung on the walls, plus there were carved geese, soft-sculpture geese, and even metal sculptures of geese.

Today, Angie Congdon sat behind the high wooden reception desk, looking cute as a button. Her blond hair cascaded down onto her shoulders, her face was serene and just this side of angelic, and she wore a yellow puffy-sleeved blouse with a long denim skirt.

Angie's face lit up with a smile when she saw Theodosia walk in.

"Ho, Miss Theodosia. What brings you to my parlor?"

"I need a favor," Theodosia said. No sense beating around the bush.

"Just ask," Angie said.

"First, a couple of questions. I want to know if a guy by the name of Bob Basset is staying here as a guest."

"The crime reporter? Yup, we put him in one of our annex rooms. He wanted a weekly rate on a room that wasn't too expensive. Said he didn't need a suite or anything fancy. Just a nice room."

"Is he there now?" Theodosia asked.

"I don't think so. But I could do a quick check," Angie asked.

"If you would."

Angie picked up the phone, dialed Basset's room, and listened for a few moments.

"He's not answering his phone so I'm guessing he's still out. Did you want to leave a note for him?"

"No. Because now comes the really big favor," Theodosia said. "I want to get a look inside his room."

Angie's brows puckered together. "Ooh . . . that request is a little out of the ordinary. Can you tell me why?"

Theodosia gave Angie the CliffsNotes version of what she'd

been up to. Cara's murder, Lois's plea for help, her investigation so far, narrowing down a suspect list, and Bob Basset being one of those possible suspects.

Angie's face turned chalk white. "You think Mr. Basset could have murdered all those women?" She was almost breathless with worry.

"He's a suspect anyway."

"The police are looking at him?"

"No, I am."

Angie hesitated, mulled over Theodosia's request for a few seconds, then opened a drawer and pulled out a large brass key attached to a leather key fob.

"Room eight-sixteen; this is my master key. But you have to hurry up and make your look-see snappy. I'll stay here and keep an eye peeled for Basset. He has to come through the lobby to get to his room, so if I see him coming, I'll call you on your cell, okay? And if I do call, make sure you skedaddle out of that room *tout de suite.*"

"Thank you," Theodosia said. "You're a good friend."

She stepped out the double doors and walked across the flagstone courtyard, where a dozen tables with umbrellas were set up. Nobody out drinking the complimentary wine or nibbling cheese today, just too much rain. But in nice weather, Angie's patio was a sight to behold. Sunshine dappling Cinzano umbrellas, palm trees swaying, giant pots of pink and purple bougainvillea everywhere, guests enjoying her hospitality.

Theodosia stepped around a woven wood fence made rich with a tapestry of curling ivy. The fence separated the annex rooms from the patio, giving those rooms some privacy.

She looked left, then right, but saw no one. No guests, maids, or gardeners were out and about.

Okay, this is it, she thought as she stood in front of room eight-sixteen and slipped the key into the lock.

It stuck for a moment, which made her heart skip a beat. Then there was an audible *click* and the door swung open.

With more than a little trepidation, Theodosia stepped into Bob Basset's room and shut the door behind her.

Ordinarily, the room would be adorable. A four-poster bed with a billowing comforter. Windows framed with filmy curtains. Furnishings that bordered on Old English. Genuine oil paintings on the wall. But today the place was a mess, as if someone had turned on a high-powered leaf blower and let it have its way. Clothes were scattered on the floor. Shirts, jackets, and whatnot had been piled on the bed. The dresser held a rat's nest of guy junk—keys, loose change, ticket stubs, crumpled dollar bills, take-out menus, a pocket knife, a matchbook, two AA batteries, a small flashlight, a baseball cap with a South Carolina Gamecocks logo, a wrapped cigar, and two pens. A pair of shoes (badly in need of polish and new heels) had been tossed haphazardly onto a side chair.

Sloppy. He's a world-class slob, Theodosia thought to herself.

She tried to shove her revulsion aside for the time being. In the back of her mind she understood she had a limited amount of time to search Basset's room. In a thriller she'd once read, the main character claimed that if you did a break and enter, you had two minutes tops. After that, the odds of getting caught skyrocketed.

Theodosia knew this was a high-risk venture so she went straight to work. Pulled open dresser drawers, looked in the closet, checked pockets on all the hanging clothes, looked in the nightstand, finally searched the small bathroom.

She didn't see a single thing that struck her as suspicious. No ropes, wire, or nylon line. No guns or knives, either.

Nothing here? Nothing at all?

Time was ticking away; time was her enemy right now.

Theodosia decided to run a second check, proceed a little slower, try to be more methodical.

The closet and dresser were still nada. Ditto the nightstand and bathroom. Theodosia stood in the middle of the room, spinning around slowly in a 360-degree sweep. There had to be something, right?

Then her eyes fell on the bed again, piled with clothes, magazines, notebooks, and a couple of cameras. She didn't relish digging through that morass of junk, but something inside her told her it might be worthwhile.

Okay, here goes.

Theodosia picked up an ugly brown jacket and tossed it aside. Found more magazines underneath. *Digital Camera, Modern Photography*, and something called *PDN*. She shoved them aside as well. Now she'd drilled down to the heart of the pile. More clothes, yet another camera, and a shoebox. She lifted the lid on the shoebox, found it was empty. She shoved a hand farther down into the pile and searched around. Wrinkling her nose, she felt for anything that might not belong there. And finally found . . . a plastic glass. Probably from the bathroom. But that was it, nothing else.

Theodosia shoved everything back into a jumbled mound—Basset would never notice that his room had been tossed—and turned to leave. She had a hand on the doorknob when her eyes caught a glimpse of something. A small wicker wastebasket half hidden by the drapes.

She leaned down to look inside just as her cell phone rang.

22

It was Angie. Calling to warn her!

Theodosia's brain bonked into hyperdrive as she quickly silenced her phone.

Do I risk looking in the wastebasket or should I get out of here now so I don't get caught?

Theodosia's burning curiosity won out. She reached in, saw a discarded yellow-and-black cardboard box, and grabbed it. She stumbled out of the room, banging her right knee against the doorframe, managing to pull the door shut behind her. Ducking low behind the woven wood fence, she prayed for a clean getaway as she sprinted down the walkway past the other annex rooms, all the time hearing heavy footsteps coming her way. And as they echoed off the uneven patio stones, the sounds drew ever closer.

Just as Theodosia heard the familiar voice of Bob Basset mumbling to herself, reminding himself to grab his wide-angle camera lens, she summoned one final burst of speed and flung herself around the corner of the building, disappearing out of sight!

Pasting herself against the stucco wall of Angie's garage, Theodosia squeezed her eyes shut and tried to breathe. Her heart banged against her ribs with excitement.

Did I just do that? Yes, I did. And for what?

Theodosia opened her eyes and stared at the crumpled box she held in her hand. It was small, maybe six by eight inches, the yellow-and-black graphics making it look almost industrial. Studying her find more carefully, she saw it was more of a cardboard wraparound label than a box.

On it were the words PROLINE TETHERING CABLE—15 FT.

Theodosia knew what a tethering cable was. It was a cord you used to connect your camera to your laptop in order to transfer data.

The question was, what had Bob Basset used the cable for? Transferring photos to his laptop—or strangling women?

"You look guilty as sin," Drayton said when Theodosia arrived back at the tea shop. "Where did you go? What did you do?"

Just as Theodosia was trying to formulate a palatable explanation for her quasi-sanctioned, still highly illegal search, the phone rang.

Drayton snatched it up, said, "Hello? Yes." He raised his eyebrows as he handed her the phone. "The boyfriend du jour," he murmured. "Looks like you are saved by the bell yet again."

"Hello?" Theodosia said.

"I have news," Riley said.

"Big news?" Theodosia's heart was still thumping from her mad adventure at Angie's.

"If you mean, 'Have we arrested our killer,' the answer would be no."

"Then what?" Theodosia said.

"Two things. The first is we traced that bouquet of dark red tea roses to Pink Lady Florist over on Queen Street. The man who ordered them paid cash, but the florist, a woman named Bibi Cooper, who owns the place, remembered the guy fairly well."

"And?" Now Theodosia was practically holding her breath.

"The owner said her customer was young to middle-aged. Good-looking, fairly well-spoken."

Theodosia let out a breath. "That description rules out Wyatt Orlock. He's old and crabby."

"And I'm guessing Bob Basset, too, since he's not exactly young or good-looking."

"Bah humbug," Theodosia said. Had her snoop and grab been an exercise in futility? "Still, you were able to question Wyatt Orlock this morning?"

"We went at him like crazy. He's a cagey old codger. Knows how to answer questions without revealing too much."

"But you don't suspect him?"

"His alibis have all checked out so far."

"So who does that leave?" Theodosia asked.

"It means we're either chasing a phantom or we're back to looking at Tim Holt, the ex-boyfriend."

"Or Nick Prince," Theodosia said. "He can be charming in a slippery-when-wet kind of way."

"Huh. I think you just don't like him," Riley said.

"No, I don't."

"Last night you mentioned something about Orlock's security guy."

"Frank Lynch," Theodosia said. "Are you going to question him, too?"

"It's in the works. We just have to *locate* the guy. I don't know if Orlock was being uncooperative or if he really couldn't remember the guy's address. Lynch isn't listed anywhere as a property owner."

"So you have to keep digging," Theodosia said. "Have you had any more luck on the unsolved cases from seven years ago?"

"Actually, the best stuff we have came from you."

"Really? That's it?"

"Sweetheart, nothing ever comes easy."

"Where were you?" Drayton demanded once Theodosia hung up.

"If you must know, I ran over to the Featherbed House because that's where Bob Basset is staying."

"At Angie's place? Sweet Fanny Adams. Did you actually, um . . . ?" He trailed off, finished his question by making a rolling motion with his hand.

"Did I snoop around inside his room? If I had done that, would you disapprove terribly?"

"Probably not," Drayton said. He turned, grabbed his notebook, and said, in a casual tone of voice, "Did you find anything? Incriminating, I mean?"

"Just a wrapper for a computer cord."

"Oh. Computers," Drayton said. He wasn't a fan. Didn't even have an e-mail account. He picked up his pen and said, "Now that we're getting down to the wire, we really should go over our plans for tomorrow's Murder Mystery Tea."

Miss Dimple was suddenly front and center. "A Murder Mystery Tea. I *adore* Murder Mystery Teas."

"That's gratifying to hear," Drayton said. "Since tomorrow you'll be playing one of the major characters."

Miss Dimple's face lit up. "I am? Which one?"

"You, my dear, will assume the role of Lady Cecily," Drayton said.

"I like the sound of that. Oh wait, will I be the killer?"

"You never know."

"What about me?" Theodosia asked. It was a relief to be talking about tea and a playacting murder as opposed to real-life violent crimes.

"You are Baroness Althea," Drayton said. He did a mock scowl. "Have you not read your script?"

"I confess I haven't," Theodosia said.

"Please try to do so before tomorrow's three o'clock tea," Drayton said. "Now, besides our two actors, I'm going to bring in Bill Boyet from the camera store down the block to be our victim. We'll have him kick the bucket at the appropriate moment and—"

"Ooh!" Miss Dimple squealed.

Drayton smiled at her reaction. "Then after I dispose of the body, our guests will be asked to pitch in and help solve the mystery of who killed Lord Bledsoe."

"How will they do that?" Miss Dimple asked.

"Each guest will receive a card that gives information and clues concerning the crime. After everyone has their turn at reading their card, they're allowed to question the suspects." He looked up. "That's the lot of us," he said.

"This is great," Miss Dimple said. "I'm getting tingles."

"After the questioning, our guests will write down who they think poisoned poor unsuspecting Lord Bledsoe," Drayton said.

"Then what?" Miss Dimple asked.

"Again," Drayton said, "you need to read your script."

"So all will be revealed?" Theodosia asked.

Drayton adjusted his bow tie. "But of course."

Once all the afternoon guests had left, Theodosia fussed about the tea shop, unpacking a carton of DuBose Bees Honey, then kneeling to arrange the jars on the lower shelves of her highboy. If she moved the cat tea cozies to the bottom shelf, she could probably fit the entire case.

A *ding-ding* above the front door caused her to turn and smile. And then smile even wider as Miss Josette, one of their favorite artisans, made her way into the tea room.

Drayton, always a proper Southern gent, hurried to greet her. "Miss Josette," he said. "Welcome. We weren't expecting you." He turned toward Theodosia. "Were we?"

Theodosia was already up and moving toward the front door. "No, but we're delighted anyway." Then, when Miss Josette set down her umbrella, Theodosia saw that she was carrying an over-sized canvas bag. Her going-to-market craft bag. "I'll bet you brought us some newly woven sweetgrass baskets!"

Miss Josette was a sixty-something African-American artist of Gullah descent. She had rich ebony skin and almond eyes and carried herself with great aplomb. Today she wore a red shawl set at a rakish angle over an elegant black dress. She wore her hair in shoulder-length twists, the better to show off diamond stud earrings.

Miss Josette also had the distinction of having two of her hand-woven sweetgrass baskets in the permanent collection of the Smithsonian, besides having won several awards given by the South Carolina Arts Commission.

"Do you have time to sit with us for a cup of tea?" Drayton asked.

Miss Josette shook her head. "I'm on my way to the Lady Goodwood Inn. I promised them two baskets to showcase in their Carolina Room. But since I have five baskets for sale, I decided to give you two first crack."

"We appreciate it, Miss Josette," Theodosia said. "We'd take them all if we could. Your baskets are so popular, our customers practically fight to get them."

Miss Josette smiled. "Good to hear. It means there's still a market for my weavings." She held up a hand with long, tapered fingers and flexed it. "Of course, these baskets are a three-hundred-year tradition here in the Carolinas and I was schooled the proper way by my great-grandmother."

"For sure," Drayton said. Like many people in the know, he had his own collection of sweetgrass baskets.

"It's heartwarming to see that crafts like weaving, spinning, and sewing have made such an enormous comeback," Theodosia said.

"Modern times, but people still appreciate the old ways," Miss Josette said.

She set her bag on a table and opened it to reveal an array of finely detailed, almost sculptural baskets—two woven trays, an oblong basket with handles, and two tall market baskets.

"See anything you like?" she asked, a hint of amusement in her voice.

"Everything," Theodosia and Drayton said together, even though they knew they could only choose three.

23

An hour later, Theodosia and Drayton found themselves at the Imago Gallery. Drayton hadn't been keen on attending the photo opening, but Theodosia had sweet-talked and arm-twisted him into it. She wanted to see Tim Holt's work and maybe get a chance to speak to him again.

"Welcome, welcome," said Holly Burns, the owner of the gallery, as she greeted them at the door. Holly was in her mid-forties, rail thin, with long, black Morticia Addams–style hair. Tonight she was dressed in a red paisley kimono top, black leggings, and stretchy nylon shoes that looked like potatoes but were probably über-trendy. A half dozen statement necklaces dangled around Holly's neck. "Come in, look around, enjoy," she enthused.

"Thank you," Theodosia murmured.

Like many contemporary art galleries, the Imago Gallery favored strict minimalist decor. That is, white walls, gray industrial carpeting, and pinpoint spotlights overhead to highlight the works on display.

The better to set off the photos and paintings? Theodosia wondered. *Or the flamboyant owner?*

The event was well underway as Theodosia and Drayton elbowed their way through the throng of invited guests who jostled in the limited space of the gallery. A DJ with a sound board played music that featured a warbling female singer accompanied by low-pitched background murmurs.

"What awful music," Drayton said. "Is the singer trying to imitate the sounds of a humpback whale?"

"I believe that's new age synthesized music."

"Ah. Well, it may be a legitimate genre, but it's still awful."

A young waiter in black slacks, a black T-shirt, and a half-shaved head came toward them bearing a tray of tall flutes filled with golden liquid.

"May I offer you a glass of champagne?" the waiter asked.

"Love one," Theodosia said as both she and Drayton accepted a glass.

"Thank you," Drayton said, then immediately took a sip. He half closed his eyes as he tasted the beverage. "Champagne, no. Prosecco, yes. These grapes are clearly not the bright, angelic product of France's illustrious Champagne region."

Theodosia was amused. "So you basically hate it?"

Drayton took another sip. "Actually it's quite crisp and good." He looked around and said, "Interesting crowd here. Most everyone's dressed head-to-toe in black. Is that because they're trying to make a quasi-artistic fashion statement or are they of the Gothic persuasion?"

"They're downtown hipsters," Theodosia said. "That's what they do to try and look cool. Besides hang out at galleries and drink cheap white wine."

Drayton's mouth twitched in amusement.

"Since we're here, should we take a look at the photographs?" Theodosia asked.

"If we must."

Besides Tim Holt's photos, the work of two other photographers was on display tonight. A man by the name of Izzy Dalton and a woman named Joshilyn Jones. Dalton's photos were crisp black-and-white, with a stark newspaper feel to them. Jones's photos were full-color, ethereal, and slightly out of focus. A lot of sunsets and misty morning low-country shots. Certainly nothing that pushed the envelope.

And then there were Tim Holt's photographs.

"Say now, some of these photos aren't half-bad," Drayton exclaimed. "I was expecting more commercial work, but Holt obviously enjoys history. See here, he's included shots of Middleton Place and Fort Moultrie."

They walked along, looking at the twenty or so photos mounted on a wall as well as on a freestanding display.

"And here's a photo of the Dock Street Theatre," Drayton said. "Holt managed to capture the play of light on the brick and ironwork facade in a manner that's quite lovely."

Holt's next few shots were of Charleston Harbor. A flotilla of J/22s skimming across the waves, their white sails billowing. A large cruise ship bustling along. A tugboat escorting a large tanker.

The composition of the photos exhibited Holt's keen eye and natural talent, but Theodosia wondered why there were so many shots of Charleston Harbor. If Holt had murdered Monica Garber as well as Cara, had he stood in the bandstand gazing out across the harbor? If so, he would have enjoyed almost the same perspective as was shown in these photos. The idea rattled her. Life imitating art?

She turned toward Drayton to mention this when her eyes locked with those of Tim Holt. He tilted his head to acknowledge contact, then walked over to greet her.

"You came," Holt said. "I didn't think you would." Tonight

he looked like a true artiste. Ripped jeans, faded T-shirt, slip-on shoes that were a cross between sandals and tennis shoes.

"Drayton and I were interested in seeing your work," Theodosia said. She tapped Drayton on the shoulder and he spun around, a quizzical expression on his face. "You remember Drayton?"

"Of course," Holt said. "It's nice to see you again."

The two men shook hands.

"I'm quite enjoying your display of photographs," Drayton said. "You've managed to capture a lot of Charleston's historic places and do it in an engaging manner."

"Thank you," Holt said.

"I found your perspective on Charleston Harbor intriguing as well," Theodosia said. She watched Holt carefully to see if there was any reaction. There wasn't. If anything, he looked awfully subdued for a photographer who should be basking in the glory of a successful opening-night party.

"You're very kind," Holt said, his voice faltering slightly.

"I'm sorry, is something wrong?" Theodosia asked.

"I think . . . after the funeral this morning I'm thinking that Cara's death has finally hit me," Holt said, moving closer to her. "Before, it felt surreal but not real, if you know what I mean. No doubt because we'd broken up in such a casual manner. But now that I've had some serious time to digest this . . . dealing with the finality of Cara's funeral . . ." Holt shook his head. "I realize that I loved her very much."

Theodosia was taken aback. Holt hadn't shown this much emotion or introspection when she'd spoken with him before. This was something completely new. Brought on by . . . what? The sad finality of the funeral like he'd said? Or a guilty conscience?

"I thought Cara's breaking up with you didn't come as a huge surprise," Theodosia said.

"It didn't at the time. But now . . . now I think we were truly meant for each other."

"Really," Theodosia said, genuinely surprised that Holt was suddenly so bereft. Or was he just a skilled actor?

Holt squinted at her. "Ours could have been a match made in heaven."

Or hell, Theodosia thought. Especially if Holt was living a secret life as Fogheel Jack.

She was about to say more when the gallery owner, Holly Burns, came spinning in like a little dust devil, tapped Holt on the shoulder, and stage-whispered, "I have an interested buyer who'd like to meet our star photographer." She threw an apologetic smile at Theodosia and said, "You don't mind if I steal this fellow away from you, do you?"

"Be my guest," Theodosia said. Because at that exact moment she'd spotted Wyatt Orlock walking in the front door. Accompanied by Frank Lynch, no less.

Of course, Theodosia thought, the Imago Gallery was just two blocks from Orlock's proposed condo development. He was a neighbor and in Charleston neighbors always got invitations. Especially wealthy, big-shot businessmen neighbors.

Theodosia watched Orlock smooth back his hair and survey the room with a haughty look. Then she nudged Drayton, who was studying a black-and-white photo of the glorious Angel Oak that had stood on Johns Island for five hundred years.

Drayton turned to face her. "What?"

"Wyatt Orlock just came in. Along with his henchman, Frank Lynch."

Drayton looked amused. "So Lynch has been bumped up from private security to numero uno henchman?"

"I'm not sure that's a promotion," Theodosia said. "And why on earth haven't the police been able to locate Lynch when the glitterati of downtown Charleston are rubbing shoulders with him?"

"Well, you can ask him yourself. Because he and Orlock just spotted us and are heading this way."

"Gulp."

Orlock walked directly up to Theodosia, making a special point to invade her personal space. His face carried a hard, knowing look that made her uneasy and reminded her of a rabid weasel. Lynch stood behind him, a human watchdog with a nasty grin.

"You," Orlock spat out. "I remember you."

"I'm not sure we've been introduced," Theodosia said, feigning ignorance and feeling discombobulated by his nasty glare.

Orlock's face darkened and his pupils contracted with barely concealed anger. "That so? Then let me refresh your memory. You plopped down at my table a few nights ago at my restaurant and started peppering me with questions. Impertinent questions, I might add." Orlock tapped an index finger against the side of his head. "I remember people and faces, particularly those that irritate me."

"I certainly didn't mean to ruffle any feathers," Theodosia said.

"You asked me about Lois Chamberlain. Then the cops showed up a couple days later and started asking me about Lois Chamberlain. And I think to myself—isn't that an amazing coincidence?" He regarded her with a smug, knowing grin. "Why do I think maybe *you* sicced them on me, girlie?"

"Why would I want to do that?" Theodosia said.

"Because you strike me as a first-class busybody," Orlock said. "Somebody who enjoys stirring the pot."

"Excuse me," Drayton said. "We don't want any trouble."

"You're gonna find yourselves in a heap of trouble if you keep meddling in my business," Orlock said.

"Why? Are you scheming to buy more buildings?" Theodosia

shot back at him. "Trying to drive a few more merchants out of their space?"

Orlock glared at her, then turned to Lynch and said, "Go get the car, Frank. I don't like the company in here. Don't care to associate with smartasses." And just like that he turned and elbowed his way back through the jostling crowd.

"The party's over," Drayton said as he watched Orlock make his retreat.

"He's a touchy one, isn't he," Theodosia said.

"You did manage to land a few sharp jabs."

"I wonder what he's up to," Theodosia said.

"Hmm?" Drayton suddenly looked flustered.

"After that bravura performance, I wouldn't trust Wyatt Orlock as far as I could spit a rat."

"So he's suddenly back on your suspect list?"

"Has to be. He's a wild card who—" Theodosia stopped abruptly and set her glass down on a nearby counter. "I think we should keep an eye on him."

"That sounds awfully ill-advised."

"You don't have to be a part of this," Theodosia said. "I'm perfectly capable of . . . Oh heck, he really *did* leave." She stood on tiptoes so she could see over the crowd. Then she grabbed Drayton by the arm and spun him around. "C'mon, Drayton."

They hurried outside, just in time to see Orlock climb into the back seat of a black Mercedes.

"There he is," Drayton said. "Leaving. Out of your hair for good. Happy now?"

"How do you like that? He and Frank Lynch are cozy as can be. The police have been wanting to question Lynch, and Orlock pretended not to know his whereabouts."

"Should we write down their license plate?"

"I've got a better idea. Let's follow them," Theodosia said as she ran for her Jeep. It was parked two cars down and, as luck would have it, headed in the same direction Lynch had driven off in.

Drayton stood there as if rooted to the spot. "Now?" he shouted after her.

"No, next Tuesday," Theodosia cried. "Yes, now. Come on, hurry up and jump in!"

24

Theodosia caught up with Orlock and Lynch two blocks away. It was easy to follow the big black Mercedes with its distinctive taillights as it sliced through traffic like a shark on the hunt.

"Don't get too close or they'll see us," Drayton warned. "Stay a couple of cars back like you always see in the movies."

"I got this, I got this," Theodosia said. She switched to the left lane, passed two slow-moving cars, then changed back.

"You don't really believe Orlock is Fogheel Jack, do you?"

"I don't know what to think anymore." Theodosia's fingers tip-tapped her steering wheel anxiously. "He *could* be. On the other hand, so could his so-called security guy / driver, Frank Lynch. I'm particularly interested in Lynch ever since I saw him skulking through the crowd at White Point Gardens the night Monica Garber was murdered."

"Yes, you did mention that to me."

"I told Riley about him, too."

"Putting this all together is getting me seriously worried," Drayton said.

"Sorry," Theodosia said.

"Say there . . ." Drayton lifted a hand and pointed. "They're turning left down Meeting Street."

"Got it," Theodosia said as she hung a left after them.

Meeting Street was fairly well traveled and well lit, with lots of shops and several fashionable hotels. Which made it a snap to keep Orlock and Lynch in their sights. Neon signs glistened off wet pavement, people ran from parked cars into bars, and there was the constant *whoosh* of tires.

But when Orlock's car turned down Tradd Street, the situation suddenly got a whole lot trickier.

"Now you need to hang back a little more," Drayton urged.

"I will. I am."

They were close to the tip of the peninsula, in an affluent residential neighborhood, where large, gracious homes sat like small principalities behind hedges, gates, and rows of palmettos. Gardens were groomed and manicured, many of the historic homes painted the colors of a French palette—almond, robin's-egg blue, pale peach.

"Where do you suppose they're going?" Drayton wondered.

"My guess is Orlock lives nearby," Theodosia said.

"In this neighborhood? You think?"

As if in answer to his question, Theodosia caught two quick flashes of red as Lynch tapped his brakes. Then the Mercedes pulled gently to the curb in front of a large three-story home that featured a gabled roof, front pillars, and a side porte cochere. Theodosia quickly pulled to the curb two houses this side of Orlock's home and cut her lights.

"Honey, I'm home," she said.

Drayton let out a low whistle. "Orlock lives there?"

"See? Now don't you wish you'd become a fat-cat real estate developer instead of a tea sommelier?"

"Not on your life," Drayton said.

Theodosia turned off her wipers and peered through the windshield. "Okay, what's happening now?"

They watched as a rear door opened and a dome light came on. Orlock stepped out into the damp night, pulled up the collar of his coat, and glanced around. Then he stepped to the driver's window and bent low, obviously talking to Lynch, who was still hunkered in the driver's seat. Thirty seconds later, Orlock hurried up the front walk and disappeared into his home.

"What now?" Drayton asked.

"I'm not sure."

"Why do you think Frank Lynch is sitting in the dark like that?"

"No idea," Theodosia said.

"You think something's going to happen?"

"Not necessarily."

Drayton was antsy. "Does it seem like we're playing twenty questions?"

Theodosia smiled. "We kind of are."

A few minutes later, a second Mercedes backed out of the carriage house that sat directly behind Orlock's house. Then it nosed through the porte cochere and turned in their direction. As the car passed under the yellow glow of a streetlamp, Theodosia could see that it was being driven by Wyatt Orlock.

"Orlock's off somewhere by himself," Theodosia said.

"Do you think that means something?"

"I don't know." Feeling a throb of anticipation, Theodosia turned her focus back to Lynch's car. "Let's see what this clown is going to do."

They didn't have to wait long.

The minute Orlock was down the block, Lynch made a hasty U-turn and took off in the opposite direction.

"Which one are we going to follow?" Drayton asked.

"Lynch," Theodosia said, gunning her engine and also negotiating a fast U-turn. "He fits the flower-shop description the best."

"Which is?" Drayton rested a hand on the dashboard, steadying himself.

"Young to middle-aged, relatively good-looking."

"You think Frank Lynch is good-looking?" Drayton asked.

Theodosia gave a harsh laugh. "Not personally. But he must be somebody's type."

"Only if there are women who are attracted to that swarthy bad-boy look."

"That might be more women than you think," Theodosia said.

Lynch headed back to Meeting Street, drove a few blocks, then seemed to meander around. They followed him down Water Street, then again when he took a right turn on Bay Street. It seemed like aimless driving. Then again . . .

"What do you think Lynch is up to?" Drayton asked. "Does this man have a plan? An actual destination in mind?"

"I don't know. Hopefully he's not out hunting."

"You mean looking for a victim? There's a terrifying thought."

"Tell me about it."

They followed Lynch as he turned down a narrow street lined with Charleston single homes, some gentrified, a few in need of repair.

Then Lynch slowed and stopped in the middle of the street.

"What's he doing? Can you see?" Drayton asked.

"Looks like he's talking on his mobile phone," Theodosia said.

Lynch started up again, driving with more authority this time. Theodosia followed him carefully down Queen Street, glancing in her rearview mirror more than once.

"What's wrong?" Drayton asked the third time she checked it.

"Just a weird feeling I have. That someone might be ghosting along behind us."

"Another car?" Drayton squirmed around in his seat and looked back. "I don't see anyone."

"I'm probably just jumping at shadows."

"Probably."

But in the light from the dashboard Theodosia could see that Drayton's brow had furrowed and that he was tapping a nervous finger against his armrest.

He's got a funny feeling, too.

Lynch turned left at East Elliott Street and cut his speed to a few miles an hour.

"Why is he driving like that?" Drayton wondered. "So slow and tentative."

"If you ask me, it looks like he's trying to locate a particular address," Theodosia said.

Brake lights flared, then Lynch stopped in the middle of the block in front of a lovely brick town house. It was shielded by a tall hedge and had decorative wrought-iron screens on all the windows. As a car approached from the opposite direction, Lynch was silhouetted in the headlights for a split second.

"Now it looks as if he's making a phone call," Theodosia said.

"But to who?"

They waited patiently for two, then three minutes. Finally, the front door of the town house opened and a woman came bouncing down the front steps. She was dressed in a silver dress and black booties and had a short dark jacket thrown casually over her shoulders. She looked as if she was off to a party.

"Oh no," Theodosia said.

"You think Lynch staked her out? That she's his next victim?" Drayton asked.

"I hope not. But we're going to be abundantly cautious and follow him closely. Like driving-up-his-tailpipe close."

"Maybe you should alert Tidwell. Or Riley?"

"I'm not ready to cry wolf just yet."

They stayed hard on Lynch's tail as he drove a few more blocks, cut over to Hasell Street, then turned down King Street, which was a one-way. And, lo and behold, pulled up directly in front of the Charleston Grill.

"Murder among the crab cakes?" Drayton said. The Charleston Grill was one of the swankier places to dine in Charleston.

A red-coated doorman hurried over to open the car's back door, allowing the woman to jump out and sprint inside.

"Holy guacamole," Theodosia said. "I think Lynch might be gigging for a ride service."

"What do you mean? Oh, you're talking about one of those companies like Huber?"

"Uber, yeah."

"I don't know exactly how those work, but it strikes me as a fine way to scope out women. If you were a driver you'd know where they lived, then you could circle back and be waiting for them when they returned home," Drayton said.

"That's a terrible scenario," Theodosia said.

Drayton nodded. "I know. But we live in strange times."

They tailed Lynch back to Orlock's home, then watched as he stowed the car inside the carriage house. Once the garage door closed, Lynch climbed a narrow flight of stairs attached to the side of the building. Fifteen seconds later a light shone on the second floor.

"He must live there," Theodosia said.

"The big question is, do you think he's in for the night?" Drayton asked.

"I kind of do."

"Good, because I've had enough of these hare-and-hound games."

"Which, unfortunately, didn't get us one bit closer to learning anything," Theodosia said.

Drayton checked his watch. "It's almost ten. We should both be getting home. We've got a big day tomorrow."

Feeling disappointed and more than a little let down, Theodosia drove Drayton home.

When she pulled up in front of Drayton's house, he said, "If you don't mind, I'm going to run inside and grab a box of props for tomorrow. Stow it in your back seat."

"No problem," Theodosia said as she shut off her ignition. "In fact, I'll come in and get it."

"It's not much," Drayton said as they walked up the sidewalk in the dark. "Just some hats, a coat, and a couple of teapots." He unlatched his side door and stepped into the kitchen, Theodosia right on his heels.

As he switched on the light, the little brown-and-white bundle that was Honey Bee came rushing to greet them, long ears flopping, tail wagging. She had to administer kisses to both of them, then back up and do her little dog dance.

"So cute," Theodosia said, yawning. "Like a little canine ballerina."

"Here's the stuff," Drayton said, handing Theodosia a cardboard box. "If it's too heavy I'll carry it out to your car for you."

"Nope, it's fine."

"Okay, drive straight home, then."

"I will."

Theodosia walked to her car, shoved the cardboard box into the back seat, and started for home. The streets were wet, but the rain had let up and there was very little fog. Maybe all the rotten weather had finally blown out to sea and they'd be done with it for good. Maybe tomorrow would dawn bright and sunny. Maybe.

Theodosia had driven two blocks when her Jeep began to buck and sputter.

What's going on?

She tapped the gas pedal, making her Jeep pogo crazily and then shoot forward.

Maybe this old bucket needs a tune-up? Or an oil change? Well, it's driving fine now, seems to have recovered.

She'd driven this particular Jeep for a good four years. It was the perfect vehicle for stowing sails, saddles, and whatnot. The whatnot being the wild raspberry and clover plants she foraged for in the pastures and woods of her aunt Libby's plantation. Nothing like South Carolina native teas.

Unfortunately, her Jeep's recovery lasted only another half block. Then there was a more urgent sputter (*A death knell? Please, no.*) and it slowed. Theodosia tromped down hard on the gas pedal again, but this time nothing happened. No acceleration, no engine noise, not even a burp.

Theodosia frowned as she rolled slowly to a stop.

Now what?

She looked around nervously, wishing Drayton was still with her. Or Earl Grey. Or anybody. It was dark, moonless, and spooky. Every tree, shrub, and shadowy spot looked like it might serve as a hiding place for someone to pop out at her.

Stranger danger? No, wipe that thought from your head.

Theodosia debated getting out of the car to see if she could fix whatever needed fixing. Or was it better to call AAA? Or Riley?

Riley won out, hands down. And as luck would have it, he answered his phone and immediately agreed to come help her.

My hero, she thought.

Some ten minutes later, he showed up.

"Somebody call for help?" Riley asked, grinning as he pulled alongside her, his driver's side window down.

"It's strange," Theodosia said. "It just stopped."

"Out of gas?"

"I just filled up a couple of days ago."

She climbed out of her car at the same time he did.

"Have you been doing a lot of driving?" Riley asked her.

"Not too much." Theodosia wasn't about to tell Riley about tailing Frank Lynch around in circles tonight. He'd have a conniption if he found out about that little adventure.

"Let's take a look," Riley said as he grabbed a flashlight from his glove box. They both walked back to check her gas tank.

Theodosia prayed that if she *was* out of gas he wouldn't think she was a ditz.

"This is a locking cap," Riley said, tapping it with his finger.

"Right. If the car's locked, the cap's locked."

"But your cap looks as if it's been tampered with. You see the scratches here?" He shone the light and traced his fingers over faint marks. "And over here? I think somebody pried this open and siphoned out your fuel." He glanced around. "To make you run out of gas right here. Where it's dark and deserted."

"Who would do that?"

Riley stared at her. "Who do you think?" He put his hands on Theodosia's shoulders and gently drew her close. "Theo, face it, somebody *caused* you to run out of gas."

"Somebody did this while I was in Drayton's house? That would mean . . ." She stopped abruptly as the reality hit her.

"That someone was following you, yes," Riley said.

Theodosia wondered about the car she'd *thought* had been following her.

"Why me?" Theodosia asked, even though her mind was already circling around the answer.

"Why do you think? Because you've been investigating on your own. Asking questions when you shouldn't."

Theodosia felt a cold chill descend on her. "You're telling me I stumbled over somebody's trip wire."

"That's an interesting way to put it, but yes. I think all your questions and snooping started to grate on someone. Worried them, made them feel uneasy."

"Please don't tell me we're talking about Fogheel Jack."

"You know somebody else who's been terrorizing an entire city?" Riley asked.

Theodosia gazed at the gas cap. So someone had been following her at the same time she was following Frank Lynch. But who? And why? Had she really bumbled across the killer?

"I need to ask you something," Theodosia said in a small voice.

Riley wrinkled his brow, looking concerned. "Sweetheart, what?"

"You questioned Wyatt Orlock, right?"

"Absolutely we did."

"And he had good alibis?"

"Creative ones anyway."

"And you never picked up a hint of anything? That he was guilty, I mean?"

"Not really. Theo, what are you getting at? Maybe you'd better just spit it out."

"I, um, figured out where Frank Lynch lives."

"What!"

"I think his apartment is directly above Orlock's carriage house."

Riley's jaw tightened. "And where is that?"

"Over on Tradd. Right by that pocket park with the two statues."

"You know this for a fact?"

Theodosia nodded.

"How?"

"You don't want to know."

Riley exhaled loudly and slowly. "No, but I can guess. Theo, you've got to stop poking your nose where it doesn't belong. I mean stop right now, this very minute. It simply isn't safe. You're putting yourself in mortal danger."

Theodosia let his words rumble through her brain. She hated to admit it, but perhaps Riley was right. Maybe she was getting dangerously close to discovering the identity of Fogheel Jack. And she'd unknowingly put herself directly in the kill zone.

"You could be right," she murmured as he opened his arms and she snuggled in close. "I don't relish being Fogheel Jack's next victim."

"Believe me, I don't want you to be, either."

Riley embraced her tenderly and they kissed.

No more investigating, Theodosia thought to herself. *Just too many crazies out there. Hard to tell the good guys from the bad guys. Maybe . . . time to turn over a new leaf?*

And that's when she heard the sirens.

Riley's head jerked up the same time hers did. "What the hell?" he said.

Theodosia was suddenly on full alert, listening, wondering. The blaring noise rose high, like a wall of sound. Then it was joined in concert by another siren. And another.

"This could be bad," Riley said. He was reaching for his phone as well as the beeper on his belt.

"Rescue vehicles? Fire trucks? Whatever they are, they're headed this way," Theodosia said. "Right into the Historic District."

Riley listened for a few more seconds. "Yeah. Sounds like the action is happening a few blocks over."

Theodosia was suddenly engulfed with terror. Her eyes widened, her heart blipped with fear.

"Oh no," she cried. "What if something's burning on Church Street? What if my tea shop's on fire!"

25

❧

"*You don't know* that—you're jumping to conclusions. The fire could be anywhere, probably blocks away," Riley said.

"But we have to make sure," Theodosia cried. "I have to be certain that it's *not* my tea shop that's burning!"

The fire was on Church Street all right. Right smack-dab in the heart of Theodosia's beloved neighborhood. But it wasn't at the Indigo Tea Shop, thank goodness.

Bizarrely enough, it was Antiquarian Books that had somehow exploded in flames. Now, windows shattered and books were blown haphazardly out onto the street, a tornado of flames shot skyward, red and orange flames that licked at overhead power lines, causing them to snap and pop.

"This is awful," Theodosia said. Her heart was in her throat as she jumped out of Riley's car and surveyed the wild scene, which included numerous fire engines, firefighters, police, and even a sheriff's car. "This is going to be another death blow to Lois."

A grim-faced Riley said, "Wait here. I'm going to try and get closer. See what's going on."

Of course Theodosia didn't wait by his car as asked. Instead, she dogged Riley's footsteps as he hurried down the block, heading for the frenzy surrounding the burning bookshop. Firefighters aimed hoses at the blaze, cops tried to help where they could, even an ambulance she hoped wouldn't be needed showed up.

Theodosia hadn't gone more than fifty feet when a wall of heat hit her like a force field, causing her to retreat. Riley made it a little farther before he ducked and turned back. He gripped her elbow as they watched from a safe distance.

Bells clanged and more sirens screeched as a fourth fire truck came screaming to the scene. Luckily, the men from the first couple of rigs seemed to be getting a handle on the fire, as they continued to squirt huge jets of water at the building.

"You don't think sparks are going to blow over and hit the tea shop, do you?" Theodosia asked. "Make it catch on fire?"

Riley shook his head. "Doubtful."

Theodosia turned worried eyes on him. "But Haley's there. She's got to be terrified." Then a horrible thought struck Theodosia. "If she even knows about this."

"Better call her."

Theodosia grabbed her mobile phone, dialed Haley's number, and got her sweet voice on the answering machine.

"Riley, Haley's not picking up. We've got to do something. Oh no, what if she's fast asleep? Took a pain pill or something and zonked out. What if she doesn't *know* what's going on out here?"

"Okay then," Riley said. "I'll see what I can do while you wait here. And this time I mean it. You stay put."

"Sure, right."

Theodosia watched as Riley sprinted down Church Street, stopping only to show his badge to a uniformed officer who was trying desperately to keep onlookers away from the fire. Then he ducked around the back of a fire truck and two smaller rescue vehicles and she lost sight of him.

Theodosia turned her attention back to the burning building. The fire was still burning like an inferno. Firefighters in flame-retardant suits worked heroically to try to save the charming yellow-brick building. Fat gray hoses lay in tangles; gluts of water ran everywhere. Down the street across from Boyet's Camera Shop, a fireman pounded with his wrench to open another hydrant.

This is bad. So bad.

Theodosia bounced on the balls of her feet nervously. She wondered if she should call Lois, then decided the police would have already contacted her. Then she started to worry about Riley. How close was he to the fire? Was he okay? Had he located Haley? What about Haley's little cat?

Finally, Riley appeared with a somber-looking Haley in tow.

"I found her wandering around outside the tea shop," Riley said. "She's okay. At least she says she is."

"I was afraid the tea shop might catch fire, too," Haley said. She was pale and shivering and looked like death warmed over.

Theodosia grabbed Haley and hugged her fiercely. Haley, whose face was smudged (from the smoke?), hugged her back.

"I was so *worried* about you," Theodosia said when she finally released Haley from her grip.

"Can you believe this?" Haley asked. "What do you think's gonna happen next? A plague of locusts?"

"It does feel like we've endured our share of bad luck," Theodosia said. "Did the firefighters knock on the door and tell you to evacuate?"

"They heavily suggested it," Haley said.

"Where's Teacake?"

"He's in his cat carrier. Leigh has him right now." Leigh Carroll owned the Cabbage Patch Gift Shop just down the street from the Indigo Tea Shop.

"Her shop's okay?"

"Looks that way, yeah," Haley said.

"I talked to one of the fire marshals," Riley said. "They're confident they can keep the fire contained, though the bookshop is probably a total loss."

"But still . . ." Theodosia said. Inside she raged as she watched the frantic goings-on. Not save the building? That would be awful.

And who was responsible for this latest catastrophe? she wondered. This fire was no accident, no short-circuiting wires or overloaded heating system. It had surely been set intentionally. Had Tim Holt been trying to make life even worse for Lois? Or was Nick Prince playing deadly games so he could rev up the stakes in his true-crime novel?

Theodosia grabbed Riley's arm and quickly whispered her thoughts to him, wild as they might be.

His answer completely surprised her.

"Neither one," Riley said in a maddeningly calm tone of voice.

"But how do you *know* that?"

Riley looked reluctant to give her an answer. Then, after some hemming and hawing, he said, "Because we've had both men under surveillance."

"What!" Theodosia practically flipped out at the idea. "I can see why you were watching Tim Holt since he's a suspect, but Nick Prince, too?"

"That was thanks to your suspicious nature," Riley said. "Your constant prodding."

"Omigosh, you actually listened to me?"

"And heeded your words. But the last report I received on both men, which came barely five minutes ago, was that neither had strayed from their homes all evening."

"Then who did this?" Theodosia asked. "Could it have been Wyatt Orlock? Or his security guy, Frank Lynch?"

"If I had to guess I'd say there's a slight possibility it could be Orlock, but only because he was trying to buy that particular building."

WHUMP!

The three of them watched in awe as a sudden explosion rocked the building and burning shingles, timbers, and hundreds more books were tossed high in the air.

"Well, maybe not the building anymore, but the land," Riley said.

Theodosia was torn with indecision. Should she tell Riley about how she and Drayton had followed Orlock and Lynch tonight? And about the curious, circuitous route that Lynch had traveled? Would it do any good? She decided no. Knowing that she'd been investigating the two men would just make him more upset. Better to keep that information close to the vest for now.

Haley, who had been hanging back, nudged her way up next to them.

"Does anyone know how the fire started?" she asked.

Riley shook his head. "We won't know anything until the fire's completely extinguished and the investigators can safely get in there to do an inspection. They'll try to determine point of origin and run tests to see if any accelerants were used."

"Look at that inferno!" Theodosia cried. "*Of course* accelerants were used. This didn't just happen on its own. Books don't simply explode. Somebody set this fire deliberately. It's arson, plain and simple."

Thirty minutes later and the fire was finally under control. There were a few hot spots, but for the most part, the excitement was over. Firefighters reeled in hoses; some started stowing gear on their rigs.

Still mesmerized by the fire, Theodosia kept pushing forward until Riley said, "I think that's close enough."

"It's getting down to charred embers inside," Theodosia said with a catch in her voice.

"But some of the walls are still there," Haley said. "And the roof. Well, most of it anyway."

Riley glanced around, saw a familiar face, and said, "A quick word, Chief?"

The battalion chief, a grizzled man in his late fifties, aimed a weary nod at Riley and said, "What's up?"

"You see anything fishy here? Any first impressions on what might have started the fire?"

"Actually, yeah," the chief said.

Theodosia pushed forward. "What was it?"

"Best guess, it was a sloppy, homemade Molotov cocktail. Probably as basic as a wine bottle filled with kerosene," said the chief.

"Hard to trace?" Theodosia said.

The chief shook his head. "Impossible."

They milled around some more, Theodosia reluctant to leave, Haley's eyes starting to droop. Then Haley turned, caught sight of a familiar face moving through the crowd, and said, "Oh no."

Theodosia followed her gaze and saw Lois Chamberlain walking toward them. She was bundled in a puffy black nylon coat, wore a pair of winter boots on her feet, and had a paisley scarf pulled over her hair. She not only looked dazed; she looked as if she'd jumped out of bed, helter-skelter-like, and put on the first thing she found.

"Lois," Theodosia said, going over to greet her, to wrap her in a hug. "I'm so sorry."

"This is unbelievable," Lois said. She rested her head on Theodosia's shoulder for a few moments, then straightened up. When she spoke, it was in a flat, defeated tone of voice. "What a perfect end to what's been the lousiest week of my life. My daughter's murder, her funeral this morning, and now my bookshop going up in flames."

Theodosia's heart ached for her. "Lois, if there's anything I can do . . ."

Lois gripped her arm and held tight. "You know there is," she said in a harsh whisper. Now her eyes blazed with intensity. "Find the person who did this. Find the monster who murdered my daughter and torched my bookshop."

"I will," Theodosia choked out. "I'll try."

"Cross your heart?"

Theodosia nodded. "Yes. If it's the last thing I do."

They walked Haley back to her apartment and watched as she retrieved her cat from Leigh. Then Riley drove Theodosia to a gas station, filled up a gas can, and took her back to her Jeep. Once he'd poured gas into her tank he said, "Promise me you'll go straight home."

Theodosia favored him with a modest smile. "I will. And thank you for everything you've done tonight."

"I meant that part about driving straight home. In fact, I'm going to follow you to make sure."

"You don't have to do that."

But he did. Waiting until Theodosia was safely inside with the door locked behind her. Then he gave a little toot of his horn and was off.

Earl Grey greeted Theodosia's arrival with searching eyes. Then he launched into a series of investigative sniffs, obviously detecting the smoke on her clothes. Or maybe her feelings of distress.

"You have no idea what I've just been through, dear boy," Theodosia said. She grabbed a treat from a ceramic Scooby-Doo cookie jar and handed it to him.

Or what poor Lois has been through. Oh dear, that woman's heart must be breaking.

Once Earl Grey had crunched his treat, Theodosia took him out into the backyard and looked around at the flowers and shrubs that should be bursting with blooms yet still remained buds and nubs.

Just too much rain. Now we need some good South Carolina heat and sunshine.

Back inside, doors locked and double-checked, Theodosia grabbed a handful of printouts from her dining table, some of the stuff she'd assembled on the past murders.

She went upstairs, took a long, hot shower, then tucked herself into her easy chair and tried to read. Maybe if she went over the information one more time she'd pick up on something—a clue, an obscure reference, anything—that would help nudge an answer into place.

Eyes burning, she tried to read, but then set the pages aside after only a few minutes.

She was just too restless, too tired, and too hyper to concentrate.

Theodosia turned out the lights, then got up and padded to the window that looked out over the alley. And straight at Nick Prince's rented house. She stared for a few seconds, then frowned.

Is that a faint shadow in that second-story window?

The shadow hovered for a few moments, as if someone might be looking back at her, then faded away.

Is Nick Prince watching me?

The idea not only angered Theodosia; it made her blood run cold. It made her want to throw on some clothes, march over to Prince's house, and bang on his front door.

And then what? Ask him—no, demand to know if he was Fogheel Jack?

Not a good idea. Better to let her investigation, the one she'd promised Lois, and the investigation the police were conducting, play out.

And hopefully lead to an arrest. Before any more women were killed.

Theodosia's brow puckered as she thought about the shadow at the window.

Before I get killed.

26

I was stunned," Drayton said. "The moment I unfolded my newspaper this morning and read about the fire at Lois's bookshop, I was rendered speechless." He stood behind the front counter wearing a fine Harris Tweed jacket, a Drake's bow tie, and a look of amazement on his face.

"Pretty shocking, huh?" Haley said. "It was even worse *being* there."

"I'm thankful I wasn't," Drayton said. "I think I would have passed out from sheer terror."

"Or smoke inhalation," Theodosia said.

"Yeah," Haley said. "It got pretty thick."

"It gets pretty thick in here sometimes," Theodosia said with a wry smile. When she'd gotten out of bed this morning she'd made up her mind to focus on positivity. To move ahead with care but also with a tenacious spirit.

"Oh you," Haley said, sniffing the air. "I know what you mean and I don't think it's one bit funny."

"Just adding a little humor to a bad situation," Theodosia said.

"Maybe so, but I swear I can still smell smoke," Haley said. She tilted her head back and sniffed. "Like burned book bindings."

"We'll light some candles," Theodosia said. She didn't smell smoke, but if a few candles would appease Haley, then she was all for it.

"Or we could spray the heck out of this place with air freshener," Haley said. "I'm pretty sure I've got lavender scented."

"I vote for brewing pots of tea instead," Drayton said. "Everyone benefits greatly from that aroma."

"Then you'd better get crackin'," Haley said as she turned and headed into her kitchen.

"You think we'll be busy today?" Drayton asked. "It looks as if part of the street is still roped off to pedestrians."

"Only in that one area," Theodosia said. "I suppose the fire marshal and the investigators are still poking around inside Lois's bookshop. Hopefully, they'll be finished in a few hours."

Drayton checked his watch. "I'm just praying that we have a few takers for tea and scones this morning. And that we don't have any cancellations for our Murder at Chillingham Manor Mystery Tea."

"I hear you."

Theodosia got busy then. Setting tables, putting out cups and saucers, filling sugar bowls, adding flatware. Oh yes, and candles. Forget the little tea lights, today she was pulling out the big guns, the pillar candles.

As she worked, she whispered a prayer and thanked her lucky stars that only one shop on Church Street had been burned. That nobody had been seriously hurt in the fire. And that no more murders would take place. Maybe cultivating an attitude of gratitude would help move things along? Help find some answers? She sure hoped so.

"So no separate morning and lunch menus today?" Drayton asked.

"That's right, it's all going to blur together into one continuous tea. Haley's got buttermilk scones, carrot bread, crab rolls with lemon aioli, a Mediterranean grain salad, and tomato soup. Plus, there are Charleston cookies and lemon bars for dessert."

"And she's finalized her special menu for our Murder at Chillingham Manor Tea?"

"She hasn't told you about it?"

Drayton shook his head. "She's been very secretive."

"Then you're in for a treat. You know how Haley adores a good themed tea."

"Hah! If Haley had her way, they'd all be themed teas. We'd be dressing in top hats and ghost costumes and old-timey britches every single day of the week."

"With valentines and pumpkins tangled in our hair." Theodosia laughed. Her mood was edging toward hopeful (knock on wood) for the first time that week.

Miss Dimple arrived at eleven, breathless, fluffy hair flying wildly, and looking uncharacteristically perturbed.

"I can't believe that adorable little bookshop went up in smoke!" were her first words.

"Sad, isn't it?" Theodosia said.

"The newspaper story said the building was a total loss. Is that true?"

"I'm no expert, but when I took a look at the place this morning, it didn't seem salvageable. The walls are still standing, but with broken windows and a charred interior it seems pretty well trashed."

"Aren't there restoration companies that specialize in fire and water damage?"

"There are," Drayton said as he joined the conversation. "But when every book is burned all the way down to its leather binding, there isn't much left to work with."

Miss Dimple bit down on her lower lip. "Oh."

"I think the only upside here is insurance," Theodosia said. "I doubt insurance will cover every single thing in the shop, but the payment will probably be enough for Lois to rebuild her inventory."

"What about her building?" Miss Dimple asked. "It's always been so charming."

"Lois doesn't own the building," Theodosia said. "She was leasing space."

"Maybe someone will buy the ruined building and restore it," Miss Dimple said. "Make it good as new."

"Maybe," Theodosia said as she and Drayton exchanged glances. She didn't hold a lot of hope that Gavin Goulding, the building's owner, would make that happen. Probably he'd try to sell it as is to Wyatt Orlock and Lois would be plumb out of luck.

Tea was indeed abbreviated this morning, with only ten people coming in for the Indigo Tea Shop's breakfast cream tea. Lunch brought in an even dozen customers.

Which was just fine with Theodosia. Because by the time one thirty rolled around and all their guests had left, she needed to start decorating for their Murder Mystery Tea.

"Okay, once I finish clearing this last table, what do you want me to do?" Miss Dimple asked.

"Make it look *mysterious*," Drayton said in shivery tones. "This is supposed to be Chillingham Manor after all."

Miss Dimple turned, a hand on her hip. "Which means what?"

"For one thing we need to turn the lights down low and light a bunch of candles," Theodosia said. "So maybe . . ." She walked to a cupboard, pulled out a stack of lace tablecloths and a silver candelabra. "Start with these."

"Create a spooky Victorian drawing room," Miss Dimple said. "Got it."

Theodosia and Miss Dimple worked steadily, setting the tables with dark plum-colored dishes and matching teacups and adding stacks of Agatha Christie books to each table.

"So far, so good," Miss Dimple said. "What else?"

Theodosia opened the cardboard box Drayton had given her last night.

"We've got a few more things here to help set the mood."

She pulled out a couple pairs of handcuffs, a dagger, two toy guns, and some old-fashioned brass keys and locks.

"Let me see those," Miss Dimple said as she grabbed a set of handcuffs and slipped them onto her wrists.

"I've also got a box of vintage hats," Theodosia said. "A lot of them are slightly Victorian-style with veils."

"We can ask each guest to wear one of the hats to help get them in the mood," Miss Dimple said.

"We also can't forget the pièce de résistance," said Drayton. He strolled over to Theodosia and handed her a small white cardboard box. Whatever was inside gave a tantalizing rattle. Like tiny glasses?

"What's this?" Theodosia asked. She opened the box slowly to reveal a half dozen small purple bottles, each one clearly marked with the word POISON accompanied by a skull and crossbones.

"Whoa," Miss Dimple said. "Now you guys are going hardcore."

"But apropos of our crime, don't you think?" Drayton said. "That's assuming you've both read your scripts."

"I *think* I've learned my lines," Miss Dimple said.

Drayton turned his attention to Theodosia. "And what about you, Baroness Althea?"

"Working on it," Theodosia said.

Drayton threw her a comedic glower. "Perhaps you should work harder?"

Theodosia held up five fingers. "Give me five minutes and I

promise I'll have the whole thing down cold. Just five minutes alone in my office."

"Go," Drayton said.

But Theodosia had only gotten through the first two pages of her script before she was interrupted by a phone call.

"Hello?"

She hoped it wasn't one of the guests calling to cancel because of bad weather.

Nope, it was Riley. Brimming with excitement and bursting with news.

"We think we have him!" Riley cried.

Theodosia, who was hunched over her desk, focused on memorizing lines, blinked and said, "Have who?"

"The killer. Fogheel Jack!"

"Holy cow, really?" Now he had Theodosia's full attention. Sitting bolt upright in her chair, she said, "Who is he?"

"It's complicated, so let me explain how this all unfolded. We went to Frank Lynch's apartment a few hours ago to talk to him—thanks to your tip last night on where he was staying or living or whatever. Anyway, the long and short of it is that the man's a complete idiot. We're standing at the door—me, Tidwell, and two uniforms—and notice that Lynch has a half dozen baggies of blow sitting right there on his kitchen table."

"What are you talking about? Drugs?"

"Yup, bags of white powder. You know, California cornflakes. Cocaine."

"Wait a minute, you busted Frank Lynch for *drug* possession?"

"I'm getting to that part. Yeah, we arrested Lynch right there on the spot. Then, figuring him for a user, possibly even a coked-up killer . . . we started grilling him. Fired all sorts of questions at him, kind of insinuating that *he* might be Fogheel Jack."

"Did he admit to it?" Theodosia asked. She had her fingers crossed, fervently hoping the nightmare was over.

"No," Riley said. "But the more we questioned Lynch, the angrier he got. And one thing led to another. Anyway, the net-net of the whole conversation is that Frank Lynch admitted to us that he was fairly certain his boss, Orlock, was Fogheel Jack."

"No!"

"Pretty crazy, huh?"

"Did he elaborate on why he was accusing him? Tell you how he figured it out?"

"Very grudgingly. First we had to get Lynch booked, then allow him to *parlez-vous* with his lawyer. Then *they* went back and forth with the city attorney and finally agreed to a plea bargain."

"Which was?" Theodosia was hanging on Riley's every word.

"Lynch and his lawyer agreed to trade information only if Lynch received serious consideration."

"And that would be . . ."

"Lynch would receive a severely reduced sentence on the drug charges in exchange for fingering Orlock for the three recent murders."

"The *three* murders? Lynch knows for a fact that all of them were Orlock's doing?" Somehow Frank Lynch's revelation felt a little too convenient, a little too slick.

"Here's the thing that clinched it. Frank Lynch swears that Orlock asked him to take care of Lois Chamberlain."

"What does that mean exactly? Take care of?"

"I'm guessing Orlock meant that Lynch should either kill Lois or set fire to her bookshop. Or both."

"But Lynch hasn't spelled that out for you?"

"We're still working on that," Riley said.

"But Lois didn't get killed—her *daughter* did. And what about the other murdered women? Does Lynch really believe—or have evidence—that Orlock killed the woman over near the university as well as Monica Garber?"

"He says yes. Probably."

"Probably? So you've gone ahead and arrested Orlock?"

There was a long pause and then Riley said, "That's the fly in the ointment. We can't *find* Orlock. Nobody seems to know where he's run off to."

"Good Lord. And I just saw him last night at the Imago Gallery."

"Thank goodness you're alive to tell about it," Riley said.

"Are you absolutely positive that Orlock's the guy? I mean, he's about as pleasant as a rattlesnake, but he doesn't strike me as some kind of wild and crazed killer. For one thing he seems more interested in real estate deals than he does in murdering women."

"You never know with these guys," Riley said. "You look at the real baddies, the psychopaths like Jeffrey Dahmer or BTK, and nobody ever caught a whiff of their extracurricular activities, either. Even their families didn't suspect a thing."

"Terrifying," Theodosia said.

For some reason she was still having trouble wrapping her head around Wyatt Orlock as a serial killer. Maybe because she'd been in such close contact with him last night? Because he'd threatened her?

"So what now?" Theodosia asked. "How do you propose to find him?"

"If Orlock hasn't already skipped town and beat feet to South America, we'll get him. I've already issued a BOLO, a be on the lookout for, and we've roped in the various sheriff's departments and state police. Law enforcement is casting a wide net."

"This is incredible news," Theodosia said.

"I told you we'd get him and we have," Riley said.

No, you almost *got him*, Theodosia thought to herself. *Orlock's still ghosting around out there. Let's just hope he's not still in this neighborhood.*

27

Theodosia walked up to the counter where Drayton was bustling about, humming as he brewed tea and lining up an armada of teapots.

"I've got good news," she said. "I think."

"Yes?" Drayton drew out the word as he flipped up the lid on a tin of Assam tea and peered in.

"I just spoke to Riley. Apparently Frank Lynch rolled over on Wyatt Orlock. Accused him of being Fogheel Jack."

Drayton's eyebrows rose in surprise. "Seriously? You mean the nightmare is over? Wait a minute. Why would Lynch suddenly decide to accuse his employer of such heinous crimes?"

"Because Lynch got caught red-handed with a bunch of cocaine?"

"That's a good reason."

"But there's a slight problem. If Orlock really is the killer, he's suddenly disappeared down a rabbit hole."

"He's gone into hiding?" Drayton aimed a finger at her. "We saw him driving away last night!"

"Maybe he's the one we should have followed," Theodosia said. "Instead of that dingbat Lynch."

"Still, if Orlock has hightailed it out of Dodge, maybe it's all the proof the police need, right? It shows that he's both a killer and a coward." Drayton lifted a lid on a teapot. "I doubt he'll get far."

"He probably won't," Theodosia said.

"Still . . . let's hope Orlock doesn't come calling on us."

"Bite your tongue."

Feeling a little unsettled, Theodosia took a quick turn around the tea room.

"Everything look okay?" Miss Dimple asked. She was arranging silverware just so, tweaking the decor on the tables.

"Perfection," Theodosia said. Yes, the Indigo Tea Shop looked appropriately British and moody, so her guests should be thrilled. Should have a high old time watching the actors perform while they tried to solve the murder mystery. Still, until this whole Fogheel Jack thing was firmly resolved, Theodosia knew she'd be walking on eggshells.

"One other thing," Miss Dimple said. "The costumes were delivered."

"There are costumes? First I've heard."

"They were brought to the back door. Along with something called a fogger."

"Seriously?"

"It's this dandy little machine. You plug it in, fill it with something called Fog Juice, and presto—swirls of fog come rolling out."

"Just what we need. More fog."

Giving a small sigh, Theodosia ducked into the kitchen to check on the food.

"Everything's coming along just fine," Haley assured her. "I'm going to pop my tea biscuits into the oven in about ten minutes, and the salmon is all prepped and ready to go."

"Our guests are going to love your menu."

"That's the whole idea, isn't it? Keep 'em happy and coming back for more?"

"It's only good business," Theodosia said. She reached for a scone, nibbled it slowly, and said, in a casual tone, "Are you feeling up to snuff, Haley? No ill effects from last night?"

"Not so much," Haley said. "I felt kinda tired and creaky when I first got up 'cause I got to bed so late. But now I'm warmed up and ready to kick it into third gear."

"Knock, knock," said Drayton.

He stuck his head in, smiled, and said, "Haley, the aromas in here are beyond tantalizing."

"Glad to hear it," Haley said as she dipped a spoon into her lemon sauce. "Now, go be tantalized somewhere else. I'm busy."

"Gotcha," Drayton said. Then he cocked a finger at Theodosia. "We need to talk."

She followed him out into the tea room. "What's up?"

"I've got good news and bad news," Drayton said. "Which do you want to hear first?"

"The good news."

"The good news is the police pulled down all the yellow-and-black tape that was strung across Church Street and pedestrian and street traffic is once more moving normally."

"Great. What's the bad news?"

"The rain's started up again. And fairly heavy at that."

Theodosia wrinkled her nose as she glanced out the front window. Rivulets streamed down the panes like erratically swimming fingerlings. "Rats."

"I concur wholeheartedly. So here's my plan. To help dispel any bad vibes caused by this nasty weather, I thought I'd serve

Dark and Stormy Tea Lattes to all our guests. You know, offer the drink as a sort of fun apology for such a dark and stormy day."

"That's a pretty clever idea. You have a recipe in mind?"

"I'm going to brew a couple of large pots of Pu-erh tea, then flavor it with bits of cinnamon, ginger, and cardamom. And, instead of using traditional teacups, we'll serve our tea in those tall latte glasses we've got stored in your office. That way we can top off our dark and stormy brew with warm frothed milk."

"I think our guests are going to love your concoction. In fact, your Dark and Stormy Tea Latte sounds so delish we might have to add it to our regular tea menu."

"All in all not a bad thing," Drayton said.

Then his head jerked toward the front door as the bell did its *ding-ding*.

"Well now, if it isn't our talented actors," Drayton enthused as the door flew open and two people, a portly man with a white beard and a stern-looking woman in her mid-fifties, stepped in. "And right on time. Come in, come in, shake off this awful rain, and we'll get you set up."

"Let me take your coats," Theodosia said as the bell *ding-ding*ed again and their neighbor Bill Boyet walked in.

With a big grin on his face, Boyet said, "Anybody looking for a murder victim?" He was husky, in his early fifties, with pink cheeks and sparse white hair. "Because I'm ready to take my swan dive."

"It's kind of you to help out," Theodosia said.

"No problem," Boyet said. "What are neighbors for, after all."

"Looks like the gang's all here," Drayton said as he proceeded to make introductions all around.

Then he explained the roles that each of them would play. The actor, John, would assume the role of Viscount Ragley, the actress, Maria, would play the Duchess of Lennox, and Bill Boyet was playing Lord Bledsoe.

After a few minutes of chatting, Drayton clapped his hands together and said, "Okay, my noble cotillion, our customers will be arriving in thirty minutes or so. Which means we need to get you into costumes and makeup. So if you'll follow me down the hallway to Theodosia's office . . ."

Drayton headed down the hall with the two professional actors and Bill Boyet following behind like eager ducklings.

"I suppose I should hustle my bustle and get into my costume, too," Miss Dimple said.

Theodosia looked down at the long black apron that covered her own T-shirt and slacks. "Guess we all need to get ready." She checked her watch. "Oops, now there's only twenty-five minutes before our guests arrive."

Not only were the costumes perfect, but the actors also slipped into their roles with ease. The Duchess of Lennox and Viscount Ragley strolled about the tea shop like veteran thespians (which they were), throwing lines at each other, ad-libbing, cracking each other up as they worked to develop personas for their assigned characters.

Method acting, Theodosia thought as she watched them. *Looks as if it really works.*

When Bill Boyet came out dressed as Lord Bledsoe, complete with red cutaway coat and curly white wig, Theodosia was in stitches.

"Oh, come on," Boyet said. "I don't look *that* bad. Do I?"

"Actually, you look quite convincing as an English lord," she told him. "Very much at home in that costume. Are you sure you've never done any stage acting?"

"Only horsing around in high school," Boyet said. "And then it was just me playing a minor bad boy in *Grease.*"

"You're a real sport to help out," Theodosia said. "Especially in light of last night's fire. I hope your camera shop didn't sustain any damage."

"Only a few drifts of noxious smoke," Boyet said. "Which was easily remedied. But poor Lois . . ." He clapped a hand to his chest.

"I know. To have your daughter murdered, then your book-shop burned to the ground . . . my heart aches for her."

Theodosia wondered in that moment if she should ask Boyet if he'd ever met Tim Holt. Then decided, why not?

"I was wondering," she said slowly, "if you're familiar with a commercial photographer by the name of Tim Holt?"

"Holt? Sure, I know him. He bought a couple of cameras from me. A nice used Rolleiflex and a Nikon Df." Boyet peered at Theodosia like a sharp-eyed bird. "Why do you ask?"

Theodosia decided to come right out and say it.

"The thing is, Tim Holt is a kind of murder suspect."

"What?" Boyet looked puzzled. "Are you talking about the Murder Mystery Tea we're doing today?"

"No, I don't mean playacting," Theodosia hastened to explain. "I'm talking about the real thing. At one time Cara Chamberlain, Lois's daughter, was Tim Holt's girlfriend."

Boyet looked shocked. "Seriously? So Holt is actually a mur-der suspect? Has he been questioned by the police?"

"Several times."

Boyet poked a finger under his wig and scratched his head. "A suspect just for the daughter's murder or for the other women who've been killed as well?"

"That's still up in the air," Theodosia said. "And, really, Holt is more like a person of interest."

"But still," Boyet said with a frown. "We sure do live in scary times."

28

Theodosia gazed in the mirror, smoothed on lip gloss, and added a touch more mascara to her lashes. Because she'd always thought her auburn hair was a little too poufy, a little too *much*, the last thing she needed was to add a bulky pompadour-style wig. Instead, she gathered her hair up, grabbed a silver clip, and pinned it into a messy topknot.

Okay, now for my dress.

Purple velvet with acres of cream-colored lace, it was a devilish thing to struggle into. The tight bodice made her gasp, the sweeping skirt was hard to walk in, and the huge puffy sleeves were just . . . huge. Theodosia had just finished getting dressed when she heard excited voices out in the tea room.

Oh wow, the first guests must be arriving!

She scurried out of her office and joined Drayton at the front door. Much to her amusement, he was wearing a dark green velvet frock coat (sans wig) and was now going by the title of Baron Cranbrook.

"Welcome, dear guests," Drayton said in faux-English tones. "Welcome to our Murder Mystery Tea at Chillingham Manor."

Two women, expectant grins on their faces, stepped inside the tea room and looked cautiously around.

"Ooh, it's all dark and foggy with only candles to light the way," said one.

"Spooky," said the second one. "With the distinct aura of an old English castle. This is going to be fun."

As the guests headed for their tables, Viscount Ragley and the Duchess of Lennox stepped in to greet them and, with great fanfare, led them to their reserved seats.

"The actors you hired are perfect," Theodosia whispered to Drayton. "They've jumped right in to help and seem to relish their roles."

"Consummate professionals," Drayton said with a knowing grin.

They greeted more guests, exchanged hugs and air-kisses with Delaine and Bettina and shop owners Brooke Carter Crockett and Leigh Carroll. More guests arrived and were handed off to Lord Bledsoe (Bill Boyet) and Lady Cecily (Miss Dimple), who held candles aloft as they led them into the tea shop proper. As the guests sat down and looked about eagerly, the duchess and viscount proceeded to entertain them, hamming it up and giving an exuberant performance reminiscent of characters at a Renaissance fair.

"You hear that?" Drayton said as peals of laughter rolled toward them. "We're off to a rousing start."

"Let's hope we can keep it going," Theodosia said.

They did.

When all the guests were finally seated and wearing the vintage hats that Miss Dimple had passed out, when there wasn't a single available seat left in the house, Theodosia and Drayton strolled to the center of the darkened tea room.

"Baroness Althea," Drayton said, inclining his head toward Theodosia.

"Baron Cranbrook," Theodosia replied. "The pleasure is all mine."

Drayton pulled out a frilly hanky and gave a foppish wave. "And to all our lovely guests, we bid you welcome."

"As you can see, we've transformed the Indigo Tea Shop into Chillingham Manor," Theodosia said. "An historic edifice located on the windswept Salisbury Plain. Here we intend to enchant you with our amazing tea and delicacies and lure you into solving a spine-tingling murder mystery."

"First order of business is to make introductions," Drayton said. "You've already met my dear cohort, Baroness Althea, but now I'd like you to meet the rest of the players." He stretched out an arm. "The Duchess of Lennox, the lovely Lady Cecily, Viscount Ragley, and, of course, Lord Bledsoe."

The characters all bowed and smiled as they were introduced.

"As we begin our tea service, please be watchful of these various participants . . . as well as the two of us," Theodosia said with a gleam in her eye. "Because not everything is as it seems. Even in the midst of our lovely tea, you must consider that danger lurks nearby. And when the time comes, each of you will be called upon to cast your vote and help ferret out the person you believe to be the murdering scoundrel."

"But first . . . food and libations," Drayton said. "Because the weather has been so dreadful of late, we're going to warm you up with a steaming-hot concoction we call a Dark and Stormy Tea Latte."

At that, Haley and Miss Dimple came out of the kitchen carrying trays laden with the tea lattes. They passed them around, getting murmurs of appreciation.

"What you have before you is a brisk Pu-erh tea flavored with bits of cinnamon, ginger, and cardamom, then topped with frothed milk," Drayton said. He took a step back, turned to Theodosia, and said, "Baroness? Care to elaborate on the feast we're about to serve?"

"Our first course today consists of authentic English tea biscuits," Theodosia said. "Served with homemade lemon curd and fresh Devonshire cream. Then we shall present you with a delightful trio of tea sandwiches—English cheddar on rye, pear and Stilton cheese on sourdough, and cream cheese and cucumber on potato bread. For your entrée we'll be serving baked salmon with lemon sauce and an English pea salad. And lest we forget dessert, our chef has prepared Victoria sponge cake with raspberries as well as English toffee bites."

A spatter of applause rose, with calls of "Amazing" and "Huzzah" and "I love this!"

Drayton lifted a hand and said, "But remember, this is a Murder Mystery Tea. So keep your eyes open for dastardly deeds as well as clues, no matter how insignificant they may seem. I warn you, gentle ladies . . . do not let your guard down for one single second."

As Theodosia and Miss Dimple placed steaming-hot biscuits on everyone's plates, Drayton made the rounds with a teapot in each hand.

"Besides your Dark and Stormy Tea Lattes, I've also brewed two additional teas for your enjoyment," he said. "English breakfast tea, which is decidedly not just for breakfast, and a lovely Lady London Ceylon."

Once the guests were happily munching biscuits and drinking tea, once the tea shop echoed with the lively buzz of conversation, Haley snuck out of the kitchen and let out a piercing scream that practically rattled the windowpanes. Then, as there was a resounding CRASH (a dead body?), she ran back into the kitchen.

The guests, who'd been smiling and talking with one another up until now, were all slightly unnerved.

"What was that?"

"Who let out that awful scream?"

"I think our murder mystery is underway!"

Drayton flipped on the overhead chandelier to reveal Lord Bledsoe lying in a heap in the middle of the room.

"Oh no, there really was a murder!" one guest cried.

"But who committed it?"

"Now what do we do?"

Bill Boyet was the perfect dead guy. He lay there silently in a crumpled heap, facedown, wig askew. Drayton ran to him, dropped down beside him, and proceeded to check his pulse. After a few moments of silence, he said, "I fear the worst has happened."

"Is he breathing?" Theodosia asked while Miss Dimple covered her mouth to stifle a giggle.

Drayton looked up, his expression registering tragedy. "He's dead. Lord Bledsoe is dead. Poisoned, I think. You see that terrible white pallor? That's a sure sign of . . . arsenic!"

"Well, don't look at me!" Viscount Ragley shouted. Which made all the guests turn and look at him.

"Still, it had to be one of us," the Duchess of Lennox said. Her eyes darted anxiously about the room. "But I wonder who among us is the guilty party?"

"We must get to the bottom of this," Drayton said, rising to his feet.

"If our tea is to continue, we also need to get rid of that dead body," Theodosia said.

"Easier said than done," Miss Dimple said in a quavering voice, adding to the theatrics.

Now the guests were watching with bated breath.

"I tell you what. We'll stash poor Lord Bledsoe in the kitchen for now," Drayton said. He grabbed him by the legs and started dragging him across the floor.

"Better yet, put him in the dungeon," Theodosia said. "Until we can send a message to the undertaker."

With the body disposed of, Drayton dimmed the lights again

and said, "I'm afraid Lord Bledsoe's murder has presented an un-expected and grisly twist to our tea party." He tugged his vest down, looked around the room, and said, "This cannot go unac-knowledged. We must determine the guilty party!"

After that much action, the guests were raring to go.

"Now what?"

"How do we figure out who's guilty?"

"Ah, you have to follow the clues," Drayton said in a calmer tone.

"And question everyone here," Theodosia added.

Drayton pulled out a stack of cards, as well as a roster of sus-pects, and passed everything around. "These cards," he said, tap-ping one, "have specific clues written on each one. You need to work with each other and exchange ideas in order to figure out who among us is the murderer. You're also allowed to question any one of us"—he indicated the five characters still standing—"while this tea party proceeds."

As Theodosia and Miss Dimple served three-tiered trays of tea sandwiches, the guests ate, laughed, and talked among them-selves about what they'd seen and who could be the murderer.

When the main entrée of baked salmon was served, they be-gan questioning the various characters.

"Were you closest to Lord Bledsoe when it happened?"

"There were two bottles of poison on our table, now one is missing—did *you* take it?"

"You, the fellow in the blue velvet coat, you don't look par-ticularly upset."

More discussion (and eating) ensued, until finally it came time for a vote. All the guests wrote their names on small pieces of paper. Then, underneath that, wrote their guess as to who might be the murderer.

Drayton collected the papers and quickly tallied them. As

Theodosia and Miss Dimple served slices of Victoria sponge cake, he made his grand pronouncement.

"It appears we have *three* guests who guessed correctly."

Everyone stared at Drayton as his eyes bounced from Theodosia to Miss Dimple to the two actors.

Then with a shout and a flourish, Drayton extended an arm, pointed to Viscount Ragley, and cried, "It was you! You are the poisoner!"

Which was Theodosia's cue to rush over to Viscount Ragley, snap on a pair of handcuffs, and lead him away.

"To the tower!" Drayton cried.

"Or at least to the kitchen," Miss Dimple said before she collapsed in giggles.

Brooke Carter Crockett, Dawn Glaser-Falk, and Jill Biatek were all winners, so they all received what Theodosia called A Tea Party in a Box. Which was basically a Brown Betty teapot, a tin of tea (in this case Drayton's blend of Dimbula tea with bits of orange and lemon, called Wisp of Spring), a jar of honey, a quilted tea cozy, and a tea strainer.

But the party wasn't over by a long shot. The guests lingered, many of them enjoying another cup of tea, which Drayton obligingly poured, while others shopped and grabbed gift items from the various displays.

Theodosia bagged up scones for take-home, fetched more gift items from her office, and rang up sales. When that was done, she thanked, hugged, and walked her happily sated guests to the front door. In fact, with all the thank-yous and goodbyes, it took a good half hour for the Indigo Tea Shop to clear out.

When the place was finally empty, when their two hired actors had changed out of their costumes, Theodosia grabbed them and said, "John, Maria, you two were absolutely splendid. The guests were gaga over your theatrics."

"You helped make this one of our most exciting event teas ever," Drayton declared.

"Happy to hear it," Maria said with a solemn nod.

"We had lots of fun," John said. "Playing it broad like that was kind of a change for us, a real hoot." He slipped on his coat and then dug into his pocket for a card. Handing it to Theodosia, he said, "Come see us sometime at the Dock Street Theatre. Next presentation will be *A Midsummer Night's Dream.*"

"Thank you," Theodosia said as she walked them to the door. "We'll do that."

She closed the door, latched it, and turned to find Miss Dimple smiling at her.

"You," Theodosia said, giving her a hug, "were wonderful. You're a born actress."

"More like a born ham," Miss Dimple said.

But by the color in her cheeks, Theodosia could tell she was pleased by the praise.

"Let me get your coat," Drayton offered. "And your umbrella. You're going to need it because it's still raining out there."

"Are you sure you two don't want me to stick around and help clean up?" Miss Dimple asked. "I don't mind."

"Nonsense," Drayton said. "You've done enough for one day."

"Besides, it's full-on dark," Theodosia said. "You scoot on home and cozy up with your kitties."

"Okay. So long, guys. See you all next week."

Theodosia, Drayton, and Haley didn't need to be told what to do. Plates and teacups were stacked into plastic tubs, then carried into the kitchen. Because they'd done this so many times, the cleanup was efficient and accomplished in no time at all.

Just as Drayton grabbed a broom, ready to sweep the pegged floors, Haley said, "Hey, big guy, did you ever get a chance to eat?"

Drayton shook his head. "Not really."

"What about at lunch?"

He shook his head again.

"Oh man, you're gonna get the low-blood-sugar blues if you don't watch out. You'd better come in the kitchen and let me warm up some leftover salmon for you."

"Or you could wrap it and I'll take it home."

"C'mon, silly, it's no trouble at all. Besides, it's still fresh. And there's lemon sauce, too."

Drayton and Haley disappeared into the kitchen while Theodosia gathered up the receipts from the front counter and walked back to her office. She changed out of her costume (ooh, those killer bodice stays) and put on jeans, a long-sleeved T-shirt, and her trusty khaki jacket. Then she sat down, cleared away a stack of tea magazines, and spread the sales slips out on her desk. As she worked, she could hear Drayton and Haley in the kitchen, talking and joking, going back and forth. It was pleasant background noise that made her work go that much easier.

And as she tallied her numbers Theodosia grew more and more pleased. Despite the rain and the terrible goings-on, the Indigo Tea Shop had enjoyed a good week. Actually, make that an outstanding week. They'd done a gangbuster business with take-out orders, and the receipts for today's Mystery Tea were the icing on the cake.

With warmer days right around the corner, and an entire flight of event teas in the works, Theodosia knew business would pick up even more.

KNOCK, KNOCK.

Theodosia glanced up from her paperwork. Somebody was knocking on the back door? Who, she wondered, was out and about at this late hour?

29

Tiptoeing to the door, Theodosia peered out through a small triangle of glass and saw the familiar face of Jesse Trumbull smiling in at her. He had the collar of his leather jacket turned up and he looked cold and wet.

"Hey there," Theodosia said as she pulled the door open, then shivered as a gust of damp wind blew in. "What are you doing out there, besides freezing?"

"Skulking down your alley in the dark," Trumbull said with a laugh as he stepped inside. "Or, rather, I was doing a quick check of the devastation at the bookshop down the way. I'm supposed to write a quick update for the media."

"Is there anything to update them on?"

"Not really. The fire marshal and his boys are taking samples for testing in the lab. Well, they *were* anyway. They finished up a while ago and took off." He glanced down the hallway. "Anyway . . . are you busy? I know you have a fancy tea going on and I don't want to interrupt anything."

"You're not interrupting a single thing," Theodosia said. "Our last guest left twenty minutes ago."

"I hope they didn't clean out your larder completely. Because if it's not too late, I'd love to grab a couple of your luscious scones."

"I think we can arrange that. Say, I heard the good news. At least I think it's good news."

"Riley called you?"

"Just before our tea party started. He was pretty excited to fill me in. Told me as much as he knew anyway."

Trumbull squinted at her. "You're referring to Wyatt Orlock?"

Theodosia nodded. "Yup."

"Yeah." Trumbull shifted from one foot to the other. "One of Wyatt Orlock's minions finally rolled on him. Spilled the awful truth."

"But I understand Orlock himself is still missing."

Trumbull waved a hand. "He won't get far. I have faith in our law enforcement agencies. They're good guys when it comes to mutual aid." He grinned, flashing a set of even, white teeth.

"I have to admit, it's going to be a relief to walk around Charleston without having to glance over my shoulder every two seconds," Theodosia said.

"I'm sure everyone feels the same way," Trumbull said. He glanced toward the tea room again.

Theodosia could see he was in a hurry. Well, of course he was. He had to head in to his office on a Saturday evening and compose a press release. Be creative on demand.

"Wait one and I'll see how many scones I can scrounge up for you," she said.

"Thanks. You're too kind."

Theo walked to the counter, grabbed three buttermilk scones from the pie saver, and placed them in one of her indigo blue take-out boxes. Then, on a whim, she stopped in the kitchen, where Drayton and Haley were still eating and yukking it up with each other, and added two biscuits and a small plastic container of jam. They'd be closing the tea shop in five minutes, so there was no sense letting leftover baked goods go to waste.

Theodosia stepped back into her office just as her mobile phone rang.

"Excuse me," she said to Trumbull. She set the box down on her desk and lifted the phone to her ear. "Yes?"

"You're not going to believe this." It was Riley again, but this time his voice was tight and guarded.

"Try me." Theodosia flashed a smile at Trumbull, who was waiting patiently.

"Our tech guys have made some progress on back-checking the e-mails that were sent to the two women at Channel Eight."

"And . . . ?"

"They're basically tracing a long string of numbers to find the geolocation of the computer where the e-mails originated."

"So you're telling me you *did* find the person who sent the e-mails?" Theodosia asked. As she spoke she glanced over at Jesse Trumbull, who was fussing with something in his jacket pocket. His keys probably. Anxious to get going.

"Not exactly," Riley said. "But here's the weird thing. Even though there are a number of intermediaries, none of the e-mails appear to have come from Wyatt Orlock's or Frank Lynch's computers."

"What's that supposed to mean?" Theodosia asked. "Wait. Are you telling me that Orlock *isn't* the killer?"

"I'm afraid that's a distinct possibility," Riley said.

"So you're back to square one?" Theodosia couldn't believe what she was hearing. After two solid weeks of investigations and task forces . . . nothing?

"No, no, with the help of the techs we're going to get our guy. It's just going to take a little more time. Whoever he was used an international resender, so it involves going through several IPs." Riley paused. "Theo, be extra careful, will you? It's possible that Fogheel Jack is still out there."

"Okay." A cold shiver started at the base of Theodosia's neck and trickled down her spine. "Be sure to call if you learn anything more."

"I will."

Theodosia clicked off, stuck her phone in her jacket pocket, and gazed at Jesse Trumbull. "That was beyond weird."

"Something I should know about?"

"I don't know if it's going to impact your press release or not, but Riley just shared some fairly big news. Now it looks as if Orlock *isn't* guilty. Or his security guy, either."

Trumbull was just this side of sputtering. "But Orlock fled town! That's got to be a sure sign of . . . and that Lynch guy . . . they found *drugs* on him."

"But apparently neither of them are the source of the e-mails sent to Cara Chamberlain or Monica Garber. They haven't found anything concrete that ties them to the murders."

"Wow." Trumbull shook his head as if this was all too much for him. Then he exhaled slowly. "Maybe the ex-boyfriend is the guy after all."

"Tim Holt," Theodosia said.

"Yeah," he said slowly. "Do you know, are they going to re-interview him?"

"Riley didn't say." Theodosia thought for a moment. "Boy . . . I sure wish I would have pushed harder on Nick Prince."

"The true crime writer? Pete mentioned him a couple of times in meetings. Said *you* were suspicious of him."

"I was. I am."

"I can see you've got a knack for this," Trumbull said. "A good instinct for pulling things together and scoping out suspects."

"Maybe not good enough. Looks like the investigation is going to hinge on what the technical crew finds. Those guy are scrambling like mad, trying to backtrack the e-mails that were sent to Channel Eight."

Theodosia turned to grab the box of scones she'd set on her desk. Just as her fingers grazed the box, she was aware of swift movement behind her.

Then a damp rag was clamped across her nose and mouth and held firmly in place by Trumbull's strong hands.

Panic exploded in Theodosia's brain. She was so stunned by this bizarre assault that she could barely breathe. When she finally had the presence of mind to take a breath, she inhaled noxious fumes that rendered her dizzy and faint.

And the last thought that went through Theodosia's buzzing head as she lost consciousness was, *Chloroform?*

30

❧

Theodosia woke up in what looked like the pit of hell. Darkness, dust, charred wood, a film of white ashes.

"Hey you, wake up." A man's voice, hollow and distant-sounding. Like it was coming from an echo chamber.

Theodosia struggled to open eyes that felt heavy as lead. When she couldn't comply, she was rewarded with a sharp slap on her face.

"I said *open* your eyes." The voice sounded closer now and more insistent.

A second slap, harder this time, brought her reeling back to semiconsciousness.

"What?" Theodosia cried. She blinked, looked around, and tried to focus as everything around her tilted viciously. Feeling sick to her stomach, she drifted off into a daze for a few seconds, until a warning sounded in her brain. A sharp little *tick* that said, *Wake up, babe, you're in big trouble.*

Theodosia's eyes flew all the way open. Still groggy, she forced herself to look around. To try to orient herself. And discovered that she was sprawled on a dirty, grimy, damp floor, with her back propped uncomfortably against a wall.

Jesse Trumbull was kneeling in front of her. Staring at her with eyes that betrayed no emotion at all.

Theodosia's lips were dry, her throat parched, and her head still spinning. "Where am I?" she managed to croak out.

She knew it was someplace dark and shadowy with an acrid stink permeating the air.

Burning? Something burned?

And then the reality of the situation hit her like a freight train. She was sprawled in the burned-out hulk of Antiquarian Books!

How did I get here?

As her brain fought to make sense of things, she was struck by a painful, gag-inducing memory of being half carried, half dragged down a dark alley. There were intermittent flashes of recollection, but most of her memory remained hazy and out of focus.

I know that Trumbull did something to me . . . drugged me? And then brought me here?

Theodosia looked around again, saw charred timbers, white ash, and wreckage everywhere. As if interior walls and bookshelves had collapsed. And that smell. So awful and acrid. Like burned rubber or . . .

Of course. All the burned books.

"What do you want?" Theodosia asked. Her brain struggled to make her mouth form the words.

Trumbull stared at her. "What do I want from you? Nothing anymore. It's what I *wanted*, Little Miss Snoop. I wanted you to quit poking your inquisitive, troublesome nose into places where it didn't belong. I wanted you to leave those murders well enough alone."

"Wait . . . what?" Theodosia was having trouble following the conversation.

"But no," Trumbull continued. "You had to go and get creative." He stood up and ever so casually picked up a hunk of charred wood. He loomed over her in a threatening pose. "You hear me?"

Going to hit me? But why? What did . . . ?

It all came screaming into focus then like a giant bolt of lightning pulsing through her brain. The murders, Trumbull's decision to move back to Charleston, his inside track with the police . . .

Jesse Trumbull is Fogheel Jack? No, he can't be!

"You can be my number four," Trumbull said in a teasing, singsong voice. "What do you think about that?"

Oh yes he can *be Fogheel Jack.*

With one quick move Trumbull tossed down the wood and said, "Get up. We've got some business to deal with."

Theodosia gathered her legs under her and pushed herself up. Felt as if she was on the deck of a pitching ship as she swayed back and forth. Then she gritted her teeth and managed to steady herself in front of him.

See. I can stand up to you. I'm not afraid. Well, actually, I'm deathly afraid. But you're a mad dog and I refuse to show fear.

"Good girl," Trumbull said. He reached a hand out, dropped it heavily on her shoulder. "Now we're making progress."

"We can forget this, right?" Theodosia stammered because she didn't have a better, more cogent idea of how to get out of what seemed like a dangerous, life-and-death situation. "I mean, I really don't care if you . . ."

Slick as poop through a goose, Trumbull pulled a piece of wire from his pocket and slipped it around her neck.

Theodosia gasped as he jerked her close to him, tightening the noose at the same time.

"Feel that?" Trumbull asked. His breath was hot and damp in her ear. "Now you know how the others felt." He gave another tug on the noose and seemed to shiver with pleasure.

"Please," Theodosia said. "Please don't . . . maybe I can help you."

"Nobody can," Trumbull growled.

"I can help you get out of town . . . make your escape," she gibbered. "Point the police in the opposite direction." She racked her brain for anything she could use.

"Is that so?" Trumbull tilted his head back, seemingly amused by her words. "Scared little girl trying to psych me out?"

"Not at all." She knew she had to come across as more convincing than pleading.

He pulled the noose tighter.

"Besides . . ." Theodosia coughed from the intense pressure. "I know deep down you don't want to do this."

"Oh but I do. This is the best part," Trumbull purred.

Theodosia stared into eyes that were dark and vacant and lost.

If I could just shimmy my phone out of my jacket pocket, she thought. *Then I could* . . . what? Somehow call 911? Set off the alarm?

They continued to gaze at each other as they did their bizarre dance, Trumbull pulling on the wire and Theodosia trying to reason with him as her hand worked its way slowly down to her jacket pocket.

"You told me you studied psychology," Theodosia said. She knew she had to keep him talking. If she could connect with him, get him to view her as a real person, not a victim, she might be able to finagle an escape. Or maybe she should try using sympathy?

"Sure, I studied psychology," Trumbull said. "Loved it, in fact. The intricacy of the human brain. I would have made a dandy clinical psychologist. Could have even worked in a prison." He winked at her. "Analyze the inmates, you know?"

Theodosia knew she was taking a chance when she said, "Did you know what you were even back then?"

"What am I?" Trumbull asked.

"A man who enjoys killing people?"

"Killing women," Trumbull corrected. He reached down, wrenched the phone that she'd managed to grab out of her hand, and threw it hard against the wall.

Theodosia groaned as he slowly pulled the noose tighter. Maybe if she could get her fingertips under the wire, help ease the horrible pinch. She tried, but little by little, Trumbull was increasing the tension, pulling it tighter, a constant slow pressure, done in incremental doses to terrify her. To give her a taste of what was to come.

Theodosia's mind was in turmoil. Was there anyone who could help her? Were there any cars rumbling down the back alley? No, everything was silent as a tomb this early evening. Customers had all gone home. Miss Dimple was gone. Drayton and Haley were busy cleaning up the tea shop. There wasn't a soul around to rescue her.

Theodosia tried to grab a quick gasp of air as she shifted clumsily.

"Stop moving," he growled. "Let me *do* this!"

She squirmed, kicking hard at Trumbull's shins, then trying to stomp down on his instep. She'd always heard those were sure-fire ways to stave off an attacker. But nothing was working and panic gripped her hard. She fought with him some more, twisting and turning, hissing at him, but the noose kept being pulled ever tighter.

Theodosia tried desperately to suck in oxygen, but her airway didn't seem to be responding. She began to feel faint and her vision closed in, fuzzy and black at the edges. All she saw were Trumbull's eyes, devoid of emotion, like two hard-boiled eggs staring at her. Waiting for her to plead with him? Waiting for her to die?

I don't want to die. Please, dear Lord, do something!

In the dim recesses of her mind, Theodosia thought she heard a door slam, but it sounded far away. She coughed again as her fingers began to tingle and her knees buckled and turned to jelly.

This is it. This is all there is. Oh, how could I have not noticed Jesse Trumbull? How could I have been so wrong? I'm sorry, Lois, I tried to help you and all I did was manage to get myself killed. And dear Riley, I'm so sorry. Please take care of Earl Grey for me.

Her hands flailed wildly, as if they were no longer part of her. One accidentally caught inside her pocket and hit the tube of pepper spray Haley had given her a couple of days ago.

Yes. Go. You have to try!

Somehow, as Theodosia continued to struggle and thrash, she managed to work the tube out of her pocket and knock off the cap. Then, with one heroic thrust, she brought her arm up and aimed the tube of pepper spray directly at Trumbull's face.

His eyes opened wide in horror as she depressed the button.

There was a WHOOSH, a peppery explosion, and then a horrific scream.

But it wasn't Theodosia who screamed; it was Jesse Trumbull. And as he shook his head wildly and gasped for air, the noose around her neck loosened a few ticks. Now Theodosia could breathe! Then he lost his grip on the wire as he dug at his eyes and howled like a werewolf with its leg caught in a trap.

"I'll kill you, I'll kill you yet!" Trumbull shouted.

He reached out blindly, flailing around, trying to slap her. Theodosia's brain, which had been ready to shut down, now felt almost . . . reanimated. Grabbing the loosened wire, she ripped it over her head and tossed it aside.

"I'll kill you!" Trumbull bellowed again.

Theodosia knew she was still in mortal danger as Trumbull

swatted blindly at her. He lunged forward and, palm open, managed to whack her on the side of the head. It was a crushing blow, one that dropped her to her knees.

What's next? she wondered. *He tried choking me. Now will he try to finish me off with a deadly beating?*

Trumbull winced as he opened one swollen red eye, gazed at her, then pulled his right hand back and powered it forward, slamming his fist into Theodosia's lower jaw.

This blow didn't just stun Theodosia; it knocked her flat and unleashed a searing burst of pain. A swift kick to her ribs yielded more pain, and an explosion of what looked like a million tiny stars danced before her eyes.

Theodosia pulled herself into a tight ball and cupped her hands over her head to protect herself. And was shocked beyond belief when a seemingly wounded, blinded Trumbull managed to grab her arm and yank her halfway across a floor that was inches thick with wet, gray ash.

Another sharp kick to her ribs made her gag in pain and practically faint. She reached a hand out, searching for the pepper spray she'd dropped. But no dice. Was there a hunk of wood—something with sharp nails sticking out—that she could use to defend herself? She flailed around again, searching—and was surprised to suddenly encounter open air.

What?

Her hands felt the edge of some sort of hole, a break in the floor.

This section of floor must have caved in during the fire.

A shadow fell on her as Trumbull let out another loud bellow. Quick as a wily hare escaping a fox, Theodosia flipped herself over the edge and hoped for the best. She tumbled downward, a slow-motion descent that seemed to take forever. Until . . .

PLOP.

Theodosia landed with a jolt on top of something that was wet and spongy and disgusting. Hot pain shot through her back like bullets. What had just happened? Where was she? She forced herself to look around and explore with her hands. She'd obviously landed in the basement and wasn't dead quite yet. But she knew she could be in another few seconds.

Books. I landed on a pile of wet, soggy books. Lois's books somehow broke my fall. Lucky books.

Or were they?

Theodosia looked up to find Trumbull leering down at her. He waggled a gun in front of his stricken face and said, "This isn't nearly as fun as up close and personal. But it'll do the trick."

Theodosia threw herself backward, desperate for cover. She needed to get behind a fallen timber, a collapsed wall, some rubble, anything that would protect her from that fatal bullet . . .

"Better say your prayers," Trumbull taunted.

Theodosia did. Scrunched behind the protection of what was probably a hundred-year-old wooden beam, maybe the only timber that was still standing and keeping the floor propped up, she closed her eyes and whispered a prayer. Hoped for a miracle. And then . . .

BANG!

A miracle happened.

From high above, the heavens opened their floodgates and rain poured down. It dampened her hair, wet her face, skimmed across her parched lips.

Rain? Is it raining?

As Theodosia tried to make sense of things, she saw Trumbull begin to sway erratically. His face went slack, his wounded eyes rolled back in his head until only the whites were visible, and he slowly sank to his knees.

Two questions drifted through Theodosia's brain, a brain that felt like cotton.

Was that a gunshot? and *Is rain dripping down?*

Whatever had landed on the tip of her nose slid slowly down to meet her lips.

Not rain. Tea. Why did tea suddenly spatter down from up above? And what just happened to Trumbull? Did he trip and shoot himself? Or commit suicide?

A moment later there were scuffling noises from up above and then a loud shout of, "Fire in the hole!"

Trumbull was suddenly spread-eagled in the air above her and falling. Theodosia shrank back again, pulling herself into a tight little ball as, a split second later, his body landed—SPLAT!—directly at her feet.

Theodosia crawled forward and stared up into darkness. "Who did that?" she called out. "Answer me, please. Who's there?"

There was a soft shuffling sound, then a familiar face peered down at her.

"Theo?"

"Drayton!" Theodosia choked out. "Is that you?" She'd never been so happy to see anyone in her life.

"At your service . . . I think." Drayton's normally slicked-back hair was askew and his jacket hung off one shoulder. Even his bow tie had come undone.

"You saved me!" Theodosia shouted. Her heart swelled with gratitude for his quick action—whatever that had been.

Then she turned to gaze at Trumbull's prone body splayed out in front of her.

"What did you *do* to him?"

"I smashed Mr. Trumbull in the back of his head and hopefully gave him a concussion," Drayton said.

"Smashed him with what?"

"A teapot," Drayton said. "Unfortunately, it was my newly acquired *antique* bone china teapot."

"How did you know I was here?"

"When I looked around the tea shop and couldn't find you, I immediately thought the worst."

"You always do," Theodosia said.

"I'm a natural-born pessimist," Drayton said happily.

"And thank goodness for that," Theodosia said as relief flooded her heart.

Drayton continued. "Seeing as how Haley had been attacked just the other day, I was suddenly afraid you'd suffered the same fate. Or been kidnapped. Or . . . worse."

"It almost was worse. Until you and your teapot saved me," Theodosia said.

"Come now, let's get you out of that . . . that awful pit."

"How?" Theodosia was a good ten feet below him.

Drayton thought for a moment. "I'll run get my stepladder. The one I use to reach the very top of my tea shelves. You stay put."

"I'm not going anywhere," Theodosia called after him.

31

Theodosia did stay put. She stood in the dark for a terrifying three and a half minutes until Drayton returned with a trembling Haley. Once they lowered the stepladder, Theodosia gingerly climbed up. Balancing on the very top step, she had to jump the last few feet to safety, one hand clutching her sore ribs.

"You're hurt!" Haley cried.

"When Trumbull kicked me I think he might have cracked a rib or two," Theodosia said. She touched her other hand to her sore neck. "He tried to strangle me, too." She paused. "Just like the others."

Haley sniffed the air. "You used the pepper spray on him, didn't you?"

"Tried to," Theodosia said, then reconsidered. "Actually, it worked rather well."

"Hot-cha," said Haley.

"We need to call an ambulance," Drayton said.

"For him?" Haley cast a disdainful glance at Trumbull.

"For Theodosia," Drayton said.

As if on cue, a peculiar warble sounded a few feet away. Not exactly a ring, more like a rang.

"That's my phone." Theodosia hunted around in the dark until she located her broken phone on the floor. "I'm amazed it's still working," she said. "Trumbull threw it so hard I figured it would be smashed to bits."

Two more sad rings sounded.

"If it's still functioning," Drayton said, "perhaps you'd better answer it?"

Theodosia picked up the phone, blew ashes off it, and said, "Hello?" Her voice sounded tentative and she felt groggy and woozy with relief.

"We found Orlock!" Riley's words burst through the phone at her.

"It wasn't him," Theodosia said. "He's not Fogheel Jack. Frank Lynch gave you a line of bull to try and protect himself from the drug charges."

"We know that," Riley said. "We just discovered that Orlock's been in Savannah for the last twenty-four hours. Arrived last night for a meeting and was vouched for by at least a half dozen people. Some big commercial real estate deal is brewing. Condos and a shopping arcade on the riverfront." Then, "Wait a minute." Puzzlement colored his voice now. "How did you know Orlock was innocent?"

"Because I found the real killer," Theodosia said.

"What? Where?" Riley was sputtering and practically screaming at her.

"Sprawled unconscious at my feet."

Riley figured it would take him at least an hour to get back from Savannah even with the advantage of lights and siren. But Detective Tidwell, who had remained in Charleston, made it to the Indigo Tea Shop in four minutes flat. Once he'd instructed his two teams of uniformed officers to deal with a still-reeling Trumbull and brought in a Crime Scene team to survey the burned bookshop, he walked down the alley to accost Theodosia.

"What were you *thinking?*" Tidwell demanded in a loud voice. He'd obviously come right from an evening at home since he was dressed in a baggy blue FBI sweatshirt, gray sweatpants, and once-white high tops.

Theodosia was sitting on the back of an ambulance that was parked directly behind the tea shop. A blanket had been draped over her shoulders and she was holding an ice pack to her injured jaw. Drayton and Haley were with her, along with two EMTs.

"I didn't have time to think," Theodosia said. "I was drugged and kidnapped and dragged into the burned hull of Antiquarian Books." She leaned forward and pressed an index finger hard against Tidwell's ample chest. "I wouldn't have been kidnapped and women wouldn't have been murdered if you people hadn't hired that *monster* to be your public information officer."

"Not my doing," Tidwell said. "Heads will roll."

"Happy to hear it," Theodosia said.

While one of the EMTs checked Theodosia's blood pressure again, Tidwell pulled out his phone and wandered away. They could hear his low-pitched grumbling.

"You're there now?" he said. "And? That's not good. Well . . . okay. At least we know we've got the right person."

Tidwell circled back to them.

"Problem?" Theodosia said.

Tidwell looked grim. "No, we've got him cold."

"You have evidence?" Theodosia pressed. "Did Trumbull take, ah, souvenirs of his victims?"

Tidwell pursed his lips. "Nothing you'd want to know about."

"No, we don't," Drayton said quickly.

"What about the two women who were killed seven years ago?" Theodosia asked Tidwell. "Are they connected?"

"It's all pending an investigation," Tidwell said. "But offhand, we don't believe so."

"Okay," Theodosia said. That was good enough for her. Her free hand crept up to her hair. It felt frazzled and wild . . . as if maybe she'd turned into a Medusa. "Haley," she whispered. "How's my hair?"

"Um, good," Haley said, a little too brightly.

"Oh dear," Theodosia said, trying to smooth her billowing waves.

"You look fine," Drayton said. "Really."

When Theodosia's teeth began to chatter, she pulled the ice pack away from her jaw and said, "Cold."

"We should transport you now," one of the EMTs said. "Your blood pressure's stable, pulse-ox is normal, but those ribs need to be looked at."

"You should go get an X-ray," Haley urged. "Make sure you're still in one piece."

"Can't go," Theodosia said.

"Of course you can," Tidwell said. "In fact, I insist."

Theodosia shook her head. "Riley's on his way. He said he'd meet me *here*."

"So we'll redirect him," Tidwell said. "It's not like the man can't follow simple directions."

"No." Theodosia was polite but insistent. "I want to wait for him right here."

Tidwell threw up his hands and spun in a circle. His mumbles were noisy but indecipherable.

Haley grabbed hold of Theodosia's hand. "Honey, you're cold as ice."

"Sweet dogs but you're stubborn," Drayton said. "If you want to wait for him, fine. But what are we supposed to do in the meantime?"

With a faint smile lighting her face, Theodosia said, "Maybe you could go inside and brew us a nice hot pot of tea?"

FAVORITE RECIPES FROM
The Indigo Tea Shop

English Tea Biscuits

2 cups flour

4 tsp. baking powder

1 tsp. salt

5 Tbsp. butter

¾ cup milk

4 Tbsp. orange juice (or marmalade)

2 Tbsp. sugar

PREHEAT oven to 400 degrees. Sift together flour, baking powder, and salt. Gently cut butter into mixture. Make a well in the center and add the milk. Stir well for 20 seconds or until all the flour is moistened. Place dough on a floured surface and knead for 20 seconds. Pat or roll dough until about ½ inch thick. Using a cutter, cut into rounds and place on a greased baking sheet. Combine orange juice and sugar and gently press mixture into the top of each biscuit. Bake for 10 to 15 minutes or until golden brown. Yields 10 to 12 biscuits.

Crab Rolls with Aioli

⅔ cup mayonnaise
1 Tbsp. fresh lemon juice
1 large celery rib, diced small
Cayenne pepper
¾ lb. crabmeat, lightly broken up
Salt
8 mini brioche rolls
8 lettuce leaves

IN a bowl, mix mayonnaise, lemon juice, and celery together. Season with cayenne pepper. Gently fold in the crabmeat and season with salt. Fill the brioche buns with crabmeat, top with lettuce, and serve. Yields 8 servings.

Haley's Cioppino

½ cup chopped onion
1 cup chopped celery
4 Tbsp. butter
2 sea bass fillets, cut into pieces
1 cup scallops
1 cup shrimp, shelled and deveined
1 cup chicken broth
1 cup tomato sauce
2 Tbsp. parsley
Cayenne pepper
2 Tbsp. sherry (optional)

SAUTÉ onion and celery in butter. Add sea bass, scallops, and shrimp. Add chicken broth, tomato sauce, parsley, cayenne, and sherry. Simmer until seafood is cooked (approximately 15 to 20 minutes). Serve in bowls with crusty bread or over rice. Yields 4 to 6 servings.

Super Simple Banana Cake

⅛ tsp. baking soda
1 pkg. yellow cake mix
1 cup mashed bananas (2 to 3 ripe bananas)
½ cup chopped nuts

STIR baking soda into the dry yellow cake mix. Now prepare cake mix according to package directions with the exception of using ¼ cup less water than is called for. Add mashed bananas and nuts to mixture. Pour into pan and bake according to directions.

Smoked Salmon Tea Sandwiches

6 slices light brown bread, thinly sliced
Smoked salmon
Cream cheese, whipped
Lemon butter

LEMON BUTTER

½ cup butter, softened
1 tsp. lemon zest
1 Tbsp. lemon juice

COMBINE lemon butter ingredients in a small bowl and mix well.

SPREAD lemon butter on all 6 slices of bread. Add slices of smoked salmon topped with whipped cream cheese to 3 of the slices. Top with the remaining 3 slices of bread to make 3 sandwiches. Cut off crusts, then cut each sandwich into 4 triangles. Yields 12 tea sandwiches. (Hint: If made ahead of time, cover with a damp paper towel, wrap in plastic wrap, and refrigerate.)

Killer Cranberry Scones

2 cups all-purpose flour

½ cup sugar

3 tsp. baking powder

¼ tsp. salt

½ cup cold butter (1 stick)

6 Tbsp. milk

2 eggs, beaten

½ cup dried cranberries

½ tsp. coarse sugar

PREHEAT oven to 425 degrees. In a medium-sized bowl combine flour, sugar, baking powder, and salt. Cut in butter until mixture resembles coarse crumbs. In a small bowl, combine milk and 4 tablespoons of beaten egg. Add to crumb mixture, stir, add cranberries, and stir again. Turn dough onto a floured surface and knead gently. Pat into an 8-inch circle. Cut into 8 wedges and place on greased baking sheet. Brush with remaining egg mixture and sprinkle with coarse sugar. Bake for 12 to 15 minutes or until golden brown. Serve warm. Note: You can also use raisins or any other dried fruit in this recipe.

Cinnamon Coffee Cake

CAKE

1 cup all-purpose flour
3 tsp. baking powder
½ tsp. cinnamon
½ cup milk
½ cup sugar
½ tsp. salt
4 Tbsp. butter, melted
1 egg

TOPPING

¼ cup sugar
½ tsp. cinnamon

PREHEAT oven to 350 degrees. Mix all cake ingredients together in a large bowl. Pour into a greased 8 × 8-inch pan. Mix sugar and cinnamon together for topping and sprinkle on top. Bake for 15 to 20 minutes. Yields 1 cake.

Drayton's Drunken Chicken

¼ cup oil
5 or 6 pieces of chicken
1½ cups white wine
2 Tbsp. flour
1 clove garlic, chopped

½ tsp. salt
½ tsp. pepper
1 large onion, chopped
8 oz. sliced mushrooms
2 Tbsp. parsley
rice

IN a large frying pan, add oil, heat, and brown chicken. When chicken is browned and partially cooked, remove from the pan and set aside. In a shaker (or jar) combine remaining oil from the pan with white wine, flour, garlic, salt, and pepper. Shake well to mix, then pour into the pan. Add chicken and onion to the pan and simmer for ½ hour. Add mushrooms and parsley and cook for an additional 10 minutes. Spoon chicken and wine sauce over cooked rice. Yields 5 to 6 servings.

Carrot Bread

2 eggs
1 cup sugar
⅔ cup oil
1½ cups flour
¾ tsp. baking soda
1 tsp. cinnamon
1 tsp. nutmeg
½ tsp. salt
1½ cups finely grated raw carrots
1 cup chopped walnuts
¾ cup raisins (optional)

PREHEAT oven to 350 degrees. In a large bowl, beat together eggs, sugar, and oil. In a separate bowl, sift together flour, baking soda, cinnamon, nutmeg, and salt. Add flour mixture to egg mixture and beat well. Stir in carrots, walnuts, and raisins. Pour batter into a greased 9 × 5-inch loaf pan. Bake for 55 to 60 minutes. Yields 1 loaf.

Blueberry Scones

2 cups sifted all-purpose flour
1 cup fresh or frozen blueberries
⅓ cup sugar
1½ tsp. baking powder
½ tsp. baking soda
¼ tsp. salt
5 Tbsp. butter, cut into pieces
¾ cup milk

PREHEAT oven to 425 degrees. Sprinkle ½ cup of flour over the blueberries and set aside. In a large bowl, mix remaining flour with sugar, baking powder, baking soda, and salt. Cut butter into flour mixture until well mixed. Add blueberry and flour mixture and mix well. Sprinkle in the milk and mix gently until dough begins to hold together. Drop scones by spoon onto a lightly greased baking sheet. Dip your fingers in flour and gently pat down the scones until about 1 inch thick. Bake for 12 to 15 minutes or until golden brown. Yields 10 to 14 scones.

Mango–Tomato Salsa on Crostini

1 cup finely diced peeled mango
2 plum tomatoes, finely diced
2 Tbsp. minced onion

1 tsp. minced serrano chili
1 Tbsp. fresh lime juice
½ tsp. sugar
1 Tbsp. chopped cilantro (optional)
Salt and pepper to taste

IN a bowl, toss the mango with tomatoes, onion, and chilies. Stir in the lime juice, sugar, and cilantro. Season with salt and pepper. Serve on your favorite crostini. Yields about 2 cups.

Baked Salmon with Lemon Sauce

SALMON

4 salmon fillets
¼ cup water

LEMON SAUCE

3 egg yolks
⅔ cup fish stock
3 Tbsp. lemon juice
4 drops Worcestershire sauce
Salt and pepper

PREHEAT oven to 450 degrees. Place salmon in a baking pan and add ¼ cup water. Bake 10 minutes per inch of thickness, approximately 10 to 15 minutes.

WHILE salmon is baking, beat together egg yolks, fish stock, lemon juice, Worcestershire sauce, and salt and pepper in a double boiler, stirring constantly.

WHEN fish is ready, plate the 4 servings, and baste with the lemon sauce. Serve hot with side salad or rice dish. Yields 4 servings.

Favorite English Pea Salad

1 large can English peas, drained
2 hard-boiled eggs, chopped
1 cup finely chopped onions
2 Tbsp. mayonnaise
Salt and pepper

COMBINE English peas, chopped eggs, onions, and mayonnaise in a bowl. Add salt and pepper to taste. Yields 4 to 6 side servings. (Note: This is an excellent accompaniment to tea sandwiches as well.)

Crunchy English Toffee

1 cup butter
1 cup sugar
3 Tbsp. water
1½ tsp. vanilla extract
12 oz. chocolate bar, crumbled
½ cup chopped walnuts (or pecans)

IN a heavy saucepan, mix together butter, sugar, and water, stirring constantly until mixture reaches 300 degrees. Remove from heat and stir in vanilla. Pour toffee mixture into a 9 × 11-inch pan and let cool for 5 minutes. After 5 minutes, sprinkle on the crumbled chocolate and nuts. When cool, break into pieces and store in an airtight container.

TEA TIME TIPS FROM
Laura Childs

Farmers Market Tea

What could be better than a trip to your local farmers market to pick up delicious farm-to-table produce for your afternoon tea? Think fresh-baked rolls, scones, or crumpets as your first course served with homemade jam. Down another aisle you're likely to find locally made cheeses, meats, and smoked fish for your tea sandwiches. Veggies are always abundant, too, so be sure to pick up radishes, cucumbers, and specialty lettuce to include in your sandwiches. It's always easy to find desserts at farmers markets— homemade pies and cookies, even candies and cakes. Often local tea blenders sell their specialty blends at these markets as well.

Bridal Shower Tea

Think elegance when you set your tea table. Fine damask linens, bone china, and silver flatware. Floral bouquets—perhaps roses, the flowers of love—are de rigueur. Candles are a must, too, as well as champagne glasses for that all-important toast. For your first course serve orange scones with Devonshire cream. Your assortment of tea sandwiches might include cream cheese and salmon pinwheels, chicken salad with tarragon, and blue cheese and walnuts. Italian Wedding Cake Blend is an elegant tea from Plum Deluxe, and you can end your tea party on a sweet note with Lady Baltimore cake or colorful macarons.

Movie Tea

Play movie trivia, pass out voting ballots for the Academy Awards, or amuse your guests with mini movie posters for place mats and stacks of movie CDs. Add a few movie magazines, cut-out stars, and mini award trophies to your table and you're ready to go. For your menu, create a Hollywood-style playbill with offerings such as Sunset Strip Scones or Tinsel Town Tea Bread. Other items on your Movie Tea menu could include Grauman's Chinese Tea, Beverly Hills Ham and Cheddar Tea Sandwiches, George Cukor Cucumber and Cream Cheese Tea Sandwiches, Paramount Pasta, Big Tuna Salad, and Rom-Com Coconut Shrimp. For dessert pass out bags of popcorn or movie candy such as Dots or malted milk balls.

Kinder Tea

Yes, your kids, grandkids, or neighbor kids would definitely enjoy their very own tea. Keep the party manageable, maybe just three or four kids, and keep it simple. Their "tea" can be apple juice, lemonade, or grape juice served in children's teacups (there are adorable Peter Rabbit tea sets to be found). Tea sandwiches can be peanut butter and jelly, apples and cheese, or even chicken salad on nut bread. Set your table with fancy plates and teacups, but caution them about taking care with such fragile objects. You could also make it a themed tea such as a Harry Potter Tea, a Lion King Tea, or even a Star Wars Tea.

Mystery Tea

Just like Theodosia and Drayton, you, too, can stage a mystery tea. There are lots of interactive mystery games and scripts to be found, so you can involve your guests as much or as little as you want. Set the stage with a darkened room, lots of candles, stacks of mystery books on your table, and props such as Sherlock Holmes hats, play pistols, knives, ropes, and bottles of poison. Begin your tea service with lavender tea bread or chocolate scones, then serve tea sandwiches such as tuna salad with cucumbers on rye, roasted red pepper with cheddar cheese on dark bread, and sliced strawberries and cream cheese on nut bread. Serve lemon meringue in small tartlet shells for mini meringue pies. Harney and Sons Tower of London Tea is the perfect tea to serve.

Passage to India Tea

India is a country of vivid colors, delightful fragrances, and amazing teas—so your tea party should reflect this. Think orange, yellow, red, and even bright blue linens. If you have some Indian fabric or an Indian tapestry, so much the better. Plates and teacups should also be colorful—a mix of patterns works great. Add some incense, ceramic elephants, and floral bouquets and you've set the mood. Because India is famous for its Darjeeling, Assam, and Nilgiri teas, those should top your list. Start your tea party by serving date scones with lemon curd, then move on to a main course of mango chutney and cream cheese on nut bread and mini samosas. A cardamom custard for dessert would be heavenly.

TEA RESOURCES

TEA MAGAZINES AND PUBLICATIONS

Tea Time—A luscious magazine profiling tea and tea lore. Filled with glossy photos and wonderful recipes. (teatimemagazine.com)

Southern Lady—From the publishers of *Tea Time* with a focus on people and places in the South as well as wonderful teatime recipes. (south ernladymagazine.com)

Tea House Times—Go to www.theteahousetimes.com for subscription information and dozens of links to tea shops, purveyors of tea, gift shops, and tea events.

Victoria—Articles and pictorials on homes, home design, gardens, and tea. (victoriamag.com)

Texas: Tea & Travel Guide Book—Annual publication highlighting Texas and other Southern tea rooms. (teablessings.com)

Fresh Cup Magazine—For tea and coffee professionals. (freshcup.com)

Tea & Coffee—Trade journal for the tea and coffee industry. (teaandcoffee .net)

Bruce Richardson—This author has written several definitive books on tea. (elmwoodinn.com/books)

Jane Pettigrew—This author has written thirteen books on the varied aspects of tea and its history and culture. (janepettigrew.com/books)

A Tea Reader—by Katrina Avila Munichiello, an anthology of tea stories and reflections.

AMERICAN TEA PLANTATIONS

Charleston Tea Plantation—The oldest and largest tea plantation in the United States. Order their fine black tea or schedule a visit at bigelowtea.com.

Table Rock Tea Company—This Pickens, South Carolina, plantation grows premium whole-leaf tea. (tablerocktea.com)

Great Mississippi Tea Company—Up-and-coming Mississippi tea farm. (greatmsteacompany.com)

Sakuma Brothers Farm—This tea garden just outside Burlington, Washington, has been growing white and green tea for over twenty years. (sakumabrothers.com)

Big Island Tea—Organic artisan tea from Hawaii. (bigislandtea.com)

Mauna Kea Tea—Organic green and oolong tea from Hawaii's Big Island. (maunakeatea.com)

Onomea Tea—Nine-acre tea estate near Hilo, Hawaii. (onotea.com)

Minto Island Growers—Hand-picked, small-batch crafted teas grown in Oregon. (mintoislandgrowers.com)

Virginia First Tea Farm—Matcha tea and natural tea soaps and cleansers. (virginiafirstteafarm.com)

Blue Dreams USA—Located near Frederick, Maryland, this farm grows tea, roses, and lavender. (bluedreamsusa.com)

TEA WEBSITES AND INTERESTING BLOGS

Destinationtea.com—State-by-state directory of afternoon tea venues.

Teamap.com—Directory of hundreds of tea shops in the United States and Canada.

Afternoontea.co.uk—Guide to tea rooms in the United Kingdom.

Teacottagemysteries.com—Wonderful website with tea lore, mystery reviews, recipes, and home and garden.

Cookingwithideas.typepad.com—Recipes and book reviews for the bibliochef.

Seedrack.com—Order *Camellia sinensis* seeds and grow your own tea!

Jennybakes.com—Fabulous recipes from a real make-it-from-scratch baker.

Cozyupwithkathy.blogspot.com—Cozy mystery reviews.

Southernwritersmagazine.com—Inspiration, writing advice, and author interviews of Southern writers.

Thedailytea.com—Formerly *Tea Magazine*, this online publication is filled with tea news, recipes, inspiration, and tea travel.

Allteapots.com—Teapots from around the world.

Fireflyspirits.com—South Carolina purveyors of sweet tea vodka.

Teasquared.blogspot.com—Fun, well-written blog about tea, tea shops, and tea musings.

Relevanttealeaf.blogspot.com—All about tea.

Stephcupoftea.blogspot.com—Blog on tea, food, and inspiration.

Teawithfriends.blogspot.com—Lovely blog on tea, friendship, and tea accoutrements.

Bellaonline.com/site/tea—Features and forums on tea.

Napkinfoldingguide.com—Photo illustrations of twenty-seven different (and sometimes elaborate) napkin folds.

Worldteaexpo.com—This premier business-to-business trade show features more than three hundred tea suppliers, vendors, and tea innovators.

Fatcatscones.com—Frozen ready-to-bake scones.

Kingarthurflour.com—One of the best flours for baking. This is what many professional pastry chefs use.

Californiateahouse.com—Order Machu's Blend, a special herbal tea for dogs that promotes healthy skin, lowers stress, and aids digestion.

Vintageteaworks.com—This company offers six unique wine-flavored tea blends that celebrate wine and respect the tea.

Downtonabbeycooks.com—A *Downton Abbey* blog with news and recipes.

Auntannie.com—Crafting site that will teach you how to make your own petal envelopes, pillow boxes, gift bags, etc.

Victorianhousescones.com—Scone, biscuit, and cookie mixes for both retail and wholesale orders. Plus baking and scone-making tips.

Englishteastore.com—Buy a jar of English Double Devon Cream here as well as British foods and candies.

Stickyfingersbakeries.com—Scone mixes and English curds.

TeaSippersSociety.com—Join this international tea community of tea sippers, growers, and educators. A terrific newsletter!

Melhadtea.com—Adventures of a traveling tea sommelier.

Carolinaplantationrice.com—Online store where you can buy heirloom "Carolina Gold" and find dozens of recipes.

Thenibble.com—A webzine of food and tea.

Shop.gourmetsweetbotanicals.com—Online store sells microgreens, tiny veggies, and edible flowers to add intense flavor and a "wow factor" to your tea sandwiches.

PURVEYORS OF FINE TEA

Plumdeluxe.com

Globalteamart.com

Adagio.com

Elmwoodinn.com

Capitalteas.com
Newbyteas.com/us
Harney.com
Stashtea.com
Serendipitea.com
Bingleyteas.com
Marktwendell.com
Globalteamart.com
Republicoftea.com
Teazaanti.com
Bigelowtea.com
Celestialseasonings.com
Goldenmoontea.com
Uptontea.com
Svtea.com (Simpson & Vail)
Gracetea.com
Davidstea.com
Teaforte.com
Silkroadteas.com
Oliverpluff.com
Piperandleaf.com

VISITING CHARLESTON

Charleston.com—Travel and hotel guide.

Charlestoncvb.com—The official Charleston convention and visitor bureau.

Charlestontour.wordpress.com—Private tours of homes and gardens, some including lunch or tea.

Charlestonplace.com—Charleston Place Hotel serves an excellent afternoon tea, Thursday through Saturday, from one to three.

Culinarytoursofcharleston.com—Sample specialties from Charleston's local eateries, markets, and bakeries.

Poogansporch.com—This restored Victorian house serves traditional lowcountry cuisine. Be sure to ask about Poogan!

Preservationsociety.org—Hosts Charleston's annual Fall Candlelight Tour.

Palmettocarriage.com—Horse-drawn carriage rides.

Charlestonharbortours.com—Boat tours and harbor cruises.

Ghostwalk.net—Stroll into Charleston's haunted history. Ask them about the "original" Theodosia!

Charlestontours.net—Ghost tours plus tours of plantations and historic homes.

Follybeach.com—Official guide to Folly Beach activities, hotels, rentals, restaurants, and events.

Charlestongardens.com—Shop and website with decor and gifts.

ACKNOWLEDGMENTS

Major thank-yous all around to Sam, Tom, Stephanie, Elisha, Sareer, M.J., Bob, Jennie, Dan, and all the amazing people at Berkley Prime Crime and Penguin Random House who handle editing, design, publicity, copywriting, social media, bookstore sales, gift sales, production, and shipping. Heartfelt thanks as well to all the tea lovers, tea shop owners, book clubs, bookshop folks, librarians, reviewers, magazine editors and writers, websites, broadcasters, and bloggers who have enjoyed the Tea Shop Mysteries and helped spread the word. You are all so kind and you help make this possible!

And I am forever filled with gratitude for you, my very special readers and tea lovers, who have embraced Theodosia, Drayton, Haley, Earl Grey, and the rest of the tea shop gang as friends and family. Thank you so much and I promise you many more Tea Shop Mysteries!

When life hands you lemons, you're supposed to make lemonade. Theodosia Browning had adopted a slightly more creative approach. She was smack dab in the middle of hosting a fanciful Limón Tea Party.

Picture this if you will: Five dozen Southern ladies dressed in gauzy florals and wearing hats and gloves. All seated at elegant tea tables in the fairytale setting of an actual lemon grove strung with hundreds of white twinkle lights. Postcard perfect, yes? Now add in a delicate waft of lemon-scented tea, large glass bowls amply heaped with fresh-picked lemons, and lemon scones served as the first course. For the pièce de résistance, a fashion show was about to begin and a camera crew was on hand to capture all the highlights of the runway. Naturally, the usual gaggle of high-strung designers, stylists, and business partners paced about nervously in the background.

A lot to contend with. Almost too much for Theodosia. It was one thing to serve morning and afternoon tea at her charming

Indigo Tea Shop on Charleston's famed Church Street, another to juggle a major event such as this Limón Tea Party.

"Grab another pitcher of lemonade, will you?" Theodosia said to Haley, her young chef and baker. "And that silver ice bucket as well."

Theodosia blew a wisp of curly auburn hair off her face as she stood in the kitchen of the Orchard House Inn, home to South Carolina's only lemon orchard. All the food and beverages were being staged here with the help of Drayton, her tea sommelier; Haley, her chef; and two additional waitstaff. And each course was (thankfully!) going out on time. Seemed to be anyway.

"That woman is driving me batty," Drayton said as he measured out scoops of lemon verbena tea. A natural orator, each of his syllables was rounded and carefully cadenced.

"You're talking about Delaine?" Theodosia asked. She gazed at him with crystalline blue eyes that were complemented by a peaches and cream complexion and an abundant halo of auburn hair. With her slender, athletic build, Theodosia always gave the impression that she was infused with energy and about to come uncoiled.

"Delaine *always* drives me crazy," Drayton said. "That's nothing new. No, I'm talking about her overbearing sister, Nadine. The woman is positively outrageous. Not only is she bullying the poor models, she's been braying out orders to the film crew. And seriously ragging that dilettante of a film director whose name escapes me at the moment. My fear is that our lovely guests might pick up on the dissonance and frenzy wafting through the air."

Haley looked up from where she was stacking lobster salad tea sandwiches on three-tiered trays. "You mean bad vibes?" Haley was sylph-like and blond, cute as a button, and in her early twenties—still easily impressionable.

"Precisely," Drayton said.

Theodosia glanced out the window over the sink and saw Nadine rushing around, waving her arms, looking as if she were jacked up on an entire bottle of Ritalin.

"Tell you what. You and Haley make one more round with scones, tea, and lemonade, then carry out the tea sandwiches. I'll go see if I can wrangle Nadine."

Theodosia, ever the peacemaker, didn't want trouble. She also didn't want Drayton to lose his cool. He was her steadfast, sixty-something tea sommelier and right-hand man, who rarely got ruffled. But today he was edging toward it. Not that you could tell. In his cream-colored silk jacket and pale pink bow tie he was the picture of a Southern gent dressed for a lovely spring afternoon. Not a wrinkle in sight, nary a hair out of place.

Walking across the grass, Theodosia tilted her face up slightly to catch the warm sun. This was such a fun idea to host a tea party in an actual lemon grove on John's Island, just a few miles outside Charleston's city limits. The Orchard House Inn was the perfect spot, a lovely plantation-style B and B with a chef's kitchen and plenty of parking. And to think that the inn's owners had actually imported all these trees, planted them, and then carefully nurtured them so that they were all producing edible fruit. Quite amazing.

Theodosia walked past the fluttering white tent that served as a temporary dressing room and where a dozen underfed models were squeezing their slim bodies into leggings and halter tops. She passed a small shed where a maintenance man in green overalls was stowing a rake and noticed the film director fidgeting with a camera on a tripod. Even though the day was warm, the director—she remembered his name was somebody Fox—wore a dark green Burberry blazer with a linen scarf looped lazily around his neck.

Theodosia smiled to herself. Like he was at the Cannes Film Festival ready to pick up an award instead of filming an afternoon tea and fashion show.

Finally, a few steps into the lemon orchard, she found the two sisters, Delaine and Nadine, locked in a heated argument. Delaine Dish was sputtering like a manic gopher, her face turning pink as she lectured her younger sister, Nadine.

"You *always* send the sportiest looks down the runway first," Delaine shouted. "Then work your way up to the more fashion-conscious outfits." Delaine was the high maintenance owner of Cotton Duck, one of Charleston's premier clothing boutiques. She was also a semi-socialite, confirmed gossip, and veteran of countless fashion shows. Today Delaine wore a flouncy rose-colored skirt with a matching, tight-fitting peplum jacket.

Nadine, grim-faced and posturing awkwardly in her yellow dress, barely acknowledged her own sister.

"Ladies," Theodosia said, breaking into their conversation. "Please don't tell me we have a problem."

Delaine spun to face her. "A problem? There's *always* a problem when Nadine's involved."

Nadine's expression turned even more sour. "You're always accusing me of being stupid," she sneered at Delaine. "Well, Lemon Squeeze Couture is *my* project and *I'm* creative director. So I'd appreciate it if you'd kindly back off!"

While Delaine was size 0 skinny with flowing dark hair and a heart-shaped face, Nadine was her polar opposite. Light blond close-cropped hair, Zaftig figure, and a temperament more mercurial than Delaine's. If that was even possible.

"Please," Theodosia said. "Let's all take a deep breath here." Yes, it may have been Theodosia's tea party, but these two ladies had the potential to turn it into Wrestlemania if they continued to go at it tooth and nail.

"B-b-but the timing," Delaine began. "With so many moving parts . . . you want everything to be perfect. The food, the fashion . . ."

"Relax," Theodosia said in what she hoped was a soothing

tone. "For one thing, the tea party is nothing to worry about. Drayton and I have done this a million times. As far as the fashion show goes, it looks as if all the models are dressed, glammed up, and eager to strut their stuff." She forced a smile. "Why don't you both take a deep breath, sit down, and enjoy the show. I have a feeling it's going to be terrific."

Nadine's waxed brows shot up as she fought to pull her pink-glossed, over-injected lips into an unhappy line. "So you say, but this is an *enormous* challenge for me. It's not just the kickoff event for Charleston Fashion Week, it's the very first time my partners and I have staged an actual Lemon Squeeze Couture fashion show!"

Theodosia sighed. Lemon Squeeze Couture was a new line of workout clothing, or as Nadine preferred to call it—athleisure wear—that was debuting today at the Limón Tea Party.

And just to throw a monkey wrench into things, a film crew had been a last-minute addition cooked up by Nadine's two business partners, Harv and Marv. They suddenly had their hearts set on a fun, bouncy fashion video that could be set to music and played on the Lemon Squeeze Couture website. Not a bad idea entirely, just a little late in the game.

Theodosia consulted her watch and waved a hand as a bumblebee buzzed lazily past her head. "Tell you what," she said. "We have ten minutes before the fashion show is scheduled to start. Delaine, why don't you check on the models. And Nadine, perhaps you could take a quick break. I know you have people from the press here, so before you speak to them maybe you could grab a glass of lemonade and . . ."

"Chill out," Delaine snapped.

Nadine, her nose out of joint because of the confrontation with her sister, walked to the back door of the Orchard House Inn.

Still steaming with anger, she hesitated for a moment, then pulled open the screen door and stepped into the empty kitchen. It was large, with lots of metal shelves stocked with stew pots, stacks of fry pans, and sheet cake pans. Acres of counter space held what remained of today's tea party bounty—extra three-tiered trays and pans mounded with lemon cream scones covered in plastic wrap. Six blue coolers that had recently held a myriad of tea sandwiches stood empty. There was also a scatter of tea tins, teapots, and tea accoutrements.

Nadine didn't give a fig about tea or tea sandwiches. What she really wanted right now was a cigarette to help settle her nerves—and who cared if this was a no-smoking zone? Who was going to know? All the tea people were running around like crazy chickens serving the guests while her silly, domineering sister was trying to take over the show and ingratiate herself with her business partners. Hah. Delaine always had been the pushy one.

Dipping into her skirt pocket, Nadine grabbed a half-empty pack of Marlboro Lights, shook one out, and lit up. She inhaled greedily, then exhaled slowly. Tried to calm her jangled nerves as well as her intense worry over the fashion show. And just as her shoulders started to unkink, just as she was beginning to relax, she heard, on the other side of the door that separated the kitchen from a rather large parlor, two people arguing.

Curious now (Nadine was *always* curious), she wondered if it might be her erstwhile business partners, Harv and Marv, sniping at each other yet again. She tiptoed over, put an ear to the door, and heard . . .

More arguing. Insistent and growing increasingly heated with every passing moment. Still, the voices were pitched so low it was virtually impossible to make out actual words.

Could they be talking about me? Nadine wondered as her paranoia kicked in big time.

She hadn't been getting along all that well with Harv and

Marv. They'd finally tumbled to her utter lack of knowledge concerning fashion and their new product launch. Once that had happened, once she'd been unmasked, it seemed as if they were *constantly* shouting and ranting at her about one thing or another. And it was upsetting to Nadine. Could she help it if she was a neophyte when it came to design and sales and marketing? Sure, she'd embroidered some of her résumé (okay, most of it), but for goodness' sake, she was *trying* to contribute. Could she help it if she lacked actual know-how about manufacturing and distribution? What about all the sweat equity she'd poured in? Surely that must count for something!

Listening harder, trying to discern exact words, Nadine leaned closer. And as she did, bumped her forehead against the swinging door, causing it to emit a loud *creak.* At that exact same moment, Nadine lost her balance and—doggone high heels!—teetered hard against the door.

The door swung open, causing her to practically fall into the parlor.

Embarrassed, cartwheeling her arms to try and regain her balance, Delaine stared at the two people and recognized them instantly. "Oh jeez," she sputtered. "I'm so sorry. I was just . . ." Before she got halfway through her apology, her eyes fell on a large black duffel bag stuffed with . . .

Oh no.

Realizing she was suddenly in serious trouble, Nadine spun about frantically, hoping to beat a hasty retreat.

Too late.

As she lurched back into the kitchen, legs churning, veins coursing hot with adrenaline, something sharp struck the back of her head. It was an exquisitely well-defined pain, almost like the sting of a hornet. The sudden assault made her cry out. Then, a millisecond later, the pain was excruciating, as if the entire back of her head was on fire. Nadine wondered what strange thing had just happened as a million jumbled thoughts spun crazily through her brain and she crashed to the floor.

And the very last thing Nadine was cognizant of before she winked out for good, for all eternity, was being dragged . . . dragged into a place that was cold and dark and sticky.